THE RANCHER

THE MEN OF WHITE SANDY

SARAH M. ANDERSON

Dedication

To the real-life masked cowboy. May he still be riding down the middle of the street in Red Lodge, Montana—without his shirt!

To my mom, Carolyn, and my Gram, Frances, for taking me on the celebratory trip to Red Lodge.

Thank you Newton Love and Annette Love Hatton, as well as the Lakota Language Consortium, for all their help with the Lakota translations in the book. Many thanks to Mary Dieterich, Amy Short and Laurel Levy for being awesome critique partners. Thanks to Dr. Theresa Newton for her medical expertise and for keeping me moving. Also, thanks to Dad for getting the video of the masked cowboy digitized! Thanks to Jill Marsal and Heidi Moore for appreciating a man in a mask. Finally, thanks to my husband and son—the best heroes ever!

Prologue

Jacob unsnapped his mask and sat it on the shelf next to his bed. His face felt different without it—foreign. Wrong. He breathed deeply, trying to enjoy air that hadn't passed over leather, but it didn't work. Never did. He couldn't sleep in the mask, but taking it off made him anxious. He didn't like being anxious.

He hadn't looked at his reflection in three years. Had no interest in knowing what he looked like now. Had gotten rid of every mirror in the ancient trailer where he'd lived his whole life. Kept the blinds drawn so he wouldn't accidentally see his reflection. He didn't want to know and, what's more, he didn't need to know. That was that.

Except when the darkness closed around him at night. Then, with nothing but the sound of Kip's gentle breathing to remind him he wasn't the only living thing left in this world, Jacob wondered what he looked like now.

He hadn't given in to that temptation. Not once. Tonight would be no different.

Although he knew the scars had healed, he still wore the mask. Logically, he knew his face wasn't about to fall off, but the mask was a constant, physical reassurance holding him together. Plus, he didn't have

1

to look at himself. No one did. The mask hid what he really was from the world.

That was the way it had to be.

On the other side of the trailer, Kip sighed in her sleep. Jacob closed his good eye and let his ears do the looking for him. He searched for sounds that weren't supposed to be there—the snap of a twig outside, the rattle of the door lock being tested. But the only sound he heard was Kip breathing. It was the only noise she made.

It'd been this way for so long—Kip being quiet, Jacob wearing a mask—that sometimes he doubted that his memories of life before were anything more than wishful thinking.

What the hell was he going to do about Kip? This was another part of his nightly ritual. It'd been three years. Three long years of trying to be a father to someone else's little girl, of trying to hide her from whatever had killed her parents. Three years of wearing a mask.

How much longer was this going to go on? How much longer could he keep her safely hidden? How much longer before the thing—man or beast, he sure as hell didn't know—came after her again?

He hadn't seen much of it before it attacked him with that knife. Just that it was tall—too tall to be a man—and covered in brown fur.

He tried not to think about the thing. He didn't want it wandering around his dreams, like it often did. If it were a good night, he'd be all alone in his sleep.

But even those blank nights left him asking the same questions when he woke up.

How much longer would he wear the mask? Hide the girl? Be alone? He knew the answer, of course. There wasn't any doubt about it.

For as long as it took. That was that.

Chapter One

Mary Beth settled into the last free table at the sidewalk café at Ronny's in Faith Ridge. In fact, as far as she could tell, it was the only restaurant within an hour's drive. The rural Illinois town she'd grown up in had been tiny, but Faith Ridge, South Dakota, was practically microscopic—and in the middle of nowhere to boot. Rapid City was almost two hours west. The state capital, Pierre, was an hour and a half north. The drive to get here had been nothing but acres of grass for miles and miles. She was tired, hungry and her butt was numb.

Hell, at the rate she was going, she was lucky Faith Ridge had a restaurant at all.

As she waited for the server, she noticed that not only was every other table filled, they were filled with women—white women, Indian women and even one black woman, but none younger than she was.

What the hell?

The waitress, long black hair hanging down her back with bangs curled high on her forehead, bopped up to the table. "Hi, I'm Robin," she said, the faint trace of accent clipping the ends of her words, "and I'll be your server. What can I get you?"

"Robin. Nice to meet you. I'm Dr. Mary Beth Hofstetter."

The young woman's eyes crinkled with a smile, which did some interesting things to the glitter on her eyelids. "Oh, the new vet. We're so glad to have you here."

Mary Beth smiled. "I see my reputation precedes me."

Robin shot her a funny look. "Well, Doc Coleman's been talking about retiring for so long, we were all just amazed when he finally announced that he'd hired a replacement." Robin took a step back, looking Mary Beth up and down. "You're a vet?"

"I grew up on a farm. I can handle everything from cattle to kittens."

Much to her surprise, Robin sat in the other chair, a delighted grin catching almost as much light as the glitter over her eyes. "Doc Coleman saved my cat, Patch. We'll sure miss him, but…" The way she said it made it pretty clear she wouldn't miss him *that* much.

"But…"

Robin leaned in, looking gleeful. "You are looking at the sum total of women in town. There aren't a whole lot of girls my age around here."

Smirking at the thought that she was about the same age as this bright young thing with cheekbones she'd kill for, Mary Beth took another glance around. "Robin, *why* am I looking at the sum total of women in Faith Ridge?"

She smirked as she stood up. "The show's going to start in a few minutes. You'll want to stick around for it."

"The show?"

"You'll see, just wait. Now, what can I get you?"

Mary Beth ordered the roast-beef sandwich, as opposed to the roast-beef platter, the beef hamburger or the myriad of steak cuts. As Robin headed back to the kitchen, Mary Beth grinned.

Deep in the heart of beef country and she'd already made a friend.

The minutes past as Mary Beth listened to the feminine buzz surrounding her. For being in the middle of the sum total of the female population of Faith Ridge—maybe fifteen strong—the women were relaxed, chatting and eating as if this were any other night. There were occasional masculine shouts from the interior of the café, where a large group of cowboys were doing their best to coach a ballgame taking place in Denver.

Just like junior high, Mary Beth mused. Girls on one side, boys on the other.

Robin brought her sandwich, carefully balancing a towel and two huge glasses of water on the tray. She set the plate and one glass down. Underneath the tray, she had a to-go bag tied up.

"I didn't order the extra water," Mary Beth began, but the buzz died around her. It was like the whole restaurant was holding its collective breath.

"Water isn't for you," Robin replied, her jet-black eyes focused up the road. "Show's starting," she added, sounding breathless.

Mary Beth followed her gaze, blinking through the streaking evening sun.

Down the center of the street, a cowboy was riding a horse, leading another behind him. As he got closer, Mary Beth could see the cowboy was shirtless. The golden light settled over his dark hat and shimmered off his bare shoulders. His front was still in light shadows, but if the rest of him was as carved as those dark brown shoulders, things were about to get interesting.

"Mmm," Robin hummed and Mary Beth swore the whole restaurant was humming in pleasure with her.

As the lone rider got closer, the shadows eased back a bit, and Mary Beth realized that there was something different about this cowboy.

He had an eye patch.

Whoa, hunk on the hoof, just like in a romance novel. But as she blinked through the angular sunlight, Mary Beth realized that the patch was far larger than the kind a pirate would wear. The swath of dark leather started at his left temple, covered his left eye and continued down over the center of his face, coming to a sharp point over his nose.

Mary Beth shook her head, but the patch remained the same. "He wears a mask?" she whispered to Robin, afraid to break the spell that gripped the café.

"Shhh," Robin hissed.

The masked cowboy rode right up to the café and stopped mere feet from Mary Beth's table before he slid out of the saddle, his leg muscles twitching through his tight jeans the whole way down. He paused for split second, clearly enjoying every female eye trained on his bare torso before he walked right up to Mary Beth's table.

"Robin," he said, gently tipping his black felt hat, its brim creased from countless such tips. His one eye, nestled between a strong eyebrow and a stronger cheekbone, swept over the scene before it settled on Mary Beth.

"Jacob," Robin practically sang. She held out the tray with the towel and the water.

6

Jacob, the masked, shirtless cowboy, gracefully lifted the glass of water from the tray before he set his hat in its place. He took a huge drink, then grabbed the towel, leaned forward and poured the rest of the water over his head.

The water rushed through his slightly overgrown jet-black hair as he stood up, his mask covered with the towel. Rivulets raced down his browned, chiseled chest before he slowly mopped them up, his gaze grabbing Mary Beth's face and refusing to let it go again.

She was sure her mouth was on the table, but she couldn't help it. Every fiber in her body was vibrating as she watched the towel trace past his pecs, down his lean abs—the muscles moving just beneath the smooth surface of his skin—and follow a faint trail of hair that ended in his jeans. The mask notwithstanding, this man was quite possibly the most ideal specimen of masculinity she'd ever laid eyes on.

A hint of a smile on his face, Jacob handed the towel back to Robin, took the to-go bag, pivoted and walked to the saddlebag of his paint. Mary Beth admiringly noted the huge tear in the seat of his pants, just under his left butt cheek. It was hard to tell what was more promising—his rock-solid chest or that flash of ass. Pausing again for just a second, he tucked the meal in the bag after he whipped out an Anthrax T-shirt that might have been black back in the 80s.

As he began to unbuckle his jeans, Mary Beth heard the entire café suck in a hot breath.

He won't. Mary Beth's brain stuttered in shock. *He wouldn't!*

The top button gave under his nimble fingers, and then the second. Mary Beth couldn't help but stare at

7

the treasure trail of dark hair that crested at an even darker line peaking just over the undone buttons.

Jesus Christ, is he even wearing underwear? She gasped, unable to look away as she squirmed in her chair.

Jacob slipped the tee over his head, tucked it in and buttoned back up. As he took his hat off Robin's tray, the whole café—the sum total of women in Faith Ridge— sighed and leaned back in their chairs. Mary Beth wondered if there were enough cigarettes in town for the collective orgasm that had just happened in broad daylight.

"So, you must be the new vet," his voice rumbled out of his superb chest, his accent identical to Robin's.

"What?" Mary Beth gaped, the wheels of her brain spinning. "Oh, yes. Yes, I'm the new vet."

Jacob crossed his arms and stared at Robin, who was euphorically beaming at Jacob. "Jacob, this is Dr. Mary Beth Hofstetter. Dr. Hofstetter—"

"Mary Beth," she corrected, finding her brain now that his fabulous body was mostly covered. She couldn't help but think of that hole over his butt—if he wasn't wearing underwear—

"Yeah. Mary Beth, this is Jacob Plenty Holes."

Jacob's black eye traveled up and down her body with an emotion that was stuck somewhere between angry and interested. "Nice to meet you, Dr. Hofstetter." His voice was so cool as to be cold. "We'll be working together."

"W-we will?" she stuttered, trying to keep her mouth from going, *Plenty Holes?* The man in a mask— who may or may not have a freaking nose—is named Plenty Holes? She barely managed to keep the brakes slammed on and almost bit her tongue.

"Jacob manages the McGillis ranch," Robin explained, the name McGillis coming out pained.

After a quick glance at the plain white building across the street, Jacob turned his eye back to the waitress. "He been by today?"

She started to shake her head no, but then her eyes went wide in fear.

Jacob didn't even move his head as he addressed Mary Beth. "Go," he ordered.

Without another word, Robin spun on her heels and was gone.

"Wait, what?" Mary Beth said, but the question died on her lips as Jacob cocked an ear. Mary Beth saw a tall white man heading straight for the restaurant. Jacob's hand stealthily dropped down to the knife that hung at his side. She had no idea what was happening. This Jacob Plenty Holes had gone from erotically enticing to confusing to ice cold in less than three minutes.

"Hey, Plenty Holes!" the man said with just enough oil in his voice to make her think of a snake wearing boots. Mary Beth could feel the whole café recoil in disgust. "You here to get that albino again?"

"Evening, McGillis," Jacob said, not moving.

Mary Beth looked at McGillis. This had to be the ranch owner. He towered over Jacob, making Mary Beth feel little bigger than a bug as she sat at the table, her forgotten roast beef getting cold. His sandy-brown hair was cut close to his head, and he had an odd smell that tinged the air around him with something close to patchouli. Standing next to Jacob in his torn jeans and faded concert tee, McGillis's clothing screamed dominance. His tan boots were ostrich, his black pants were perfectly creased and around the neck of his crisp blue shirt sat a bolo tie that had an honest-to-goodness diamond in the center of a black onyx medallion.

He was a good-looking man, although probably in his fifties. But there was something in his eyes that reminded Mary Beth of Brian Greevy and the way he would smile at her when she threw herself in between him and her mom. Everyone thought Brian was such a great guy. Even her mom had been convinced Brian was a winner, if only Mom could have done what he wanted, when he wanted it. Only Mary Beth had seen him for what he was—a coward hiding behind a bully's fists. Skeevy Greevy, she'd called him.

Buck McGillis and Skeevy Greevy didn't look anything alike, but their eyes told her everything she needed to know. She'd refused to be afraid of Greevy. She wasn't about to be afraid of Buck McGillis.

So she swallowed down her dread and met his gaze straight on. He owned the major ranch near town. Mary Beth knew that she'd have to work with—work for—this tyrant of a man. Man, she wished she'd brought her knife to dinner.

"Well, now, what's this?" McGillis drawled, jerking his waistband up and down like he was screwing his zipper. She'd seen lots of farmers and cattlemen hitch up their pants, but his agonizingly slow pace was just plain wrong.

Then he bent over to get a good look at what passed as her cleavage in her V-neck T-shirt. "Haven't seen a pretty little thing like you here before." He jerked his head towards Jacob. "Enjoy the show? I got a better one. You'll have to see it some time," he said as he gave the pants one final tug.

Jacob's mouth opened, but Mary Beth beat him to

the punch. "That's Dr. Pretty Little Thing to you, Mr. McGillis," she bristled, casually resting her hand on the steak knife on the table. It was no Bowie knife, but it'd do. "And I hate to disappoint you, but I don't sleep with clients. I'm afraid I'll have to pass on everyone's show."

As McGillis's smile hardened, Mary Beth caught Jacob cocking his eyebrow, looking almost amused. But the look quickly vanished into impassable stone as McGillis sat down at the table.

"Doctor? You're the new vet?" He looked her up and down before his face began to warm into something that might have been seductive if it hadn't been so mercenary. "Have dinner with me tomorrow night. Take you out for a ride around the ranch. You'll like it, better than that," he said with jerk back towards a stone-faced Jacob.

The I-don't-sleep-with-clients thing went whistling right past him. Okay, she thought as she leaned forward on her hands, batting her eyes, draw the line early. "Oh, Mr. McGillis," she cooed.

"My friends call me Buck," he replied, his eyes trained on her cleavage.

"Buck? Why that's an interesting name," she giggled as she broke out the dazzling smile. A quick glance to the left revealed the shocked look covering Jacob's face. He was properly befuddled. She giggled again.

McGillis's eyes fluttered as he tried to hitch his zipper up again. Yes, proper befuddlement had occurred all the way around. "You like it?" he preened. "I picked it out myself."

"Well, I'm not sure it really fits you," she drawled, tracing a finger on the tablecloth. She caught Jacob's mouth flop open before a look of rage wiped out the shock.

"No?" McGillis replied, his honeyed voice making him sound pleased with himself.

"No," she cooed again before going for the jugular. "I think you overvalued yourself by at least fifty cents."

McGillis stood up so fast that his chair flew into the street. "You little—"

"Dr. Hofstetter!" Robin screeched, carrying a huge chocolate confection that had an honest-to-God sparkler flaming out of the top. "Here's that chocolate bomb you ordered."

She'd done no such thing. But Robin's actions made it blisteringly clear that the whole restaurant had been listening in. McGillis looked from Mary Beth to Jacob before he leaned in close to Mary Beth. She caught the movement of Jacob grabbing his knife as she did the same.

"No one says no to Buck McGillis," he snarled.

"Bill Coleman hired me. I don't sleep with clients. I castrate calves. If you've got a problem with that," she snarled back, slamming the butt of the knife back onto the table, "you just feel free to find another vet. It's your call."

McGillis smiled, a joyless thing that didn't fit on his face. He stood up straight, brushed invisible lint off his shirt and slowly looked her up and down again. "Another time then."

"I'm not going anywhere, Mr. McGillis," she replied, looking as mean as she could despite the cold chills he sent racing down her spine. She wasn't afraid of him, she reminded herself. She wasn't afraid of anyone, but especially not the jerks of the world.

The big man gave her a joyless grin before he turned and casually strolled back towards a spotless black Jeep as if they'd just been shooting the breeze instead of threatening each other. The vehicle's windows were tinted, but as the Jeep rolled past the restaurant, Mary Beth could feel Buck's eyes on her—even if she couldn't see them.

As he drove past, Jacob's two horses shifted nervously from where they'd been drop-tethered, and Jacob patted their necks as he stared at her. "You don't want to make an enemy of Buck McGillis, Dr. Hofstetter."

"I don't want to be treated like a play toy, Mr. Plenty Holes." The horses calmed at his touch, and God help her, all she could think about was the show. "You're not suggesting I give in just to make nice?"

"No. Just steer clear." He caught her gaze and held it. His eye was so black it was almost blue, and Mary Beth felt like if she wasn't careful, he'd pull her in with just one eye. "Just be careful."

"Jacob?" a woman's voice—older, clear and authoritative—called out from across the street. "We're ready."

Mary Beth watched as he crossed the street. Robin had misspoken. One woman in Faith Ridge hadn't been watching the show.

"Who's that?" she asked the shaken waitress.

"Mrs. Browne, the school teacher." Robin collapsed in the chair she'd just set back at the table.

Mrs. Browne looked every inch the old West schoolmarm, her gray hair pulled back into a tight bun, reading glasses perched on the edge of her nose. She was holding the hand of a small child nearly lost behind the folds of her voluminous skirt.

Mary Beth leaned to the right, trying to get a better look at the child who seemed to be—

White.

Milk-white skin, shock-white hair.

McGillis's barb came back to her. *You here to get that albino again?*

Mary Beth rubbed her temples. In the course of less than fifteen minutes, she'd nearly orgasmed watching a one-eyed, masked cowboy put on a strip-show shower in the middle of a street, managed to piss off her biggest client who just happened to be the town bully, and now she watched as said masked cowboy took the hand of an albino child, long white hair practically glowing in the early dusk. Mary Beth could see the purple-tinged eyes never move from the ground as Jacob led him? Her? Mary Beth couldn't tell, but then Jacob was boosting the child onto the bare back of the second horse.

In one fluid movement, Jacob sprang up onto his horse's back as if the five feet were nothing.

"Robin, Dr. Hofstetter." He touched his fingers to his hat. "Ladies," he replied to the remaining gawkers at the café.

And the masked cowboy rode off into the sunset, leading a horse carrying an albino child behind him.

The moment he was out of sight, the café began to buzz again, and Mary Beth's mouth kicked into overdrive. "What the hell?" she asked Robin. "Does he have a nose or not? And was that albino kid a boy or a girl? And do I need to start packing a weapon?"

Robin sighed as she got up to clear a table. "Where are you staying?"

"Dr. Coleman set me up in a little house up on Beech—"

"Oh, yeah, Junior Malley's old place," she said as if that would mean anything to Mary Beth. "Ronny and I live two houses down."

"Well, after you get off work tonight, you can come over and tell me what the Sam Hill just happened here."

Chapter Two

The knock on the door—swift and solid—made Mary Beth jump. She grabbed her Bowie knife off the table. Better safe than sorry. "Who is it?" she yelled, hoping she didn't sound as panicked as she felt.

"Dr. Hofstetter? It's me, Robin!" Robin yelled back.

Mary Beth's shoulders sagged in relief. "Just a sec." She stowed the knife back in the sheath and opened the door.

Robin grinned and held up a six-pack. "I brought a housewarming gift."

"How old are you again?" Mary Beth scolded as Robin sauntered past her. *Jeez, I sound like my mother.* She shuddered.

"I turned twenty-one two months ago," Robin giggled, sounding more like a teenager than an adult. She popped a can's top and handed it to Mary Beth, then opened one for herself. "But we're not here to talk about me. You were drooling all over Jacob."

"Everyone was drooling all over Jacob," Mary Beth shot back. "So tell me why everyone drools all over Jacob."

"Oh, where to begin?" Robin asked as she took a drink.

"Start with the mask part and go from there."
Mary Beth sighed as she collapsed on the one spot of
the couch that didn't have a box of books on it.

"The masked cowboy." Robin sat cross-legged on
the floor.

"Has he always worn the mask?"

"No. He lost his face about three years ago."

Recent. He was probably still having depth
perception problems, like that one-eyed horse that kept
walking into doorframes back in vet school. "What
happened?"

"He said he got into a brawl at the bar in Sturgis
over a girl."

Right. Sturgis. Mary Beth remembered they were
less than three hours away from motorcycle heaven.
"You don't sound like you believe that."

"I don't." Robin took another drink. "You should
have seen him back before he had to wear that mask. I
mean, he was Indian perfection on a horse. Hair almost
down to his ass, face carved of stone—the rest of him
carved of stone—man, he was freaking perfect.
Number one hunk on the rez." Her eyes got dreamy at
the memory.

Mary Beth was feeling a little dreamy herself.
"You knew him?"

"He played football with my oldest brother,
Ronny—the one who owns the café—and my second-
oldest brother, Randy, at the consolidated high
school."

"Sure," Mary Beth said, trying to sound like she
knew that.

"God, how I lusted after him. He and Ronny and
Randy would come over after practice and race their

17

horses up and down before they jumped in the pond out behind our house and—" She shivered, but the room seemed several degrees warmer to Mary Beth. "You should have *seen* him."

"I think I saw enough today. How old is Jacob?" Honestly, it didn't really matter. What mattered were those abs and forearms and *especially* that trail of hair. But she was curious.

"Twenty-six, I think. Ronny turned twenty-seven last fall, and Jacob was a year behind him."

Damn. She had three years on him. But now was not the time for self-pity. Now was the time to pump Robin for all the info she could. "So you don't think he got into a brawl?"

"I know Jacob, and he doesn't drink. He's one of those Indians who believes the white man's alcohol is the ruination—" she pulled the ruin part of the word out, like she was calling pigs "—of the tribe. Very righteous."

Righteous? A man who nearly pulled off a full monty in the middle of town was *righteous*? "Really?"

"Sure. Helped us get a loan from the tribe so we could buy the café."

"Your brother knows about the show?"

"Of course he knows about the show. Ladies' hour, he calls it. Trust me, in this town, there's no way we'd make it if we didn't get the business Jacob pulls in every night during the summer."

"So that's why he does that? He's helping a friend?"

"Sure, part of it," she shrugged, taking another swig. "But…"

Mary Beth slid off the couch, getting down on Robin's level. "But…"

"I think it's because of the mask. He didn't do it before. I think he thinks that if everyone's looking at that rock-hard body, no one will see his messed-up face."

"Distraction." Her mind reeled. Of all the coping mechanisms, that had to be one of the more *unique* ones she'd ever heard of. It was like he was hiding in plain sight.

"Absolutely. And you saw all those women." Robin giggled. "You should have seen yourself gawk at him. He likes you, you know."

"Wait, what?"

"He only undoes the top button, but today, he undid two. He was showing off for you."

"Whoa. *Whoa.*" Mary Beth repeated, finishing her bottle as the image of his black-blue treasure trail ending at the horizontal line of thicker hair floated before her. *That* was flirting around these parts? "So how well do you, um, know him?"

Robin smiled dreamily. "He kissed me, really kissed me for my sixteenth birthday. I swear, I would have given it up to him right then and there in the middle of the party. But he just stepped back, tipped his hat and said, 'Robin,'" her voice dropped into a reasonably good impression, "just like he does every night at the café."

She wasn't going to be jealous. That was an order. "He doesn't do that in the winter, does he?"

"Any night it's over sixty, he's out there." As Robin worked through the beer, her accent got a bit thicker, but it was a lovely sound. Completely different from the Midwest drawl Mary Beth was used to.

Only another three months to watch the show. She couldn't help but wonder how many buttons he'd undo tomorrow. Was hoping for three being greedy? "Is he married?"

Robin smirked, her eyes knowing. "You like him too."

"Let's be honest. I like parts of him." They both giggled. "I don't know anything about him."

"Which is why we're here," Robin replied, sweeping her arms out to encompass the entire living room crowded with boxes. "No, he's not married. He dated this girl from the rez in high school pretty seriously, but she was a lot older than I was, so I didn't really know her. I think she married someone else and they got off the rez. Maybe they moved to Pierre or something." She shrugged.

"That's it? He had a high school sweetheart, he kissed you when you turned sixteen and he puts on a striptease every night in the summer?"

"That's it." She got a greedy look in her eyes. "It's almost like he's uncharted territory just waiting to be discovered. God, I'd love to discover what he's got in those pants."

Mary Beth whistled, more to keep from saying something that her mother would have said than anything. "But back to the mask. If he didn't get messed up in a bar brawl, how did it happen?"

"No one knows, except maybe that little albino." Robin shrugged, getting up to fetch two more beers. "He was gone for a month or two, and one day he rides into town wearing the mask and leading her to school on that broken-down nag. No one had ever seen her before. Mrs. Browne said that he said she was his daughter."

"So she's a girl?"

"That's Kip. She's always wearing the same blue

pants and a baggy T-shirt." Robin twisted the caps off both bottles and handed one to Mary Beth. "It's like he's trying to hide her or something."

"How do you hide an albino in the middle of Indian country?" But the moment she said it, she realized it was just like what he was doing with the mask and the show—hiding in plain sight.

Why would anyone do that?

"I don't know. He won't tell anyone where she came from or who her mother is—not even Ronny."

"She just appeared out of thin air? How the hell does that make any sense?"

"It doesn't," Robin agreed. "She seems pretty slow too. Mrs. Browne says she just sits in her chair all day long, staring at whatever is in front of her."

"Autistic?"

Robin nodded. "Mrs. Browne is a nice lady," Robin went on. "She really cares about Kip, but I don't think she understands that girl at all. At least she keeps Kip in the schoolhouse until Buck goes by."

"Okay, that's the next thing. What is up with Buck McGillis?"

"Mr. Faith Ridge? He's a bad man, Dr. Hofstetter. You stay clear of him."

Mary Beth looked at the suddenly gloomy young woman drinking her third beer far too fast. "How bad?"

"You heard the man. No one says no to Buck McGillis."

"I can't stay clear of him," she moaned. "He's the biggest client we have—he's like three-fourths of our entire business."

"He owns everything. He doesn't own the town proper, but Faith Ridge is like a bowl in the middle of a huge ranch. He owns most of the land around the town on this side of the White Sandy."

"Who owns the rest?"

"The Lakota tribe." The word Lakota came out strong and proud, the accent even thicker as she stressed the *ko*. "We used to own everything, a long time ago," Robin patiently explained. "The McGillis family has been chipping away at the edges of the reservation for decades, maybe longer."

"So why does Jacob work for a slime like him?"

"To keep a Lakota hand on the land. Did you know that Jacob is the grandson of a powerful chief?"

Mary Beth shot her a smarmy look. "You didn't tell me that until right now."

"Well, a Plenty Holes has been running this tribe for a long time. Jacob is the first to step away from the Council."

"Because of Buck? Why?"

"It's not a big secret, although I wouldn't say it to Buck's face if I were you." She winked. "Jacob's a smart fellow. Went to college, got one of them—oh, you know—masters in something business—"

"An MBA? He's got an MBA?" Indian perfection on a horse with an MBA. Almost too good to be true, she mused.

"Yeah," Robin slurred, the beer finally working on her tiny body. "An MBA. He probably figures if he can just outsmart ol' Buck there, he can steal the land back. He cut his hair and got hired. Worked up to manager real quick like too."

Mary Beth wondered what was more dangerous—outsmarting Buck or working for him. "Robin, why aren't you at college?"

"I wanna go. I really do. But Ronny needs me at the café. Our parents died a while back, and Randy and Ricky went off and married white chicks." Mary Beth winced, but Robin kept going. "They don't come back around much anymore, so it's like it's just me and Ronny. I really worry about the big lug."

"Robin," Mary Beth said, sounding a whole lot like her mother again, "you should go to college. If Jacob can do it, so can you."

She beamed, her eyes blinking at slightly different speeds. "You really think?"

Mary Beth nodded with an enthusiasm that was only a little forced. She knew next to nothing about Jacob Plenty Holes, and not a whole lot about the sloshing young woman sitting before her. But it was obvious that Robin wanted to go, and who was she not to help her?

"Well," she murmured into her beer, "I do have the forms for Sinte Gleska University."

It sounded tribal. Not Ivy League but then again, not everyone needed Ivy League in this world. "Perfect. I'll help you fill them out."

"Really?" Her eyes popped wide open in excitement. "You will?"

"Sure. That's what big-sister types do. We nag little-sister types until they do what we think they should."

"Deal." Robin grinned.

This was the Robin who had watched Jacob's show, humming in pleasure next to her. But there was that other Robin, the one who'd bolted in terror the moment Buck McGillis had showed up. "Robin," she asked the goofily grinning young woman, "why did you bring me dessert tonight?"

23

The grin died as she got up and got the last beer, swigging half of it before she sat back down. "No one says no to Buck McGillis," she said, her eyes scrunched up tight.

No one says no to Brian Greevy. The words slipped out of the small box in her mind where she kept them locked away, and she remembered the way he'd said it as he backhanded her. She'd been sixteen when she'd come home from a date to find Skeevy Greevy alone in the house, Mom out buying more beer for him. He'd pinned her down and hit her, but Mary Beth had refused to go down without a fight. She'd kneed him in the crotch and then done it again, just for good measure, before she'd gotten a kitchen knife and called 911.

She'd gotten rid of Skeevy Greevy. Mom had finally found the backbone to leave him after that. They'd bounced around for a while before Mom had gotten a job as a nurse and finally got her life back under control—all because Mary Beth had dared to say no to Skeevy Greevy.

Mary Beth had thought that she'd left all that behind her. But now? *Jesus, what the hell have I gotten myself into here?*

Robin was still sitting there, her eyes shut. Mary Beth's heart broke for her. Mary Beth might have fought her way out of a shitty situation, but Robin hadn't been able to. That much was clear. "Jacob came by to do the show and saw the bruises under the makeup. He's a smart fellow. You'll like him a lot," she repeated. "He figured what had happened, and since then he's kind of kept an eye on me. God, I wish he didn't look at me like I was his kid sister." She took another drink.

"Christ on a crutch, Robin, are you okay?"

"Sure. Just a few beers. No biggie," Robin said, answering the wrong question. "I don't have to work until eleven tomorrow. Say…" her eyes popped open, "… you want me to go get some more? Won't take me long at all."

"No, you're going home now," Mary Beth said as firmly as she could while she hoisted Robin up. "You need to sober up and get your college applications together, and I need to unpack." And figure out what the hell I'm going to do about this fine mess I landed in.

"I guess." Robin pouted. "Hey, you'll come to the show tomorrow, right?"

Despite the long-buried memories and Buck McGillis—despite the damn fine mess she'd walked into—Mary Beth couldn't help but smile. "I wouldn't miss the show for the world."

Chapter Three

Mary Beth spied the slightly stooped older man standing on the steps, his grey hair blending with the grey morning light. For a second, she hesitated but decided against carrying the knife in with her. Somehow, packing a blade didn't seem to be a part of making a good first impression, so she shoved it in the glove box and hopped out of the truck.

"Dr. Coleman?" she asked, although the answer was obvious.

"Dr. Hofstetter, so glad to meet you in person." He smiled as he held out his hand. While he looked a bit frail, his grip was still the grip of a man who held onto animals for a living. "Please, call me Bill. Did you like the house?"

Mary Beth thought back to the shag rug, lava lamp, and avocado-green appliances. "It's a little Brady Bunch, but otherwise, I love it, Bill. Perfect. Do I have you to thank for the groceries?"

"My wife wanted to make sure you were comfortable." Bill leaned in close, an impish grin on his face. "Leslie is looking forward to Florida this winter. Our son and his family are down outside of Tampa."

"I like what I've seen so far. I imagine that she'll get there before Christmas. And call me Mary Beth."

"Of course. Come in and meet Fran. She's my everything assistant."

A grumpy-looking older woman, her hair in a permanently curled helmet and her orthopedic shoes peeking out from behind a low desk, scowled when Mary Beth walked in. The scowl looked familiar, and Mary Beth realized that Fran had been at the show.

"Hello," Mary Beth said as she stuck out her hand. "I'm Mary Beth Hofstetter."

"I know that," Fran snipped as she stared at Mary Beth's hand. "You made quite a scene at the café last night. I told Bill all about it."

Whoa, unpleasant. Mary Beth winced as she pulled her hand back.

"Now, Fran, be generous. She didn't know who she was talking to."

"She does now," Fran snipped again as she answered the phone.

"Bill, I can explain," Mary Beth muttered as they headed back to his cramped office off the small operating room.

"No need." He motioned to an empty chair. "While Fran is a bit of a sourpuss, she's a darned good assistant. You'll be surprised how fair she is. She told me you handled yourself quite well."

"Well, if you call insulting the biggest client handling myself, then yeah, I handled myself well."

Bill gave her a kind smile. "You'll get the hang of it. Now, Fran does all the scheduling and secretarial stuff. She's in charge of billing, but you need to tell her what you did. She knows what we charge. Costs are different for cattle, horses and buffalo."

"Buffalo? We care for buffalo?"

27

"Didn't I mention that? The Lakota keep a small herd on the edge of their reservation. There's not a lot I can do for them—the buffalo aren't what you call tame, you know. But every now and then one gets wrapped in barbed wire or the like," he explained. "If they are properly sedated, it's just like working on a big, hairy cow."

Maybe Bill wasn't quite as sharp in his old age as his grip foretold. How could he forget to mention buffalo?

"Now," he continued as if buffalo were no big deal, "Friday is the small-animal day at the clinic. The one day of the week we see dogs and cats and the like. Can you handle ferrets?"

"In the plural?"

"Mike Nolan raises ferrets. Sells some for pets to stores in Rapid City. Ranchers like to have them in the barns too. I see a lot of ferrets."

Suddenly, she wished she'd taken that exotic pet class. But she was a large-animal vet. Who knew she'd need to know ferrets? "What do you do for a ferret?"

"A lot of neutering and de-scenting. I'll walk you through the operations. Not terribly complex. Mike does a good job raising them. Saturday I'm on call, but I only go to the office for emergencies. Mondays are at-large days. Everyone else's horses, any buffalo emergencies and the like. Tuesday, Wednesday and Thursday are at the McGillis ranch. Over 10,000 head of cattle."

Mary Beth whistled. "That should keep me out of trouble." For years to come.

"Actually, I spend more time with the ranch horses than the cattle. Jacob's got the skills to do almost

28

everything the cattle need, but the horses require a higher level of care. They get a lot of work, and we do a lot of preventative maintenance. Everyone's got horses out here. Best way to get around."

"I have no problem riding. But… about Buck." She hated the feeling of having opened her big mouth a bit too far. Even more, she hated how damn familiar that feeling was. Would she ever be able to keep quiet? "How badly did I stick my foot in it last night?"

"Seems pretty clear. He came onto you, you rebuffed him—what was it Fran said? 'I don't sleep with clients, I castrate calves'?"

"Yeah." She couldn't stop the blush that moved up. "Best I could do on short notice."

"It's a good stance. Men outnumber women five to one in this town."

"But he's our biggest client, and I insulted him."

"Well, yes," he chuckled, "I'd not do that a whole lot more, but frankly, I rarely deal with him. Haven't much for the last seven, eight years. He spends most of the day either holed up in his house with some shady lawyer or riding the boundary of his property. Jacob Plenty Holes basically runs the place."

Mary Beth blushed again.

"Fran said you met him as well." Bill smiled, looking just like a grandfather should.

"It is a small town, Bill."

"His land management is a step up from McGillis's last guy too. That dope was grazing the place flat, but Jacob keeps the fields irrigated and rotates the herd. We use a lot less wormers now. It keeps the parasites manageable."

"So he really is smart," she marveled before she

shut her mouth. *You sound like a smitten teenager*, her brain scolded her.

His eyes wisely smiling, Bill replied, "He keeps better books too. He pays on a monthly basis," he added. "The McGillis check on the thirtieth, and Jacob's check is on the fifteenth. After we get those, we pay bills, put some aside for Fran's weekly paycheck and order the next round of supplies."

She was missing something, she just knew it. "His check?"

"Jacob is quite a businessman," he said, the admiration undisguised. "He breeds mustangs for rodeos. Pays McGillis for some of the land, keeps the rest on the tribe's land next to the ranch. His horses are as tough as nails and quick too. The Lakota are big horse people."

Mary Beth's mouth opened—force of habit—but for once, nothing came out. She was having a little trouble reconciling the man in the mask and the ratty T-shirt and the holey jeans with someone who had an MBA and ran a horse-breeding business on the side. Again, she was struck by the thought that he was hiding. Not necessarily from her—she'd barely met him—but from someone. Or something.

"It's a small town. Everyone knows everything about everyone." Bill sighed, picking up a picture of him and what had to be his wife a good twenty years ago. "Leslie's looking forward to Tampa. Says no one will know who we are. I have trouble imagining that, though."

A perfect opening to talk about something other than the fool she'd made of herself last night. "When are you leaving?"

"Two weeks before Christmas, if we can get everything squared away."

"It's seven thirty!" Fran screeched from the front.

"Going!" Bill hollered back. "Come on. It's a ranch day. I'll show you around."

By the time Bill drove through the formidable stone gate with the name *McGillis* worked in iron at the top, Mary Beth knew the names, birthdays and favorite toys of all seven of his grandchildren. Clearly, Leslie wasn't the only one excited about Tampa.

Bill pulled up in front of a large barn abutted against several huge lots. Jacob Plenty Holes stood against the barn door, his paint horse drop-tethered next to him, and two other horses tied to the fence nearby.

Perfection next to a horse. He looked every inch the cowboy he was, his hat pulled down low to shade his eye, one boot kicked back and resting on the door, thumbs stuck in his belt loops. The only difference was that instead of a six-shooter, there was a knife that had to be close to nine inches long tied to his leg.

Her thoughts spun as they walked up to him. *At least he's dressed this time*. The maroon flannel shirt was cuffed up to his elbows, revealing muscular forearms tanned from long hours in the sun. At the sound of their footsteps on the gravel, he slowly lifted his head, his eye trained on her the whole way up.

The mask seemed bigger now, but Mary Beth reasoned that it was just because she was really looking. There were three straps holding it to his face—one where it began at the left temple, one that continued the diagonal back under his right ear and

31

another strap that went just below his right eye and over his right ear. He didn't need a whole lot of help to look rugged and mysterious, but the mask sealed the deal.

I wonder what a man with no face looks like. I wonder if he's wearing underwear. I wonder if he knows I'm picturing him naked. Her thoughts cascaded as he spoke.

"Morning, Bill, Dr. Hofstetter," he said coolly as he tipped his hat towards her.

"Morning, Jacob."

"Please," she added, trying not to think of his underwear status. "Call me Mary Beth."

"Where's your knife?" he demanded.

That shook her brain firmly back to reality. "What?"

Jacob angrily cocked his eyebrow as Bill chuckled. "Your knife. You should have one."

"I didn't tell her she needed one on the first day, Jacob. I imagine she's just going to get the lay of the land."

Jacob pursed his mouth into a narrow line, his long face growing harder. There wasn't a whole lot of his face visible, but the parts she could see said nothing but barely contained anger. "You should have one."

"I do," she defended. "I just left it in my truck."

Glaring at both of them, he undid the ties at his thigh in one quick gesture. "Wear mine."

"Now, Jacob," Bill scolded.

"No, she needs one. McGillis isn't the only jerk around here. You know some of those guys he hired are barely better than thugs. Someone as beautiful and delicate as she is?" Jacob scowled at Bill, completely ignoring the high scarlet blush that swamped Mary Beth.

Holy cow, that may be the best line I've ever heard—even if he didn't say it to me. Her brain swooned.

"She's got to draw the line in the sand early before any of Buck's knuckleheads get the wrong idea," Jacob continued.

"You sound like my father," she snipped as she grabbed the blade from him. God bless her mouth. It always covered for her, and she had the feeling that it was going to be doing a lot more of that today. Even if she didn't exactly remember what her father sounded like, Jacob was being more patronizing than her uncle Hank had ever been.

His knife was a lot heavier than hers, with a beefy handle she could barely wrap her hand around. She nearly dropped it as she tried to fit it along her leg.

"I'll do it," he grumbled, kneeling before her. Aside from the *beautiful* comment, he showed absolutely no awareness that she was particularly female in any aspect. It was almost like he was mad that she'd shown up.

Mary Beth held her breath as he completely encircled her thigh with his fingers, drawing the rawhide cord between her legs. But for a man who seemed as gruff as he did, Jacob's touch was surprisingly gentle, like he was used to handling fragile things. The mere thought made Mary Beth start sweating as he pulled the cord taut.

He stood and stepped back just as three cowboys emerged from the side of the barn. "Whooee! Looks like Doc Coleman brought us a present," the tall one with red hair whooped. The two other cowboys hung back, already looking uncomfortable as the redhead winked and blew a kiss to Mary Beth.

Ugh, she mentally recoiled. This would have to be one of Buck's knuckleheads, for no honest cowboy would talk to a woman like that. Mary Beth had spent a long time on farms and ranches, and not once had any man ever treated her like a party favor. The most she normally got out of a cowboy was *ma'am*. At least the other two hands looked like they were watching a car wreck.

Jacob shot her a look before he turned to the men. But before he could open his mouth, Mary Beth asked loudly, "Dr. Coleman, are those the ones?"

"The ones?" Bill asked, eyeing her warily.

Jacob pivoted back towards her, the look of amusement she'd briefly caught last night outside the café dancing at the edge of his mouth. "The ones?"

"Yeah." Mary Beth nodded, taking a step in the direction of the confused cowboys. *Don't drop it*, she thought as she unsheathed the knife. "The ones you wanted castrated this morning. You said you needed to fix a couple of animals. They fit the bill."

All three cowboys froze. The one who looked Native turned beet-red as the other white man took a panicked step back. Mary Beth could see they weren't the problem. Not Buck's knuckleheads, and she felt bad for grouping them with the redhead.

She didn't feel bad for the redhead. The blood drained from his face as his eyes shot wide with a real fear. "You're the new vet?" He seemed to shrink before Mary Beth's eyes.

She slid the knife back in the sheath, amazed her shaking hand hadn't dropped the heavy blade. "Dr. Hofstetter, gentlemen." She quickly crossed the distance between them, firmly shaking their hands as she glowered at them. "I look forward to your cooperation."

The Indian almost smiled as the other two quickly scurried back to the barn. "Jacob, *awánin'iglaka yo*," he said over her head as he turned and disappeared behind his cohorts.

"*Níš-eyá tanyán awánin'iglaka yo*, Tommy," Jacob shouted back.

"Wait, what?" she asked as Jacob led the palomino over to her. She saw that Bill had slung a pair of huge nylon saddlebags over both horses. "What did he say? What did you say?" Mary Beth stiffly mounted up, hoping she wouldn't stab herself in the leg doing so.

"It's Lakota, our language," he said as he led their group away from the barn. "Tommy Yellow Robe's an old buddy of mine. You should castrate him last. Definitely do Paul—the redhead—first. He could use the rest." She thought she saw the corners of his mouth curve up, a definitive crack in his frozen demeanor. "You're riding Jezebel there."

"You gave me a horse named *Jezebel*?" So much for that line in the sand.

The terrain changed and they headed down a steep gully. Bill trailed behind them. If she kept her eyes pointed forward, she could pretend she was alone with the masked cowboy. On a horse named Jezebel. Had he done that on purpose? "Where are we going? And what did Tommy say again?"

She could see Jacob's shoulders shaking with glee. Not always stone-faced, she thought.

"You've got some mouth on you. Do you always threaten to castrate people?"

Mary Beth rolled her eyes at his back. "Only the ones who need it," she replied. Both men chuckled.

"We'll be there in a bit. Bill's convinced me to move to electronic tagging instead of branding," he called back as they forded a trickle of a stream.

Tagging. Mary Beth felt some tension ebb out of her shoulders. She'd been helping tag cattle for years on her Uncle Hank's farm. Those summers out on the farm—and away from whatever jerk Mom was dating—had saved her. She shuddered to think of where she'd be if she hadn't had those months of freedom and safety. "My uncle never had the stomach for branding," she absent-mindedly said to herself.

"What?"

"Oh, nothing. Tagging is good. Like accessorizing cows with earrings."

Jacob twisted in his saddle, shooting her the oddest look. *Yeah*, she nodded. *Probably not a man who accessorizes much.*

There was a break in the forest before them, and suddenly Jacob's paint shot forward.

"Hey!" she called out, but Bill clucked behind her.

"He's just going to let the hands know we're here," he cautioned. "You think you can handle tagging and vaccinating?"

"Been doing it for years, Bill. I told you that on the phone," she reminded him, a bit irritated that he would question her skills within earshot of the cowboys.

"Oh, that's right."

The horses walked into a meadow tall with prairie grass. Ringed with ancient pine forests and a small pond in the center, the meadow probably looked as it had for hundreds of years.

Beautiful. Mary Beth tried to take it all in without looking like a tourist. *Just beautiful.*

Jacob came racing back towards them, expertly pulling up just before his horse crashed into Jezebel. When the dust settled, he was sitting there almost grinning at her, his horse perfectly parallel to hers.

"Jesus, Jacob!" she hissed even as the girly part of her brain realized he was showing off.

"Come on," he said with his eyebrow arched in challenge. "We've got four hundred head to do today."

Almost three times the number she'd done at home with Uncle Hank. Jesus, this was a lot. Knucklehead cowboys, Buck McGillis, a cowboy in a mask *and* that many cattle, plus random things like ferrets and albinos.

But then she saw the four cowboys standing around waiting for her and Bill to get started. If four hundred head was what it took to prove herself, then she'd do four hundred head. In one day. And she'd do it with a smile.

Of course, smiling was easier said than done when a girl had cows stepping on her, cows pooping on her, cows head-butting her. And with the cowboys wrangling the next cow before she'd had the chance to catch her breath? The morning passed in an unending swirl of mooing, fur and hooves.

What few moments she did get were filled with an odd silence. Usually, ranchers joked and talked—

anything to pass the day a little faster. Not this lot. Aside from the occasional heads-up or shout when a cow broke loose, they worked in near silence. It was such a foreign thing that Mary Beth found herself wondering how much of it was her fault. She'd promised to castrate at least three of those present. She had to stop doing that. Or, at the very least, come up with a better defense.

Every time she looked up, she saw Jacob. She only caught him watching her a few times—maybe three, total. Half the time, his mask was the only part of his face she could see. But even then, something about the way he moved… it was like every part of his body was keyed onto her movements. No matter where he was, she *felt* his presence.

Or maybe that was just the lingering sensation of his hands on her thighs. That was always possible too.

Uncharted territory. That's what Robin had said, and Mary Beth could see what she meant. The hired hands didn't show many signs of familiarity. In fact, the only thing she'd heard to signal that he even talked with other humans was the conversation he'd had in Lakota with Tommy. Otherwise? It was as if he existed on a separate plane from the rest of the mere mortals. It wasn't that no one dared to challenge him, although she doubted anyone would. It was that no one dared even *look* to him.

At one point, a calf broke loose from Paul, the redhead cowboy. She lunged and wrestled it to the ground. The next thing she knew, Jacob was next to her, holding onto the calf.

"Can you handle this?" he asked. His voice was quiet, so Mary Beth doubted anyone else could hear him.

Still, she bristled. She was not about to stand for having her abilities questioned, no matter how intimidating Jacob could be. "I've got him—or did you miss the part where I caught him all by my little ol' self?"

He stared at her—actually stared—for a three-count, and in that moment of eye contact, Mary Beth saw the mask slip. Not the physical leather mask, but the front that made him so unknowable. He gave her a look that could have been amused or could have been something else—something *interested*.

Heat flared between them. This *was* interest—it had to be. Hell, yes, she was interested.

But then Paul was apologizing for losing the calf and Bill asked Mary Beth to look at something and the calf kicked. The moment was gone.

She couldn't be sure it'd been there at all.

Jacob let his mind wander as his paint, Mick, followed the familiar route down to the town.

What on earth was he going to do about Dr. Mary Beth Hofstetter?

He'd known from the moment he laid eyes on her she was trouble, and it had taken all of five minutes to prove that suspicion right.

Like he didn't have enough with Buck McGillis to worry about. Had to go add Dr. Mary Beth Hofstetter to the mix.

Didn't help that she was beautiful. It would have been so much easier if she'd been the size of an ox and twice as ugly.

But no. Her light-brown hair falling in natural waves around her perfectly curved shoulders, her gray-blue eyes flashing as that mouth of hers—oh, Lord, that mouth the color of barely ripe strawberries—cut a swath of destruction through every man who even looked at her funny.

And to top it all off, she knew what she was doing. Lying awake in bed last night, long after Kip's even breathing gently filled their tiny, ancient trailer, he'd hoped that maybe she wouldn't be able to cut it and would bail after a week. Hell, most people would have bailed after Buck threatened them.

Not her. She'd handled those cows like she'd been doing it her whole life, because she probably had. She may be delicate looking, her long fingers awkwardly wrapped around his knife handle, but she was plenty strong. When that calf had broken loose from Paul, she'd grabbed it before Tommy could even move and wrestled it to the ground, bare handed—better than most of the kids did at the rodeos.

He had to give her credit. Her little introduction to Paul had been quite effective. No one had probably ever threatened to castrate him before.

All in all, she was hell on horseback.

Mick paused just outside the first house, and Jacob stripped his shirt off and shoved it into the far saddlebag. Sue, Kip's retired Mustang, shifted nervously as she waited to finish the trip down and get her rider.

"Calm down, Sue," he scolded as he picked up Mick's reins. "We'll get her soon enough."

Finally, after a long breath, he gently squeezed Mick's side. "Showtime," he muttered to himself, unable to stop from wondering if she'd be there or not. She wouldn't have had a lot of time, he thought. Maybe she won't make it.

He rounded the corner, trying to pinpoint her at the café, but at this distance it wasn't easy. It wasn't until he was past the first house that his depth perception kicked in and he could gauge where the café was. After a few moments, everything came into sharp focus and he saw her.

Her hair, still wet from the shower she must have raced to get in, hung in dark damp waves, pulling in the fading light until she practically glowed. As he got closer though, he couldn't help but notice her face. Her lips were glistening in the evening sun.

She'd put on lipstick.

Jacob sat up a bit straighter in the saddle as Fran caught his eye and shook her head in warning.

Good old Fran. Ugly as a tumbleweed and twice as prickly. Why couldn't Bill have hired someone like that—someone he didn't have to protect, who didn't remind him of what he'd lost—someone instead of Dr. Mary Beth Hofstetter?

Tonight, he only undid the top button. He could tell by the way Robin's eyes were shooting between him and Mary Beth that she'd told the new vet all about the show, and he wasn't about to set that tongue wagging again.

Besides, it had been idiotic to undo the second one yesterday, even if it had been worth it to see every single jaw drop.

She was *tough*. She met his gaze as he undid his pants, her eyes never dipping below his face.

Oh, hell—was she staring at the mask?

He almost undid the second button just to make her look away.

Thankfully, as he put his hat back on, she finally shifted those eyes that weren't quite grey and weren't quite blue back to Robin, breaking his panic. He forced himself to take a deep breath.

"He been by?" he asked as the sexual tension melted from the content women. This was the only time he'd ever seen Fran without a frown, even if it did feel like he was stripping for grandmothers. But the café kept Ronny clean and Robin out of trouble. He'd do anything for the Benge family, after all those years they'd taken pains to make him part of their family. Including show off for little old ladies.

And now, Dr. Mary Beth Hofstetter.

"He drove by about twenty minutes ago," Robin replied, visibly relieved as her gaze danced down to his pants and back up.

Ignoring the unspoken button question, Jacob somberly nodded to Mary Beth. "He must have found out she threatened to castrate Paul, Benny and Tommy today and decided not to push his luck."

"Jeez, Jacob, do you have to spread it around?" Jacob had to bite his inner lip to keep from laughing at Mary Beth's self-induced fluster. Then he noticed the warm blush spreading across her face, giving her a heated glow that melted his amusement into something deeper, and he remembered that he'd actually said *delicate* and *beautiful* out loud. In front of her.

In a split second, he resolved to keep his mouth shut from here on out. Shouldn't be too hard. She was just a white woman.

"Yeah, I heard," Robin replied with a wink, calling him back to his present reality.

"From who?" Mary Beth demanded, the blush creeping down her neck and towards the ivory tank top with the dangerously scooped neck.

42

Where the hell was Mrs. Browne?

"Paul called you a ball-buster at the two-beer mark," Robin giggled.

"Line in the sand," Jacob said as he actually grinned, immediately forgetting his self-imposed moratorium. When was the last time he'd actually grinned at someone? A real, honest-to-God grin, not the fake one he pulled out for Ladies' Hour?

Had to be at least three years.

"Thanks for the knife, by the way. Made a big impact." When her gaze met his, something changed about her that took her from embarrassed to smoldering, like she was some sort of angel or something.

He opened his mouth to make a *small* comment, but before he could form the words, a voice from across the street cut him off.

"Jacob? We're ready."

Oh, thank God. Mrs. Browne was finally going to save him from himself. Jacob felt his grin die as he pivoted. Within seconds, he was holding Kip's hand.

"How was she today?"

Mrs. Browne—unchanged after all these years except for the gray hairs—smiled gently as she shook her head. "The same, Jacob. Always the same." Mrs. Browne tenderly patted Kip's head. "Have you thought any more about what I said? If you took her to Rapid City…"

"I can't just up and move, Mrs. Browne."

The frown moved the corners of her mouth. "Sooner or later, Jacob, you'll need to do something about her, or when she gets to high school…"

Jacob fought the urge to roll his eye. They had

this same conversation every day. Mrs. Browne had taught every student in this valley for the last thirty-five years, but Kip was something out of her realm of expertise, and she made no secret of it. Almost a year ago, she'd come to Jacob with information on a specialized school for autistic children in Rapid City, convinced that Kip could get the care she needed there.

The only problem with that plan was that Kip wasn't autistic.

Jacob nodded as she repeated the benefits of the school—again. He appreciated Mrs. Browne's concern, but there was no way he was leaving the land to McGillis.

No way.

"We'll see you tomorrow," he finally said, interrupting the kind old teacher.

Mrs. Browne sighed in frustration as she patted Kip's head once more. "Tomorrow we'll start on *Stormy*, okay, Kip?"

"Thanks again." Jacob smiled as he turned back to the patiently waiting horses.

And into the questioning gaze of Dr. Mary Beth Hofstetter.

She looked at Kip differently than most people did. Most people just stared at the pair they made, as if they weren't sure which was weirder—the guy with a mask or the albino kid.

But Mary Beth—she leaned over the table like she was trying to catch Kip's eye. Like she was looking past the whiteness and trying to see the girl underneath, when Jacob had done everything he could think of to hide that girl underneath.

It was almost as unsettling as knowing she was looking at his mask.

Quickly, he hefted Kip onto Sue and mounted up himself. In his haste to get away from Dr. Mary Beth Hofstetter, he forgot to tip his hat to the ladies as he urged Mick into a fast trot.

"Hold on, Kip," he muttered back to the girl as she loosely hung onto Sue's mane. "We've got to go."

Mary Beth carefully studied the masked cowboy and the albino girl as they trotted off down the street. Jacob fascinated her, no doubt, but Kip—Kip was another matter entirely. Aside from the oddity of an albino in the flesh, there was something about her that almost called out to Mary Beth.

Kip reminded Mary Beth of the wounded baby bunny she'd saved from a coyote when she was about nine. The poor thing didn't make it, but she'd kept it alive in a shoebox Granny had stuffed with a tea towel for a day. It'd been afraid to move.

Kip looked like a wounded bunny, terrified and hurt, and all Mary Beth wanted to do was wrap her up and keep her safe.

She couldn't shake the feeling that Kip needed her, not after Kip and Jacob disappeared down the street, not after she walked home and not after she turned out the lava lamp that was her nightlight.

Something was going on in Faith Ridge, and she had the feeling she was going to find out what it was, one way or the other.

Chapter Four

The routine was easy to pick up. Fridays were the easy day of office visits with dogs that had gotten into the garbage and cats that had gotten into fights. Mike Nolan showed up regularly with an ever-increasing number of ferrets, but Bill gave her several books on ferret care to study. It really wasn't too hard to pick up. Her first attempt at a ferret neutering was a complete success.

The ranch days were more of a challenge. While Jacob showed flashes of playfulness during the show, tentatively flirting with her and Robin at the same time, on the ranch he was all business. And the more of his hired hands that were around, the colder he got towards her. Some days, the most she heard out of any of them was "Ma'am," from Tommy Yellow Robe, always accompanied by a tip of his cowboy hat. Jacob seemed to scowl when his friend said it, but he never did or said anything about it.

Line in the sand, Mary Beth had to keep reminding herself. But somehow, that didn't stop her from slipping on the slinky bras and barely there panties underneath her cowgirl flannels and work jeans on the days she was due at the ranch.

After she'd proven herself with the tagging on the

first day, Bill was more and more content to send her out there alone. First it was one day a week, then two, then all three. Bill was only making the trip to the ranch once or twice a month as summer peaked to help when they had a large number of cows to preg-check.

She spent a lot more time working on the horses when she was by herself. A few cowboys apparently didn't know how to cool an animal down. They nearly lost a stunning quarter horse to colic when a cowboy let the horse eat sand, but Jacob managed to keep the animal on its feet until Mary Beth got the tube threaded up its nose and its gut cleared.

Jacob fired the cowboy who'd let the horse eat sand. "I told you, knuckleheads," he muttered as Tommy Yellow Robe escorted the cussing ex-cowboy off the ranch.

"Not all of them," she replied, looking him dead in the eye.

"You'd be surprised," he responded, his face still.

That's how it was. When they were on the ranch, around the hands, he was unreadable, the epitome of the strong, silent cowboy. At the café, Mary Beth saw about three minutes where he showed hints of being a regular guy—except for the mask—interested in regular-guy things like the opposite sex and food. But as soon as Mrs. Browne called his name, the regular guy disappeared again, and he got as unreadable as Kip.

Mary Beth wanted to know more about the mysterious girl, but she sensed that Jacob might take any approach as a threat, and the way he handled his knife on the ranch made it clear that any threat would be quickly dispatched. So she kept her distance, trying to figure out Jacob on the ranch and Kip from her table at the café.

47

Aside from Jacob's cold work demeanor, the ranch days were pretty much what she'd hoped they'd be. She never saw Buck, although she kept an eye out for him at all times. But the horses and cows kept her busy.

The ranch horses—sturdy, efficient, trained animals—did indeed need a lot of maintenance, and Mary Beth enjoyed working on them. But she was itching to see the mustangs Bill had told her about. Finally, one Thursday after they'd spent the morning on the ranch horses, Jacob saddled up Jezebel and pointed the horses away from the normal trail to the pastures.

"Where are we going?" she finally asked after about two miles had melted behind them.

"Mustangs," he replied without looking back.

Undeterred by the gruff reply, she kept going. "Bill said you were quite the businessman." She marveled as they rode past a young Lakota riding bareback. It almost looked like he was guarding the place.

"We aren't ignorant savages, you know," he scoffed, a trace of irritated emotion creeping past the cold exterior.

She glared at the side of his face, but he didn't see it. "Never even crossed my mind."

The mustang—a spectacular young stallion named Tahalo—had all the classic symptoms of bowed tendons, but it wasn't advanced. "Okay. No biggie," Mary Beth soothed the jittery animal while she looked at the immaculate barn. "I'll inject dextrose, an irritant solution, compounded with lidocaine. That will restart the healing process."

"A solution? Bill used to pin-fire them."

"I think we've moved beyond hot metal spikes, don't you?" she snipped. "If this doesn't work, I can split the tendons, but that's major surgery, and he's not far gone. This should work, as long as you wrap him properly and slowly reintroduce him to exercise. It may be a year before he can do barrels again." She couldn't help herself. Trying not to smirk, she added, "You can still stud him. He won't have any problems."

Jacob actually blushed but was saved by another young man walking past the stall, his long hair gathered into a loose tail that flowed halfway down his back and a nose that looked like he'd stolen it directly from an eagle.

"*Wanhínmayaya hwo?*" he asked Jacob, his eyes barely flitting to Mary Beth.

It seemed like half of these Lakota guys never even looked at her. Mary Beth hadn't decided if it was because she was a woman or if she was white, but either way, it was starting to get on her nerves. And every guy she'd seen around here looked like he was barely 18. Invisible and ancient, she grumbled silently. And dumb. It was really starting to grate when they all talked about her in Lakota, no matter how beautiful the language was.

"*Hiyá, Dave, tanyán naúnninpe ló,*" Jacob replied, and with a tilt of his head, the young man was gone.

Mary Beth shot Jacob a sharp look, her hands on her hips.

"I hire the young ones for the horses," he said simply in response. "Tommy started out here. That was Dave. One of the best. He helps run the local rodeo."

"You train the new guys on the mustangs instead of the cows?" she asked incredulously.

"Horses are a part of the tribe." He began to caress the stallion's nose with long, even strokes.

Mary Beth watched his careful hands running over the fur with a steady, even pressure as he continued, "Cattle aren't. I only take on the ones who are capable of understanding the old ways."

That snapped her attention away from his powerful hands. She bent over to ready the syringe and decided to ask what the old ways were, but as she stood, she saw that Jacob had Tahalo in a near trance.

"We need to tie him so I can do the injections," she said quietly, afraid to break the daze Jacob had cast.

"No, we don't," he replied. "Just be calm."

"Are you sure?"

He nodded as he began to whisper in Lakota in the horse's ear.

Hesitantly, Mary Beth knelt beside the animal. Horses didn't like this because it hurt. She couldn't blame them—who did like needles under tendons?—but *not* having the horse tied was an invitation to being squished by a one-ton animal in pain.

"Okay," she muttered to herself, preparing to jump out of the way when the stallion reared. But as the needle sank deep, the horse didn't move. His muscles barely even twitched as she completed the series of shots that normally sent horses into spasms of panic.

When she stood, Jacob's eye was trained on her while he continued to stroke the animal's face. His black-blue eye looked deep into hers as his fingers steadily rubbed the horse's fur. Mary Beth froze, feeling as paralyzed by his gaze as the horse had been by his touch, and suddenly aware of her frilly green and pink panties.

"Are you done?" his voice was low and quiet, seeming to vibrate not from his mouth but directly out of his chest. She could barely nod as he held her captive with his power. "Then get out of the way."

The order broke the spell he had her under. She gathered her bag and quickly moved out of the stall.

In an instant, Jacob was beside her. A second later, Tahalo sprang back to life, whinnying and shaking as the pain suddenly hit him.

"What just happened here?" Mary Beth asked. "Are you some sort of horse whisperer or something?"

Dave walked back through leading a colt. "*Yuš'ínyeyaya hwo*?" he demanded, his eyes laughing.

"*Kitányela.* Dave, *Thahálo awányanka yo*," he said as he picked up Mary Beth's packs and walked out to Jezebel.

"Okay, can I tell you how much it irritates the hell out of me when you do that?"

"Do what?" he asked, his eye laughing at her.

"When you and all your friends talk about me in Lakota. I'm going to start cussing in Arabic every time you do it."

That pulled him up short. "You cuss in Arabic?"

Mary Beth stuck her chest out a bit. "Quite well, too."

He stared at her for a moment, but she didn't flinch.

"Okay, I'll bite." He slung his leg over his horse. "Why does a white woman like you know how to cuss in Arabic?"

"It's complicated," she easily parried, mounting Jezebel.

Jacob looked out over the grassland they had to wind their way back through. "I've got about half an hour."

"Oh, sure, I tell you and the whole town knows it."

"I promise. I won't talk."

"Not to Tommy?"

"Not even to Tommy." He sat back in the saddle, patiently waiting.

She knew he wouldn't. If only because of the mystery that surrounded Kip, she knew he'd keep her secrets just because she asked him. Everything about Jacob Plenty Holes said he was a man of his word. "My cousin, Annie, is Iraqi. My uncle married an Iraqi woman during the Gulf war—the first one and then couldn't get them out when he left. He couldn't find them for a long time, then she showed up at our farm about twenty years ago, after her mom died."

"Now that I wouldn't have guessed," he said, sounding sympathetic.

"She got her citizenship and married a neighbor guy from up the road. They've got three kids running around the farm, just like I used to do. She's my best friend."

Jacob turned to look her up and down again. "Not that complicated."

"Try living it," she snorted. "It was very complicated for a long time. Only took a few years for some people to stop referring to her as a terrorist."

Jacob was silent, and Mary Beth realized that perhaps she'd overstepped her bounds. The rumors of his life indicated that, whatever the truth was, his life was far more complicated than hers had ever been.

"Okay," she said lightly. "Your turn."

"My turn what?"

"*Quid pro quo*. I tell you something no one else in town knows, and you tell me something no one else knows."

"This isn't *Silence of the Lambs*, you know."

"One thing. That's all I'm asking."

"Fine," he grumbled, his face unreadable behind that mask. "You can ask one thing."

"What happened to your face? You didn't really get into a brawl, did you?"

"That was two," he said, his voice short and clipped.

"Well?" she demanded.

"What?"

"Aren't you going to answer me?"

Slowly, he pivoted his head as he stared at her, his eye hard and dangerous. Mary Beth shrank back from the barely buried rage that churned beneath his calm exterior. "I said you could ask. I didn't say I'd answer," he replied before he kicked Mick into a full gallop across the plains.

"*Ya khara*," she muttered as she raced to keep up with him.

Jacob could hear her cussing behind him. At least he assumed she was cussing. He didn't recognize what she said, but her tone made it clear that, whatever she'd just called him, it wasn't flattering.

Up in front of her, where she couldn't see him, he let his face crack into a smile. Damned if he wasn't almost having fun. Yeah, he should have tied Tahalo. It was risky, bordering on stupid, not to. And Jacob never took stupid risks. Calculated risks, yes. His whole life these days was a calculated risk. But stupid?

Why hadn't he tied the horse?

Probably had something to do with the way the vet—the vet who did *not* sleep with clients—had

53

looked up at him, her eyes wide with a sense of wonder. She'd been impressed. With him.

In the last three years, he'd scared a few people, intimidated more than a few and made a whole bunch of ladies swoon when he rode around without a shirt.

But this was different. She hadn't been impressed with his muscles—not just then anyway. It wasn't what he looked like. It was what he did.

What was more, she'd trusted him. She could have demanded he tie the horse up—threatened to castrate him if he didn't. But she hadn't. She'd taken him at his word. No second guessing, no suspicion. Just faith that he knew what he was doing.

He knew he should be worried about this—about her. But right now, he felt good. Today was a good day.

Or at least it was until he broke through the trees that surrounded the barn. When he saw the cop car parked next to a corral, anything good about the day disappeared. The law, such as it was around these parts, didn't venture out to Buck's personal fiefdom without a damn good reason.

Jacob scanned the rest of the property. It was late in the afternoon. The rest of the hired hands were already drinking their day's wages at Ronny's or headed home to their families. The show wouldn't start for another hour, maybe. Buck's mansion was dark. The land seemed quiet.

Except for the cop who got out of his cruiser when he saw Jacob and Mary Beth coming.

"Who's that?" Mary Beth had spotted him now too. For once though, she didn't sound full of the normal bravado. If anything, she sounded nervous.

For some unexplained reason, Jacob felt the pull to protect her. Which was ridiculous considering who was waiting for them.

By now, they were within earshot of the cruiser. "Afternoon, Jacob."

Jacob waited until he and Mary Beth were on the ground before he did the introductions. "Sheriff, this is the new vet, Mary Beth Hofstetter. Doc, this is Sheriff Tim Means from the White Sandy rez."

"Nice to meet you." Whatever uncertainty Jacob had heard on horseback was gone, buried beneath her usual take-no-prisoners attitude. She gave Tim's hand a hell of a firm shake.

"Likewise." Tim shot Jacob an amused look over Mary Beth's head—he had a good foot on her. But then he got serious. "We need to talk."

Damn, but Jacob hated that statement. Tim had been out here several times over the years. It was never a social call. He'd arrested a few cowboys for a few violent crimes, questioned a few others. Tim was a good cop, something that earned him a fair amount of suspicion. Jacob knew the feeling, even if he didn't entirely trust the man himself.

As always, every time Tim popped up, Jacob's thoughts turned to Kip. Was she okay or had something happened to her? Had Tim caught wind of a new clue? Or—and this was the worst thought of all— had he come to tell Jacob that he was taking the girl away?

"In private," Tim added, dismissing Mary Beth.

The effect was immediate. Mary Beth's eyes narrowed as she looked at Jacob. What, did she think he was going to ask her to stay? Not happening.

"Well. Nice to meet you." Her acid tone made it clear that she thought it was anything but. At least she hadn't threatened to castrate him, right?

She shot Jacob a look that could melt metal before taking Jezebel's reins and leading the horse into the barn.

"I can get her," Jacob called after her.

"She needs to be rubbed down. You're busy," came the short reply, which was closely followed by that phrase again, "*Ya khara.*"

It was an odd feeling, knowing he'd done something to offend her and not being sure what else he could have done. Hell, it was an odd-enough feeling knowing that he'd just offended her. He couldn't remember the last time he'd cared if he'd pissed someone off or not.

Tim followed him into the small front room that served as his office. Wasn't much—four feet wide by six feet long, a narrow desk shoved up against the window, a filing cabinet in one corner, hay and sawdust on the floor. Barely enough room to get the door closed behind Tim, but Jacob sat in his chair and slid over until his back hit the filing cabinet. Tim got the door shut with inches to spare. "Problem?"

"Problem," Tim agreed. "When was the last time you were on the rez?"

"Can't recall." A look of disappointment flitted across Tim's face, like he expected better of Jacob. Well, he could shove his *better*. Jacob was busy. "Months, maybe."

A tense silence stretched between them. "You heard about what happened a few weeks ago?"

"Nope."

"Mass food poisoning. Church picnic at St. Francis and everyone who had the beef got sicker than a dog."

The St. Francis Catholic Church and School was on the south side of the rez, a ways away from Faith Ridge. "Anyone die?"

Tim shook his head no. "Got a new lady doctor out there, she figured out what it was and got it nipped in the bud."

Something wasn't right. Why would the law be here for a case of bad burger? "So?"

Tim didn't respond immediately. Instead, he checked out his nails and looked out the window. As if he could make Jacob sweat. "Doesn't Buck McGillis have the contract on providing beef to the church?"

Jacob switched on the computer and called up the file. "Yeah." And then, as much as he hated to defend Buck, he added, "But that doesn't prove anything."

"This was on the scale that the Bureau of Indian Affairs is getting involved. They'll have warrants, so be ready for them."

Now it was Jacob's turn to let the silence stretch. No love lost between Tim and Buck. Just because Robin Benge had never pressed charges against Buck didn't mean that Tim didn't know about it. But prosecuting a white man for raping a Native woman was damn-near impossible. Tim seemed to know about everything that happened on or near the rez, with the exception of the murder of Fred and Susan Two Elks.

The problem was no one ever pressed charges against Buck. Tim kept hoping he'd get his breakthough, just like Jacob did.

A break like supplying contaminated beef to a

church? He checked his records again. "We sent two cows to the butcher. Everything's in order on our end."

Tim didn't say anything. Jacob got the distinct feeling there was something else. "What?"

"What if the problem wasn't on your end?"

"What do you mean?"

"Someone saw something. Said it was in a field near the White Sandy, halfway between here and, well…" Tim paused, looking uncharacteristically unsure of himself. "Well, honestly, I don't know where."

"This *someone* didn't tell you where?"

"Only that he saw some people slaughtering some cattle in the middle of the night, in the middle of a field, in the middle of nowhere. And they were armed."

Suddenly, Jacob had a good idea who the unnamed witness was. "Was this *someone* able to identify Buck?"

"No. Just that he'd caught them doing it twice. And that he lost a couple of horses—whatever happened in the fields appears to have contaminated the grass."

Nobody Bodine—that had to be who Tim was talking about. And if Nobody was actually talking to Tim? Nobody was a menace to society. True, a menace who was good with horses, but that didn't change the fact that Nobody was a convicted killer. Tim had been the one to arrest him for that fatal brawl in the bar. If those two were actually working together on something… "How bad was it?"

Tim paused, looking tired. "It hit the kids real hard. We almost lost a few of the little ones."

Again, Kip—so small, so vulnerable—appeared in his mind's eye. "When will the BIA be here?"

"They're still getting their house in order, warrants, just cause—test results."

"What do you need from me?"

"You know this range better than anybody. Any missing cattle, any sick cattle—any suddenly dead cattle—I need to know."

Tim first, BIA second. Jacob understood. Justice was a hard thing out here. That much hadn't changed since the old days of the Wild West. Buck might be able to weasel his way through the legal system—he could buy all the lawyers in the world. But if Tim could deal with things before it got to that point, well, it'd be a victory on its own.

Just outside the window, a movement caught Jacob's eye. It was Mary Beth, hauling her huge medical saddlebags out to her truck and stopping to rub Mick's neck. "Hang on," he said, managing to push past Tim and get the door open.

Mary Beth was just getting into the cab of her truck when he caught up to her. "I need you," he said before he realized those were the exact words that were going to come out of his mouth.

"Oh?" She tried to jerk the door closed on him, but he used his shoulder to keep it open. "Did you also need me to muck the barn or water the horses?"

"No. I need a vet." He thought that was the right thing to say, but the look on her face went almost blank. Just a little anger colored the edge of her cheeks. "The sheriff and I need a vet."

Seemingly against her will, she exited the vehicle. "What's the problem?"

There really wasn't room in the office for all three of them, but he didn't want to have this conversation out in the open, just in case Buck came back. Tim stood aside and let her enter. Jacob motioned for her to take the chair.

"What's the problem?" she repeated, not bothering with social niceties this time.

Tim dug a slip of paper out of his back pocket. "Do you know what Campylobacter jejune and E. Coli are?"

"I can see how you'd think I might not have heard of them. I've only spent the last eight years studying animal medicine."

In these close quarters, Tim didn't have to turn his head far to shoot Jacob a wide-eyed look of surprise. *Yeah*, Jacob wanted to tell him, *she's got a hell of a mouth on her*.

"Would a bad infection be enough to kill a horse?"

All of Mary Beth's bitchiness disappeared in a heartbeat. "What happened?"

Tim laid it all out for her—the *someone* who'd lost his horses and seen strange activities in some distant field, the food poisoning at the church picnic, the massive infections the new doctor had only just managed to stop.

For the first time since she'd shown up in Faith Ridge, Mary Beth didn't say anything. She just listened, her eyes fixed on Tim and the slip of paper.

"So if I see any signs of contagion, you want me to collect samples and... what? Save them for the authorities or give them to you?"

"Jacob will hold onto them until I can get here."

At this, Mary Beth almost—but not quite—rolled her eyes. "I can assure you, I can keep stool samples and blood work just as safe as the next ranch manager."

Tim leveled a lawman's stare at her, but she didn't crack.

"I trust her," Jacob said, more to her than to Tim.

Whatever he'd said or done to piss her off earlier disappeared in the heat of the gaze she turned his way. He almost felt like he was back at Ronny's, watching her watch him put on a show. That hint of a blush—that was anything but professional.

Tim cleared his throat, breaking the moment. "We don't know who's behind this or what really happened," he went on in an extremely diplomatic tone. "The area where the slaughter could have occurred is something of a no-man's land. It could be any rancher between here and Rapid City."

Mary Beth arched up one eyebrow. Diplomacy or not, she understood exactly what Tim was saying. "I'll be sure to keep an eye open at any of the ranches I visit."

Tim tipped his hat. "Dr. Hofstetter."

The three of them managed to get out of the office without stepping on toes. For a second, Jacob thought she was going to wait Tim out, but then she climbed back into her truck. Would she go home and shower? Would he see her at the show?

Would he get back to having a good day?

God, he hoped so.

"So that's the new vet," Tim said, his Lakota accent ten times stronger.

Jacob tried not to bristle at the good—and probably harmless—humor in Tim's voice. "Yup."

Tim gave him a sideways look. "Don't imagine she gets along that well with Buck."

Had Tim heard about the confrontation at the restaurant that night? "Not particularly."

61

"Do you really trust her or…" The question was as loud as if Tim had spoken the words. *Or are you just hitting on her*?

Jacob's first reaction was to go on the defensive. She was a damn fine vet and, as far as he could tell, seemed to like children. At least she was interested in Kip. Besides, their relationship was strictly professional.

But he didn't say any of that. "Doubt she'd stand by while animals die." Tim nodded and headed toward his car. "Besides the BIA, will anyone else be asking questions?"

The sheriff paused, one hand on the door. "Nobody else should," he replied with a slow grin.

Jacob watched the cruiser head down the drive. Damn it.

Nobody was going to come looking for him.

Chapter Five

Sure enough, a few nights later, Jacob was sitting on a rickety lawn chair while Kip changed into her nightshirt inside the trailer when a part of the shadows separated from the trees that surrounded his trailer.

Instinctively, Jacob reached for his Colt .45. He didn't wear it to the ranch—Buck wouldn't allow that. But here? Hell, yeah, he was armed.

The shadow seemed to materialize into a man before his eyes. Jacob set the gun down on his leg— easy enough to reach, but not in a position where he might accidentally shoot anyone.

A man, all compact muscles and ugly scars, moved toward the side of the trailer—Jacob's bad side. Jacob hated that. He knew that Nobody Bodine didn't like to be seen, but if the man was going to go to all the trouble of coming to talk to him, the least he could do was stand where Jacob could see him.

"Tea?" Jacob asked, mindful of the traditions.

Not that Nobody gave a rat's ass for traditions. "No." And then, after another moment he added, "Thanks."

Well, that was something. Nobody didn't talk much. Even when he showed up at the mustang barn with a horse he wanted to sell or trade, he usually kept things to one word at a time.

"Could you see who it was?"

In response, Nobody moved to Jacob's good side. He hiked up the sleeve on his right shoulder, revealing a scabbed wound. "Couldn't get close," was all he said.

Jacob nodded in appreciation. Collateral damage. Better a shoulder than a face. "Where?"

Nobody didn't retreat back to the shadows. Instead, he held his ground as Jacob looked at the man. The flesh wound had taken something out of the big man. He looked more drawn than normal, slightly less dangerous. "Clearing, half a mile north of the buffalo valley where the White Sandy bends."

"I know it." It was a hell of a long ride out that far, but not impossible. "How many times?"

"Twice. Lost two horses." Nobody sounded downright depressed by this fact. As far as Jacob knew, Nobody didn't have anyone except his horses. "Smelled. Buffalo wouldn't go near it, but there was something there the horses liked."

Jacob mulled over that information for a bit. Horses weren't known for their self-preservation, not like buffalo were. "We got a new vet—a good one. If the horses show symptoms again, let me know. She can help."

Nobody looked pained at this suggestion. Jacob couldn't decide if it was because of the *she* or because Nobody didn't rely on anyone for anything. But he nodded all the same.

"She took care of Tahalo," Jacob offered, knowing that the stallion had been one of Nobody's favorite horses. So far, Jacob had bought three horses off of Nobody, midnight deals done in the dark.

Nobody's horses kept Jacob's bloodlines true. Of course, he had no idea where Nobody got his horses. Best not to ask.

"Yeah?"

"She knows her stuff. I trust her." It had been one thing to say that to Tim in front of her. It had almost felt like he had to prove it to her right then. But now? She wasn't around to hear him, but he said it anyway.

Just then, the door to the trailer opened and Kip stood there, looking as blank as ever in an old shirt of Jacob's that she slept in. This was their normal routine—it meant she'd brushed her teeth and was ready for bed—but it appeared to scare the hell out of Nobody. He took two steps back and all but disappeared into the shadows.

This made Jacob nervous. Nobody was the rough sort of man who got shot and stabbed, who'd done time for killing a man—even if it was involuntary manslaughter, it was still killing. He was not the sort of man any sane person wanted around a child, especially a vulnerable girl like Kip. Moving slowly, Jacob put his hand back on his gun. Shooting Nobody wouldn't stop him, but Jacob would put a hell of a hole in him if he tried something.

Kip lifted her gaze, looking somewhere between Nobody and the setting sun. This was the only time Jacob saw her with her eyes raised—the only time she seemed to be aware of the world around her. Every night, she looked for the sun before it set. She'd always liked the sun.

Nobody paused halfway between being there and not being there. One day, Jacob might figure out if the man actually was a shapeshifter or if he was just that damn good, but it wasn't going to be today.

"Yours?" Nobody asked, his voice quiet and unexpectedly gentle.

"She is now."

Jacob could almost feel the worry coming off the big man from several feet away. Finally, he said, "Keep her safe."

The tenderness with which he said this took Jacob by surprise. He wouldn't have figured Nobody Bodine for having a soft touch around children. "I will."

Nobody took another step forward. Even a man like him was curious about an albino Indian. Looking as thoughtful as Jacob had ever seen him—which was to say, less mean than normal—Nobody added, "Does Rebel know about her?"

Rebel Runs Fast? "The medicine man? I don't know. I don't go to the rez much."

As he watched, Kip's eyes seemed to focus on Nobody's scarred face. The big man and the small girl stared at each other. Both were creatures apart—not in the tribe, not in the world but just hovering between the two, invisible to everyone else. Could she really see him? Was that a gift she had, something she'd inherited from her grandmother, or was there something else? Damn it, if he only knew what to do about her...

Then Kip dropped her gaze and Nobody stepped farther back into the deepening shadows. "Call the clinic if you need Rebel." Already, he sounded farther away. Even though Jacob was concentrating all of his effort on watching Nobody, the man still disappeared before his eyes. Maybe he was a shapeshifter after all.

"Will I need him?"

He didn't get an answer.

"She's in good shape," Mary Beth said as she finished palpating the mare.

Jacob had selectively bred one of his two mustang stallions to the hardiest of McGillis's mares on the ranch and charged McGillis for the stud fee. Although he only got a foal, maybe two, a year, he had created another self-sustaining herd. Jezebel was one of those crosses from about three years ago, and Jacob had told Mary Beth that when she got a bit steadier, he'd cross her with Tahalo down the road.

Again, Mary Beth found herself marveling at how much planning went into everything Jacob did on both sides of the fence line. Nothing was accidental. She wondered if Jacob even knew what the phrase "by the seat of your pants" meant. She had the distinct feeling that if anything ever went off script, he might just flip out, although she had no idea what that would look like.

But somehow, she managed not to say this to him, or even to Robin. The trick was to stay focused on the animals. "She's got another seven months."

"Good, good," Jacob replied, grinning as she stripped the shoulder glove off. "You got time to look at that colt? I don't like the limp."

"Go get him," she replied as she returned his smile. She liked that smile. She liked seeing more of it. After almost a month and a half, he was finally showing hints of his evening playfulness during the day. And in the two weeks since the sheriff had shown up, she hadn't seen a single thing out of the ordinary.

With a barely perceptible nod of his head, Jacob pivoted and was gone. Mary Beth sighed as she leaned against the munching mare. "Does he like me, or am I imagining things?" she asked.

The mare whinnied at her. "Yeah. Probably imagining things," she agreed as she began chucking her stuff out of the stall. With a small groan, she hefted the nylon bag over her shoulder and headed out.

And right into the barrel chest of Buck McGillis.

Shit, she thought as he took a step forward, forcing her to take a step back into the stall. But her mouth covered for her. "Mr. McGillis! Haven't seen you much in the barn!"

"Why, hello, Dr. Pretty Little Thing." His gaze slid down her chest. "You're as good a reason as any to come out and check on my investments," he said, drawing the last word out as he reached out to touch her arm.

Jesus, where is Jacob when I need him? She tried to slip past his barrel chest. "Mr. McGillis," she cautiously cooed, but she wasn't fast enough. He latched his fingers on to her biceps, refusing to let go even as Mary Beth practically dragged him into the middle of the aisle.

"I'm still waiting on our dinner," he drawled, dragging her back toward his chest. "It's time for you and me to get... together."

"Mr. McGillis," she replied, trying to keep the panic out of her voice as she wondered how she could pull her knife on him if he had that arm, "it's against clinic policy to be involved with clients. I have to decline."

"I don't take no for an answer, Dr. Pretty Little Thing." His smile could be something friendly, except for the hard edge to his eyes that grew harder as she tried to pull away from his iron grip. With his other hand, he took her bag off her shoulder and dropped it in the aisle in a quick movement before he grabbed her other arm and pinned them to her sides.

Don't beg. He wants you to beg. That's what Skeevy Greevy had wanted—to put the pain in his ass firmly in her place. Mary Beth had come too close to convincing Greevy's meal ticket—her mother—to leave him. That she'd been a pretty teenager hadn't hurt, but it'd never been about lust. Just power. No one said no to Skeevy Greevy.

She felt the same fear that had nearly paralyzed her thirteen years ago as Buck's grin turned mean. Not about lust. Just proving that he had the power here. Mary Beth's hand scrabbled for the knife in the sheath, even though she knew she couldn't get it drawn.

"Knives? Please, Dr. Pretty Little Thing. Let's try to keep this civil."

The condescension—that's what pushed her past the fear. By God, she would not just stand here and let a man *use* her. That's not who she was. He had her arms pinned? So what. That left her legs free and clear.

At the exact moment she drove her knee up, Jacob yelled, "Watch out!" A horse burst between them, knocking Mary Beth free from McGillis's terrifying grip and into a stall door. She bounced right onto her butt in the middle of the aisle, a small cloud of hay dust floating around her as Buck began cussing at the top of his lungs. She had no idea if she'd managed to crush his nuts or not, but the effect was the same. She was free of him.

"Goddammit, No Nose, what the fuck is wrong with you?" he howled from the other side of the hall.

Immediately, strong hands were under her arms,

gently lifting her to her feet. "Are you okay?" Jacob asked, his eye darting between her and Buck.

"That shit-for-nothing horse of yours nearly killed me!" Buck yelled, his voice echoing throughout the tall barn. The echoes that bounced back took on a distorted sound, making him sound like something from a horror movie.

Be okay, Jacob's eye said. *Be okay.*

"I'm, uh, I'm fine," Mary Beth stuttered, her head still spinning. She looked up to see Tommy Yellow Robe appear out of nowhere, grab the bucking horse's lead and calmly circle him into an easy stop.

"*Hé únthunyan hwo?*" Tommy called out, sounding surprisingly aggressive.

"*Únthunye šni s'elél,*" Jacob yelled back.

"Goddammit, you know how much I hate it when you assholes don't speak English! This is America. Learn the fucking language," Buck snarled. "And No Nose, if you can't control my animals, I'll just have to get myself a new manager, won't I?"

Jacob dropped his hands away from Mary Beth's arms and took two steps in front of her. "I'm sorry, McGillis. It won't happen again."

"It better fucking not," he screamed as he stalked out of the barn.

"*Ínš tanyán he?*" Tommy demanded.

"*Enháš thimá yín kte kin él étunwan yo,*" Jacob ordered. Tommy dropped the horse's lead and lit out of the barn.

"Okay, I hate to be forced to agree with the likes of that man…" Mary Beth said as she sat back down in the straw.

"Tommy wanted to know if you were okay, and I

told him to make sure Buck went into the house," Jacob quickly explained as he sat down next to her. He reached out as if he was going to stroke her hair like she'd seen him stroke the stallion but quickly drew his hand back. "I don't want him to lurk."

Old memories collided with new ones. Part of her wanted to wail in pity. Why were there assholes? And poor Robin. No horses had galloped to her rescue. No one had saved her. Mary Beth's stomach turned. She'd worked so hard to get away from Skeevy Greevy— away from anyone that could hurt her. And where had that gotten her? Working with—she refused to say *for*—a man who considered her body an *investment*?

"Breathe," Jacob calmly ordered as she ducked her head between her knees. "In through the nose, out through the mouth."

She focused on the sound of his voice and was surprised when a sense of calmness filled her. The horror of the moment faded away, replaced with more of a sense of amazement at the whole stupid situation. How did he *do* that? Damn, but he was some sort of hypnotist. He had to be.

Finally, the nausea passed. She looked at him. "Jesus, Jacob, what just happened? I mean, what the *hell* just happened?"

"It was my fault," he said softly. "I shouldn't have left you alone. Not when he's around. It won't happen again."

"How can you be sure of that?"

"I won't let him hurt you," he simply said, and she knew he wouldn't. How weird was that? She wasn't one to trust a man, with the lone exception of her Uncle Hank—but Jacob was different. Understatement of the

71

century, what with the mask and—did Buck call him No Nose? Did he have a nose under there or not?

But her thoughts turned back to Robin, of the way she shut down whenever anyone mentioned Buck. Of the way Jacob tried to look after her. "How many women are you protecting from Buck McGillis?" she asked as she rubbed her bruising arm.

It was an odd thing to see such sorrow wash over his normally blank face. "I won't be late again."

More than just Robin. Was he counting that little girl who probably wasn't his daughter too? "It wasn't an accusation," she said as he turned away from her.

He paused, not looking at her. "I know. Just a fact."

The horse snuffed as it lifted a piece of hay from the ground. "Jacob," she asked carefully as her mind ran back over the flurry of motion that had saved her from McGillis, "did you let the horse go?"

"No."

She shot him her cut-the-crap look—never as good as her mom's, but it got the job done.

"I didn't let him go," he protested.

"I've never seen you lose control of an animal."

He sheepishly shrugged.

Realization dawned on her. "You drove him down the aisle?"

He leveled his eye at her, unreadable as always. "Worked, didn't it?"

For the first time since she'd run into Buck, Mary Beth smiled. "I didn't cost you your job, did I?"

"First, *you* didn't do anything. Second, I make him too much money for him to fire me. Third, he's all talk."

"I don't know about that," she replied, scrambling to her feet. "Not a lot of that seemed all talk to me."

"I'll give you that. He's all talk with men," Jacob corrected. Mary Beth giggled, and he looked at her like maybe she'd hit the ground too hard. "What?"

"'This is America—learn the language,'" she snickered. "He's not too smart, is he? Lakota is more American than English is. You guys were here first."

"Yeah, you're okay. The mouth still works."

Tommy cleared his throat. She hadn't heard him come back into the barn, but suddenly there he was standing next to Jacob. "He's in the house."

"Hey, Tommy." She smiled, trying to act like the whole thing had been just another day on the ranch. "Thanks for your help."

"No problem, Doc." He blushed, looking more like the slightly shy guy he normally was. "Next time, threaten to castrate him."

She laughed out loud, and even Jacob chuckled. "I'll do that, thanks."

After that, Jacob never left her alone while she was on the ranch. From the moment the cab door opened, he was within line of sight, never taking his eye off of her until she climbed back in the Ram at the end of the day. Even then, he stood there and watched her until she drove around a curve in the road.

But instead of a claustrophobic closeness, Mary Beth felt unusually safe around him. Aside from when he'd grabbed her by the armpits and hoisted her onto her feet, he hadn't touched her. He was close enough to defend her, but not close enough to give anyone, including her, the wrong idea. Sure, some days he still didn't do more than grunt in response to her questions, but he was always there.

Mary Beth guessed it worked, because aside from the roaring of the Jeep past the café just before the show every night, she didn't see Buck McGillis again.

But just seeing his Jeep cut a swath down Main Street was enough to make her sweat.

Chapter Six

One cloudy morning in late July, Bill sent her up to the ranch alone. "Got a bit of a head cold," he explained as he reached for the tissues on his desk.

"No problem, Bill."

"We were going to preg-check those cows," he said before he blew his nose.

Nothing new there. "Jacob will have the chute, right?" The chute was a rickety steel contraption that was probably older than she was, but it kept the cows contained. Mary Beth always felt badly for the poor cows, but preg-checking was an important job. And besides, she was usually covered in manure from head to toe by the time she was done. The cows got their revenge.

"Right. And Fran has packed extra shoulder gloves," he sniffed, unsuccessfully trying to breathe through his nose.

"I'll be sure to thank her," she replied, quickly escaping before Bill shared any of those germs with her.

As usual, Jacob was leaned against the barn with Mick drop-tethered next to him and Jezebel tied to the fence. "Mary Beth," he said with a touch of the fingers to the brim of his hat. "No Bill today?"

"Head cold," she replied with a shrug as she hefted the saddlebags out of the truck bed. "He said we'd be preg-checking. Is the chute here or out on the range?"

"Can you do it on the range?"

Mary Beth couldn't help but roll her eyes. "Yes, I could see where you might think I wouldn't be able to handle preg-checking cows after all these months. Seriously, Jacob."

His eyebrow edged up just a bit as he almost smiled. God, Mary Beth thought, what a piece of work—uncharted territory just waiting to be discovered. And then her brain decided this was the exact moment to revisit the question of his underwear.

But she didn't want to fold first, so she jammed her hands onto her hips and glared back at him, ignoring the fact that she was blushing.

Finally, he broke the silence. "The cows are up on the south edge of the ranch. Close to the rez," he replied, gracefully gliding up onto the paint's back. Then he looked at her as if he were trying to tell her something.

Close to the rez? Were they checking to see if a field had been used to slaughter cattle? She didn't know. She only knew he wouldn't tell her. Then he turned his face away.

"Then let's get gone," she said, relieved he wasn't giving her that look—half-amused, half-pissed—anymore.

The trail wound far away from the parts of the ranch she'd been to, deeper into the hills. Like most of their rides, Jacob was silent, but he was acting a bit odd today. He kept turning around in the saddle like he was going to say something but then seemed to think better of it.

Finally, he pulled his horse to a stop and waited for her to come up next to him.

"Yes?"

"Have you seen the buffalo yet?" Jacob blurted out. Was he blushing?

"No," she admitted, trying not to stare at the unexpected sight of the masked cowboy looking nervous. "Bill seems to think that if I sedate them enough, it's no big deal, but I thought they were monster huge."

He grinned, and Mary Beth melted just a bit. "You want to see one?"

"You hiding buffalo out here too?"

"Nope. There's a small herd on the rez. We aren't far."

Something about the offer made Mary Beth want to giggle. Almost like he was asking her out, but instead of to a movie it was to go buffalo watching. She couldn't help but wonder if this was flirting.

"We won't get trampled or anything?"

"I promise," he replied in all seriousness, "I won't let you get hurt."

It was the second time he'd made that promise. As she watched him canter up over a small hill, his body moving in perfect harmony with his horse like he'd been born in a saddle, she wondered if it wasn't already too late to make that kind of promise.

They rode on for another half hour, slowly climbing higher into the plains, farther from the ranch—and from everything else—than Mary Beth had ever been.

"Where are we?" she asked as he finally slowed down and slid off his paint.

"The center of the world," he smirked as he grabbed her around the waist and easily lifted her off Jezebel. For just a second, his hands lingered, settling on her hips as he turned her to look out over the ridge they'd climbed.

Okay, this officially counted as a date. His right hand trailed up her back while the left pointed out over the Great Plains. Every spot he touched positively tingled with a pleasure so acute it almost hurt.

"See?" he murmured, his mouth only a few inches from her ear. "Down below."

The whole vista was nothing short of stunning. The buffalo were huge, but if they'd even noticed the humans a hundred feet away, they didn't seem to care. She'd never been so alone with Jacob. She could kiss him now and no one would know.

Mary Beth's heart began to hiccup as she tried to focus on the enormous dark shapes gliding through untouched grasses instead of the overwhelming desire to kiss him. As he lightly swept his fingers over her shoulder and down her arm, leaving a trail of goose bumps in his wake, she decided that she wasn't getting back on that horse until she'd found out whether or not he had on any underwear. She was tempted to throw herself at him—that's what she would have done at any other time, with any other man—but somehow, she knew he would have to be the one who made the first move. Otherwise? He might just shut down on her, be as unreadable as ever.

Suddenly, he tightened his arm around her as he gasped. Yes, Mary Beth thought. This was it. He'd made his move, now she could make hers. But then, unexpectedly, he pulled away from her. "We've got to go."

She stumbled back. "Huh?"

As he mounted up, he pointed west. It was only then that she saw a huge wall of clouds quickly advancing. "Storm's coming," Jacob yelled as the wind surged up.

"Yeah, thanks for the weather bulletin," she snapped as the cloud opened up, furious that she'd missed her chance to find out what kissing a man in a mask could have been like. *Great. Just what I need.*

The wind and the rain were coming down so fast that the horses were beginning to flounder. Then the wind shifted direction, furious and demanding as the hail began to pelt them.

"Jacob!" she yelped as the hail grew from peas to dimes.

In response, he turned Mick around and darted over a hill. "Come on!" he hollered back to her.

Mary Beth urged Jezebel on faster, trying to dodge the hail that was now up to nickels. She didn't know where they were going. They were nowhere near the ranch, and she hadn't seen another sign of life in the last hour and a half. There couldn't be anything else out here for miles.

Jacob rode through a narrow creek that was already dangerously rising as the trees bent to the will of the wind. But as they crested another hill, Mary Beth was shocked to see a small dark house tucked in a stand of pines appear out of nowhere.

"Quick!" he howled against the wind, throwing himself off Mick and racing the horse to a small lean-to against the house. Mary Beth did the same, but there wasn't enough room or protection from the hail for all of them.

"Can we go in?" she screamed as the hail battered the tin roof.

Jacob actually paled as he seemed to debate it. But as lightning struck a nearby tree, he flipped a switch on a generator she hadn't noticed, grabbed her hand and raced the twenty feet to the front door.

It was unlocked and he pulled her inside and slammed it against the furious elements. The wind buffeted the door, threatening to push it open again, but it held fast.

Mary Beth groped around for a second before she found the light switch. As the florescent light flickered and then hummed to life, she saw they were in a one-room cabin with one small bed against the near wall and a larger one in back. A short counter with a sink and a narrow oven encompassed the kitchen, and a sturdy farm table sat in the center of the room.

Everything was clean and neat, if covered in dust. It didn't look like anyone had been in here for a long time.

Then she noticed the deep-brown stains covering the floor. Three distinct stains glared at her against the light pine floor. The one between the table and the small bed was huge. Between the table and the door was another large stain, and just off to her right was a smaller blot, the edges marking an irregular pool.

"Blood?" she gasped, realizing there could be nothing else that left that kind of mark. When Jacob didn't answer her, she spun around and said it again. "Blood?"

Jacob's terrified appearance confirmed her suspicions. He was wheezing, his one eye wild with fear as sweat beaded on his brow. The extreme panic he was caught up in led to only one possible explanation.

Jacob knew whose blood stained the floor.

"Jacob," she said quietly as his head swung around to hers, his eye still wild in terror. She knew that look. She'd seen that look in Uncle Hank when the PTSD overwhelmed him—usually when anyone shot off fireworks. Jacob was having a flashback. "Jacob," she said again, keeping her voice low and steady, "tell me what you see."

"The blood—blood everywhere," he gurgled, shaking violently.

"Tell me what happened, Jacob. Let it go," she soothed like he was a panicked, wounded animal.

"I tried to stop it, but it slit her throat. Jesus, there was so much blood," he cried, the pain twisting his body towards hers.

She caught him as he tried to burrow into her. "Whose blood, Jacob? Yours?"

"Susan's. Susan died here, and I couldn't save her. I was too late for Fred, but I thought I could save her." He wept into her hair. "And it killed her. It laughed as it killed her, and then it came for me. Oh, God," he sobbed as she held him up.

It came for him? Jesus Christ, is this where he lost his face? Trying not to panic, she did her best to keep her voice calm. "I'm here, Jacob. What killed her?"

Suddenly his back went stiff and his eye furious. "You aren't supposed to be here. No one is supposed to know about this," he choked out as the grief transformed into rage before her eyes.

Okay, this is normal, she tried to reassure herself as his body went steel hard against hers. Displacement. No problem. Uncle Hank used to do this too. Just a flashback.

The wind blew the door open, throwing her into his inflexible arms. He slammed her back into it, shutting the door with her body as he returned from his own personal hell. His breath was hard and fast as he stared her down, mere inches between them.

Good, she thought. *He's coming out of it.*

But then his eye began to dart back to the bloodstain next to them.

"No, don't go back there, Jacob," she demanded, taking his face in her hands. "Stay with me. Just stay here with me." She skimmed her hand over the worn leather of his mask, and the growl that sprang from deep in his chest flattened her even harder against the door.

If she could keep his attention, he wouldn't slip back into the flashback—and her hands on his mask *definitely* had his attention. "I want to see what a man with a mask looks like underneath," she said in a breathy whisper, relieved to have something he could focus on with exquisite, if enraged, clarity.

At least he's not panicking, she thought as Jacob knocked his mouth against hers so hard that her head bounced back against the door. The stiff leather nose of the mask dug into her cheek before he tilted his head a bit and shoved his tongue into her mouth. The surprising ferocity sent a thrill through her.

Okay, she thought as she opened her mouth farther, drawing his tongue in, if it's distraction sex you want, it's distraction sex you'll get. As she looped her leg around his, pulling him into her, she tried to touch the mask again. "I want to see," she whispered when he pulled back, his chest heaving in an erotic rage.

"You shouldn't be here," he growled, grabbing both her hands and smashing them over her head. "These things are not for you to know." With each word, he banged her hands against the door with an extra bit of force. "These things are not for you to see."

Mary Beth supposed she should have been scared. All the times she'd been with men, she'd chosen timid, cautious guys too shy to do much but come at the third thrust. Guys she could control. Guys she could dominate. Guys she could take or leave.

But now here she was being savagely kissed by an-honest-to-God cowboy—an Indian with a mask, to boot—as if she were the enemy and sex were the weapon. He had control, at least of her body, but she still had him right where she wanted him. The combination of power and powerlessness was intoxicating. As he raked his tongue through her mouth again, Mary Beth decided she was far too excited to be scared.

"What things do you want to see, Jacob?" she growled in his ear, testing to see how firmly he held her hands as she arched her back, pushing her breasts into his chest. "What things do you want to know?"

He snarled at her as he quickly put both of her wrists in his left hand. Then the mother-of-pearl buttons on her cowgirl shirt were popping apart as he ripped through them, leaving her covered with nothing but her red silk Victoria's Secret bra.

"You ride horses in that?" he barked, momentarily distracted by the flash of overt femininity.

"I didn't wear it for the horses." She wiggled one

hand free and ran it through his mop of hair until she hit the patch strap. Before she could even begin to trace its path back up to his face, he growled again, grabbing her hand and completely flattening her against the door with the force of his kiss. Despite the soaked clothes, the heat rolling off him had her melting in all the best places.

"That's right," she panted, beginning to feel like she was losing control of the situation—of herself. "You wanted to know. You wanted to see." He savagely grabbed one breast, expertly kneading the nipple through the silk.

Mary Beth was definitely losing control of herself as her head began to spin. No man had ever touched her like this, with this naked, aggressive need. Already, she was more turned on than she could ever remember being with any of the others. The way he pawed at her made the tingles on the top of the bluff look like child's play. This—this was for grown-ups only.

"Yes," she hissed as he bent his head and bit down on the silk. "Feel me. Taste me. Know me."

"Shut up, just shut up," he growled as he released her hands to yank her belt free and strip her pants down to her knees.

As he traced around the edge of the matching red silk panties, Mary Beth caught his face with her hands and pulled him back up to her lips. But instead of trying to get under his mask again, she slid her hands down to his belt and slid it free as she quickly undid those promising buttons.

He really wasn't wearing any underwear. He was rock hard under her hands, his eye briefly rolling back into his head as she traced the length of everything he had to offer. But then that erotic rage snapped his head forward and he spun her around, pressing her into the door.

"You shouldn't be here," he panted as he fumbled out of his pants. "I shouldn't be here."

"Shut up," she demanded, spreading her legs as far as she could with her pants around her knees. "Shut up right now or I'll rip that mask—"

She didn't get any farther. The panties were no match for him. He burst into her, sliding all the way in, all the way up, filling her as no one and nothing ever had before. The power of the unexpected orgasm shook her like leaves on aspen, and that was just from the first thrust.

"*Oh!*" she moaned as she shivered from the safety of his arms.

He froze. "What? *What*? I didn't—I thought—"

"Jesus Christ, Jacob," she begged, "don't stop! Oh God, please don't stop!"

With a hungry, guttural moan, he slid in and out of her. He grabbed her hands and moved them back up the door until they were over her head again. But instead of holding them there, he traced back down the length of her arms until he came to her breasts again. He slipped his right hand under the silk cup of her left breast, kneading it with the same savage intensity he had just seconds before.

With his other hand, he followed the curve of her waist down to her hips, then over to the hair that covered her sex. With a flick of his thumb, he found her clit and began to rub the nub in small circles.

If he hadn't been holding her up, she would have lost her footing as the second orgasm shook her violently. "*God*!" she screamed this time, unable to control herself under his maddening touches.

He growled with satisfaction behind her, pushing harder and deeper with each thrust. His hips knocked into hers so hard that her forehead was again bouncing off the door, but she didn't care as she arched her back, driving her breast more into his hand and raising her bottom up to meet his every demand.

Then, with one final deep thrust, he froze in silence, his fingers pinching the tip of her nipple, his thumb pressing against her clit, finally surrendering to the promise of freedom she'd offered him. While he came quietly, she couldn't help but buck in ecstasy one final time with another "*Oh*!" Suddenly, he was gone from her, leaving her barely able to stand.

"Jesus Christ, Jacob," she gasped as she rested her slightly sore forehead against her forearm. "Jesus Christ."

He staggered against the door beside her, his eye closed. "I didn't want to hurt you. I just wanted you to stop talking," he said in a rush. She looked over to him and could see that while the sex had definitely distracted him from the horror house they were in, he was still worried.

He was worried about her.

She smiled, wrapping her hand around his waist and pulling him closer so she could kiss his forehead. "Cowboy, anytime you want me to stop talking, you just let me know."

"Didn't anyone tell you I was the Indian?" He smirked as he turned away from her and began to button up his pants.

Mary Beth pulled what was left of her red silk

panties out from between her legs and shoved them into her pocket before she pulled up her own pants. As she started to snap the buttons on her shirt, she realized he was watching her, so she turned to him and slowed down, letting her fingers linger over her curves.

"Are you sure you're a doctor?" he asked, sounding a little pissed. The erotic part of the erotic rage had faded, leaving a mildly unpleasant post-coital grump. "They teach you that stuff at doctor school?"

The wind rushed up again, pushing the door open and knocking her back a step, but he caught her before she stepped on the bloodstain. He shot a sorrowful look at the remains of death, but he didn't slip back into the panic. Thank God, she thought.

The door now open, they could see the storm was blowing out. It wasn't raining anymore, and blue sky was showing behind the angry clouds rushing on to their next unfortunate destination.

Jacob stepped out into the rain-cleaned air, away from the horrible past he couldn't forget and the sex he wasn't sure he wanted to. He stood with his eye closed, letting the wind ruffle his hair. The breeze was lifting the pain from his soul, but in its place was overwhelming confusion.

God, he wished Susan were here. Susan would be able to tell him what to do about this new mess he'd just screwed his way into.

The first mess he'd screwed his way into in over eight years.

He heard Mary Beth clucking to Jezebel. "Oh, sweetie, you're soaked," she soothed, and Jacob couldn't help but smile.

Even after *that*, she was still concerned with the animals.

He suspected he knew what Susan would say. Susan would arch that eyebrow of hers up and say, "If you like her, you should go after her," just like she'd said in ninth grade right before he'd mustered up the courage to ask her to the dance.

Susan had been right then, and she'd be right now.

But this was different. This wasn't high school, and he wasn't an awkward, lonely kid with a crush anymore. And Mary Beth had already told every single man in town that she didn't sleep with clients. Hell, she'd threatened to castrate half of them.

God, he missed Susan.

He tried to focus on Susan back in high school, not Susan dying. He didn't want to dishonor her memory, but hell, it was a little too late for that.

It was too late the moment I kissed her in there. What the hell was I thinking?

And he didn't have any idea what to do next. What if she wanted a relationship? What if she wanted to see his crummy little trailer?

Holy hell, what if she wanted him to take the mask off?

The mere thought pissed him off even more. Mary Beth had gotten under his skin in a vulnerable moment and she could screw everything up. If he was going to start thinking with his dick, there was no telling what would happen with Buck. And what about Kip? His first job was keeping the little girl safe—not taking the pretty vet against a door, of all the crude things to do.

He couldn't tell who he was madder at—her or himself.

Focus. Focus on the animals.

He turned towards Mick. Mary Beth was right, the horses were soaked, but they didn't seem any worse for wear. Good ol' Mick had already found some grass to eat.

As they sopped off the saddles, Mary Beth looked at him and batted her eyes just like a girl wearing a red bra would. "That was really good, you know."

He snorted but couldn't stop himself from cautiously peeking at her over the edge of his mask to see if she really meant it or if she was just mocking him.

She froze, and he knew he shouldn't have looked. *Here it comes*, he thought as he braced himself.

"You know that, right? You know you were amazing?"

He shrugged, determined not to give her any more leverage.

"Jacob, haven't you done this before?"

He snorted again. "Not like that. I assume you have."

She recoiled in shock and he could have kicked himself. Shit. Only making it worse.

But after an agonizing second, she shrugged as she casually replied, "I've had my share of men. And just so you know, I'm on the pill and I've been tested. I usually use condoms…"

Condoms. God, when was the last time he'd thought about condoms? "Didn't have one in your pack there?" What the hell was wrong with him? Was he intent on pissing her off?

89

"Wasn't planning on this today," she retorted, but she wouldn't let it go. "I have to say though, *this* was definitely a first for me."

So much for not giving her any more leverage. She had him right where she wanted him. "A first?" he cautiously ventured.

"Jacob." She sighed, his name rolling off her sweet tongue like she was born to say it, "I didn't know I could come like that. You…" she leaned over, tracing her soft fingers down his face, away from his mask—almost like it didn't matter when she'd threatened to rip it right off his face moments before, "… you are amazing. Absolutely amazing."

He couldn't stop the grin that took hold of his mouth, wrestling the corners up. Amazing. Could it really be that long out of the saddle didn't matter?

For just a second, he forgot about being mad at her and being mad at himself. He even forgot about the terrible house where Susan and Fred had died. He forgot about his face and Kip and even Mick standing in wet mud.

All he could think about was her touch, her taste, her feel. Had he really lived for eight years without this in his life?

Finally, her fingers trailed off his skin and reality crashed back onto him. They had to get away from this house before Tommy came looking for them, and they had to get the horses back to the barn before they got too chilled. The creek would be too swollen to cross here. They'd have to go south.

As much as he wanted to kiss her, he turned and led Mick out into the clearing. Mary Beth wordlessly followed.

Maybe she won't ask. Maybe she'll let it go. He snorted. *Aw, who am I kidding? This woman never shuts up.*

And she didn't. As she swung that long leg he'd only gotten a glimpse of over Jezebel's back, she asked, "You? You've been tested?"

"I had a lover, once," he coldly replied. This would definitely kill whatever she felt for him, and quick. But he wouldn't lie to her. He owed her that much.

Mary Beth thoughtfully nodded, no doubt recalling all the gossip Robin had joyfully shared as fast as she could. "What happened to her?"

Jacob looked up to the sky, daring it to rain again. She was going to hate him for this, he just knew it. He already hated himself.

"Well?"

"She died," he finally answered, careful to keep his voice perfectly level. "On the floor in that little shack."

She shot up in her saddle like she'd been hit by lightning, something between guilt and pity all over her. Guilt he could understand, but the pity just pissed him off all over again. Without waiting for her reaction, he kicked Mick into a trot.

For a second, she didn't follow, and he couldn't decide if he should just leave her there or go back for her. *Of course I can't leave her*, he grumbled to himself. But he couldn't take being pitied. He didn't have time in his life for pity.

After a moment, he heard her kicking Jezebel into motion, and seconds later, she was riding besides him.

"Jacob," she started, her voice shivering.

Jesus, he thought. *Don't cry. I can't handle the crying*.

But she choked down a sob and simply said, "I'm sorry."

Jacob nodded as he guided the horses south, looking for a crossing of the now-swollen gully. Maybe that was the best he could hope for, if only she'd drop it.

And for once, she stopped talking as they followed the edge of the roaring gully. *Maybe she doesn't hate me*. He tried to be optimistic, but he was afraid to look back at her, afraid to see if she was crying or furious or staring at him with that awful abject pity.

His mind raced through all the possible outcomes.

McGillis. Kip. The hands. The gossips—especially Robin. The tribe. The *Waka Sica*.

No matter what the variable, it still ended badly. At best, he'd break her heart—or she'd break his. At worst—

Well, he'd already lost Susan.

Finally, he reached an incontrovertible decision.

I can't risk it.

I can't risk her.

The thought nearly broke him down, but he tried to take heart that this was the most honorable thing to do. Honorable and right weren't always the same thing, and it was up to him to decide.

He chose honorable, even though he knew she'd just hate him again.

It took about an hour before he got to a point where the horses could brave the current. Without a word, he turned Mick into the ice-cold rushing water and forded the stream, the frigid chill cutting right through his not-quite-dry jeans.

Mary Beth only hesitated a moment before she followed him in. The water was quickly at her thighs, and he knew she had to be freezing. But Jezebel was out the other side in less than a minute.

Now, before they got any closer to the ranch. "No one knows," he said, his gaze unforgiving.

She cocked her head to the side, looking a little confused. "Not even your sheriff friend? Wasn't there an investigation or something? Did they ever catch who did it?"

"No. No one knows."

The way she looked at him should have scared him. If she shot her mouth off to the wrong person at the wrong time...

"No one has to."

"No one knows," he repeated more forcefully.

She stiffened her back, temporarily mastering the teeth-chattering shakes that gripped her. "And no one else will."

"Jacob! Dr. Hofstetter! You out here?" Tommy's voice cut through the timber.

"Keep it that way," he replied as he kicked Mick toward the waiting cowboys.

And away from her.

Chapter Seven

The show ended unceremoniously one mid-September day. A few women had gathered at the café, their teeth chattering over steaming cups of coffee as they waited.

Mary Beth sat with them.

It didn't matter that Jacob hadn't said more than six words to her since that absolutely insane afternoon one month ago, she told herself as she sipped her tea. It didn't matter that he wouldn't even look at her when anyone else was around. It didn't matter that when they were alone, riding out on the range to check on his horses or on cattle in a distant field, he only responded to her in grunts. It didn't matter that he looked at everyone but her during the show.

Didn't matter. He was just a man, and she could take him or leave him, just like she'd left every other man she'd ever bedded.

Yeah, right, she fumed at herself as she waited for him to appear. *He was never yours to take or leave.*

What was more, it didn't matter that in that month of sexual frustration, she'd given up on her vibrator and the dull little pop of release it offered her—too much like the little pop she'd always gotten out of any other roll in the hay. Now it didn't release a damned thing, not compared to the screaming ecstasy Jacob had effortlessly awakened in her. It didn't matter that she might never get that ecstasy back again. Didn't matter.

She saw Bill less as he let her shoulder more of the responsibilities of the practice. Some days, the only person who talked to her was Fran—and that was to boss her around.

Mary Beth knew that if she hadn't had Robin to tease her about her makeup and gossip with over beers at the café Saturday nights, she'd be completely alone out here, surrounded by people who didn't want her here.

People like Jacob.

The most she'd gotten out of him had been when he'd called her out to his horse barn late one night. One of the foals was breech, and as they silently worked to save both animals, he'd lost some of the cool-cowboy demeanor.

"Robin said you were helping her with her applications," he'd tentatively begun as the newborn foal tried to find her legs.

"I was, but she missed the deadlines," Mary Beth had grumbled, somewhat amazed he was talking. *Maybe the miracle of life loosens him up*, she'd mentally sniped, trying not to be as big of a bitch as he was being a jerk.

"She'll go when she's ready," he'd tried to reassure her as he lightly rested his hand on her shoulder. "You can't force her to do something she's not ready for."

For a millisecond, she'd let his touch set her blood on fire. But if that was his idea of an apology for being a jerk, she'd realized as her anger rose up, he could shove it. "Yeah, I know all about that the hard way, but thanks for the tip, Jacob," she'd snapped. *So much for not being a bitch.*

In the faint barn light, she hadn't been able to tell if he was mad at her for mouthing off or just amused, but it had been the first flicker of real emotion she'd seen in nearly a month.

But then Cole had padded through the barn, and Jacob had gone all unreadable again.

And that was it. In the whole month, the longest month of her life, *that* was the most he'd said to her to even hint that he acknowledged her existence outside of calving and vaccines. He still watched her like a hawk, and she supposed she was grateful that he hadn't cast her off to Buck, but it was hard to muster up the gratitude when all she wanted was to wring his neck.

Mary Beth shivered again, more from the confused emotions than the gust of chilled air blowing down the street. How could she even describe the best sex she'd ever had, in the world's *worst* place to have it? It didn't seem possible to think of something so earth-shakingly wonderful having occurred in the same room where two people had been slaughtered and Jacob permanently maimed by... by what? *It*? Something that laughed as it killed with a knife? She had no idea.

Mary Beth had pieced together a theory about that hidden house and the people who'd lived and died there. He'd loved the woman, Susan. She'd been his one and only, until she'd married Fred. Robin had said she thought they might have moved to Pierre after that, but they hadn't. They'd gone off the grid until Jacob had found them.

That left only two options. Either he'd gone to win Susan back, or…

Robin had said that maybe Kip was the only one who knew what happened to his face. Kip, the girl no one knew existed before she just appeared. Kip who didn't talk and didn't see.

It all connected back to Kip.

But she didn't know why, and with Jacob answering her in only monosyllabic grunts, there was no way to find out. She couldn't just walk up to the silent little girl with weirdly purple eyes and say, "So, did you see what took his face?" That was no way to make friends with a kid.

And frankly, she was beginning to wonder if she really wanted to know. She wasn't Native. She didn't speak the language, and her attempts to cuss in Arabic were met with icy glares or head scratches. Except for dinner at the café, beer Saturday nights and occasional shopping runs to Rapid City—except for Robin—she didn't feel like she much belonged here at all.

If this was her new start, maybe she would have been better off with vanilla-pudding Greg. But that thought just made her even madder as she chugged the rest of her tea. She didn't need Jacob to take care of her because she didn't need any man to take care of her. She was the one in control. She was the one who walked. Every time.

"Are you sure you're okay?" Robin asked as she refilled Mary Beth's mug. "You look pissy."

"I'm fine. You're the one who didn't mail off the applications on time," Mary Beth snipped.

"Let it go, Mary Beth," she snipped back.

"Fine." She forced an unnatural smile. "It's gone, okay?"

Robin hugged her tray to her chest as she looked Mary Beth up and down. "You know what you need? You need to get laid."

Mary Beth almost fell off her chair. "Excuse me. In public here."

"Uh huh," Robin giggled. "I bet I know just the man too." She nodded down the street as Jacob rode into view.

Not only was he not shirtless, he was wearing a long duster coat that draped out behind him and nearly covered Mick's haunches. His legs were invisible and his chest was completely bundled against the rapidly dropping temperatures.

"Oh, I hate it when summer ends." Robin sighed. "Tell him I'll be right back with his dinner."

"No! Don't leave me alone out here," Mary Beth shouted after her.

"You aren't alone," Jacob's deep voice rumbled from in front of her table.

"Oh, you're talking to me today? What's the special occasion? Is it my birthday, or are you just deigning to speak to the lowly creatures?" she barked out before she could stop herself.

He looked at her coolly, his eye holding her gaze.

"Ignore her, Jacob. She's extra pissy tonight," Robin sang as she came back out with his to-go bag.

"*Robin*," Mary Beth screeched as Jacob let a lazy grin play out over his face.

"She's sorry the show is over for the season, that's all." Robin giggled as Jacob took his dinner.

"Later? I'm going to kill you, Robin," Mary Beth muttered as she tried to kick her best friend's shins.

Jacob's face went hard. "I heard she was pissed at you, not me. Should've mailed your apps in, *Šišóka*."

Now it was Robin's turn to blush. "Jesus, it's like you both think I'm thirteen or something."

"No," he slowly replied, his eyebrow arching with glee, "I remember you at thirteen. This is worse."

"Screw you, Jacob," she hissed before she stalked back into the kitchen.

"Well. Glad to see I'm not the only woman you have that impact on," Mary Beth said as she glared at him.

His gaze softened a bit as he took a deep breath. "Mary Beth—"

"Jacob? We're ready." Mrs. Browne stood in the doorway of the school, Kip nearly invisible in the bright light that flooded out of the doorway.

Without another word, he turned and picked up the girl who probably wasn't his daughter and lifted her onto the old mare. He touched his fingertips to his hat and then they were gone in the cool night, leaving Mary Beth alone.

Again.

He was still wearing the coat the next morning as the winds whistled down the hills and slammed into the broadside of the barn. The air cut right through Mary Beth's jeans, left exposed below her barn coat.

Great, she thought as he hefted the bags out of the truck. One more thing to buy. At least she'd planned on running up to Rapid City this Sunday with Robin. She wouldn't have to make the extra trip.

"Where we going today?" she asked as they swung up on their horses.

"Mustangs," he replied as he rode away from her.

"Right. Mustangs. A whole word that time," she muttered, kicking Jezebel after him.

The wind was at their backs for the quick twenty-minute ride out to his barn. Dave was waiting for them, a worried line crossing his normally unreadable brow.

"What's the problem?" Mary Beth demanded as she dismounted.

"They're all blowing snot everywhere, holding their heads funny. Half of them won't eat," he replied as he led her into the barn.

"Strangles."

"What?" Jacob demanded.

"It sounds like strangles. A strep infection." She took one look at the first horse and nodded.

"Didn't you vaccinate them for that?" Jacob asked. Was he accusing her of making the animals sick?

"It's not a hundred percent foolproof, but it's usually good enough. I don't understand it at all." She shook her head, just as confused as Jacob. "I can take cultures to be sure, but that mucous will start to turn green in a few days."

"Already has in Bell," Dave said with a nod to the next stall.

Poor Bell. But then, she already felt bad for the horse that was officially named Hell's Bells. "Dave, I'm sorry, but the whole barn has to be sterilized—walls, buckets, tack, everything."

Dave nodded as Jacob said, "Go ahead and bring in Lisa and Alex."

"I'll get Gary too."

Jacob shot him a questioning look.

"Look, I know he's only eight, but he's got what it takes. Cleaning tack is a good place to start him," Dave explained. It was by far the longest speech he'd ever made, and it was in English.

"Do it."

"Warm compresses to the ones that seem to be having trouble breathing," Mary Beth went on. "Most of them will be better in a week or so." She turned to Jacob, somewhat surprised to see him smiling at her. For a second, it threw her. First, it had sounded like he almost wanted to apologize last night, and now, after a long summer, he was smiling at her again, in front of Dave no less. "Uh," she stuttered, trying to remember what she was going to say. "The disease might make it past the lymph nodes in some of them. If any of them start really laboring to breathe, call me immediately."

Jacob and Dave nodded in unison.

"Clean the whole barn, isolate the ones who aren't symptomatic yet, and watch to see if any of them turn," she reminded them. "I'll take some cultures."

Jacob whistled, and Jezebel slowly plodded into the barn.

"I didn't know she did that," Mary Beth exclaimed as Dave headed out to round up his help.

Jacob looked a little guilty. "I've been training her."

She dug out her culture swabs and latex gloves. "You have?"

He nodded, that grin still smiling out at her from beneath the mask. "I thought you might like to have a trained horse."

Good Lord, she thought as she began swabbing

snot from pained horses. *He's been training Jezebel? For me? Is this how cowboys apologize for being jerks?*

Bell was in bad shape, and Mary Beth was worried the strangles had already gone to the next level, so she broke out the high-powered antibiotics and the intravenous fluids. A few others needed fluids too, but the rest of the herd just looked like it had the common cold.

Something just didn't add up. "How did they get this? This is a vaccinated, closed herd and none of the ranch horses have had any symptoms," she puzzled out loud as she cleaned out another mustang's nasal passages.

"Not sure. Cole said he thought he heard strange hoof beats a few nights ago but didn't see anything." Jacob went on, "That might be... nobody." But he seemed genuinely confused by this statement. "That couldn't be it though."

He wasn't the only one confused. Mary Beth stared at him, wondering what the hell he was talking about. Did he know who'd ridden in—or not? "Surely someone wouldn't try to infect them on purpose?"

Jacob shrugged. "I'll have Cole look around some, see if anyone left a trail. And don't call me Shirley."

Mary Beth tried to roll her eyes at him, but she couldn't stop the giggle that escaped. "You sound like Robin."

"She's right about you, you know."

Now that pulled her up short. There was no way he should have been able to hear Robin say she needed to get laid.

"You have been pissy recently."

Oh, thank God, not a getting-laid discussion—or

was it? "You do realize that I spend most of my days with either you or Fran, and neither one of you has been very nice to me recently? Fran I can understand. She's not very nice to anyone, but you?"

His eye softened as he took that familiar deep breath. "Mary Beth..." he began, but again was interrupted by Dave calling them back to look at a pregnant mare.

"Yeah," she muttered, pushing past him as she stripped off one pair of gloves and slapped on another. "I've got work to do."

Two hours later, Mary Beth had exhausted her supply of gloves, saline and culture swabs. She was nearly out of antibiotics and syringes. She and Dave walked through the barn with his young recruits as she patiently explained what needed to be cleaned and how to prevent re-infection.

"This is important, kids," she reminded them, looking down on the young faces. Lisa was the oldest of the three, nearly as tall as Mary Beth was and nearly as quiet as Kip. She was Alex's older cousin, and they were both somehow related to Dave. Gary barely came up to her waist, but he paid the most attention. "The first rule of being a good cowboy is caring for your animals."

"Roy Rodgers told me it was to be neat and clean," Jacob yelled from Bell's stall where he was holding hot compresses to her swollen throat.

Lisa rolled her eyes as the boys snickered. Mary Beth shot the stall a dirty look. "That works too!" she shouted back. "In this case, it's the same thing. Jacob's counting on you guys, so you better not let him down."

"Dr. Hofstetter?" Alex piped up.

"Yes, dear?"

He giggled. "Did you really almost castrate Tommy Yellow Robe?"

Gary snickered again as Mary Beth went purple. Even Lisa blushed as she whacked Alex on the shoulder.

"That's enough," Jacob thundered from the stall, and the kids scattered to different parts of the barn.

"Is that what everyone knows me by on the rez?" she asked as she wandered back into Bell's stall. The poor mare was nearly leaning all her weight on Jacob as he held the compresses to her throat.

"Mostly," he replied as he looked at her fading blush. "Alex will tell everyone you turned bright red. That'll be something different."

"Lord," she muttered as she took Bell's temperature. "Down a degree."

"Good. Can you come back tomorrow?"

"If it won't piss McGillis off," she shrugged.

"We'll come here last. Might be a long evening though."

"What about Kip?"

He looked surprised at the mention of her name, but it quickly disappeared. "Dave is trustworthy. He'll keep an eye on you while I go get her."

"That's fine," she responded nonchalantly, even though her curiosity was up. First he was talking to her again, and now Kip was a part of the conversation. He'd never talked about her at all. A new thought occurred to her. "Jacob, where was Kip when the mare was breech?"

His face was blank as he shifted the horse off his shoulder.

"Aren't you going to tell me?" she prodded.

His lips disappeared into an angry line. "Fine. She was asleep in the tack room."

"You brought her to the barn?"

"I don't leave her, not at night." And with that, he turned and walked away, leaving Mary Beth more confused than ever.

That afternoon, after Mary Beth had driven off the ranch, Jacob sat in his office staring at his phone. On occasion, Nobody had visited the barn late at night, unseen and unheard, only a new horse in a paddock in the morning to tell that he'd been there. If Cole had thought he'd heard something in the dead of night, it could have been the big, silent man.

But that didn't fit with the man whose whole life was taking care of horses. Jacob didn't trust Nobody much around people, but around horses? It wasn't possible that Nobody would infect the mustangs, even by accident.

Which left what other options? The barn's location was on a need-to-know basis—if you didn't need to know, you didn't know. Jacob trusted his hands—Dave and Cole and even Lisa and Gary were all reliable.

Who else could have infected his horses?

Jacob thought about calling Tim, but what could Tim do? If Cole couldn't pick up a track, there wasn't a hope in hell that Tim could.

He opened his desk drawer and pulled out the aged, thin Yellow Pages that covered most of the rez and surrounding counties. The White Sandy Clinic and Hospital was listed. Honestly, Jacob wasn't sure if he needed a medicine man. Sick horses needed a vet, not a sweat lodge. But something about the whole situation felt *off*. More off than they had in the last three years. He hated the feeling.

It'd been years since he'd done anything spiritual. Hell, before that night when Susan and Fred had died, he hadn't given the spirit world much thought at all. He'd been busy. The last time he'd talked with a medicine man had been... well, he'd gone on a vision quest when he was thirteen. Hadn't seen a damn thing. Afraid to disappoint his grandfather, he'd made up a story about seeing the land from above, soaring with the eyes of an eagle.

That had been long before Rebel Runs Fast had taken his place. Rebel's world and Jacob's world didn't cross much.

Still, if Nobody trusted the man, maybe Rebel was a man who could be trusted. Maybe Rebel would be able to talk or communicate or something with Kip. Or at least tell Jacob if Kip really was as special as she looked.

Before he could talk himself out of it, Jacob dialed the clinic. The phone rang, then rang some more before a machine answered it.

"You've reached the White Sandy Clinic," a crisp female voice announced. "Our office hours are between eight thirty and four thirty." Jacob glared at the clock on his computer—four forty-five. Damn. "If this is an emergency, please call 605-555-6829. Otherwise, leave a message and we'll return your call."

He hung up. This wasn't an emergency. At least, he didn't think it was. Hell, he didn't know what to think anymore.

All he knew was that he didn't like this, not one bit.

Chapter Eight

The next day, Jacob was waiting for her as usual. The winds had let up a bit, but Mary Beth was thankful she'd broken down and put on the long underwear. Sexy, no, but warm, yes.

"We need to get to the mustangs first. Dave's worried about the pregnant mare," he said as he slung her pack onto Jezebel and the extra one, with what would normally be a three-week supply of saline and penicillin, over Mick's back.

"Did anyone pick up a trail?"

He paused for a moment—thoughtful, but not as confused as yesterday. "No."

She nodded as they took off for the barn without another word.

The horses beat a steady staccato as they raced back to the edge of the ranch. Without the wind, it seemed to take an extra few minutes to cover the prairies and stands of trees, but finally the barn was in sight.

At the exact moment she saw Dave step out of the darker interior, Jezebel whinnied in pain and bucked sharply to the left. Completely unprepared for the wild motion, Mary Beth went butt over shoulder and landed squarely on her back.

As the world stopped spinning, she caught a dark motion coming directly at her and she rolled out of the way.

"Jezebel!" Jacob hollered as he grabbed the mare's reins. "Jesus, Mary Beth, did she step on you? Are you okay?"

"Fine, just fine. Like a roller coaster," she wheezed from the ground.

Jacob threw Jezebel's lead to Dave and was on the ground in a heartbeat, cradling her head in his arms. "Can you move everything?"

"You act like I've never been thrown before, Jacob," she sputtered, wincing as a sharp pain cut through her left shoulder. "Let me sit up and I'll see what's what."

Carefully, he pushed her into a sitting position, the worry on his face undisguised.

She wiggled her toes. "Toes, check. Legs..." she moved them back and forth, "... check. Ribs—"

Jacob's hands moved over her ribs, gently pressing at all the joints starting on the back and working his way to the front.

"Uh, okay," she stuttered, going pink as his hands skimmed just below her teal bra, "got it. Ribs, check. All good there."

"Arms? Neck?" he demanded.

"Neck," she said as she gently rotated it, "check. Head still attached."

"Arms?"

Mary Beth couldn't remember the last time a man had looked at her like Jacob Plenty Holes was looking at her right now. Worried, sure. She'd taken a hard fall. But there was something deeper behind that, something that she couldn't quite make out.

"Arms?" he repeated with more insistence.

"Uh," she tried to pivot both of them, but the pain radiated back up through her left shoulder and she sucked in air.

"Arms no good?"

"Right is okay. Left is—let me think," she paused, hoping the stars would vanish from her eyes while she tried to recall the human anatomy she'd taken as an undergraduate. "Left is probably a separated shoulder."

"Do you need to go to the clinic on the rez? The ER?"

"In Rapid City? No," she chuckled as he slid his arm around her waist and lifted her to her feet. They began to hobble towards the barn. "If I recall, the best thing to do is to rest it up for a few weeks. You've got ice in the barn, right?"

Jacob nodded and hollered for Lisa to get some ice.

Jezebel whinnied in pain, and Mary Beth snapped back to attention. "So what happened? Dave, could you see?"

He shook his head. "She stepped on something. Her foot is bleeding."

"Damn it," she and Jacob muttered at the same time.

The sad group slowly made it to the barn. "We can't leave her here tonight—she'll get the strangles," Mary Beth said as Jacob held the wounded mare's foot for her while she inspected it for the offending object. The wound was small and clean. "She shouldn't even be in the barn."

"Well, you can't ride her back, and you can't take

any of the mustangs," he countered. "They're all contagious."

"Have Dave stand her in some Epsom salts while I look at the mare," she ordered. "Then we'll wrap her and walk her back. I've got an extra boot in the pack. If we go slow, she should be okay."

"What about you?"

"What about me? I said I'll walk her back."

Jacob scowled. It was a damned intimidating thing. "You just separated your shoulder and you're going to walk her back?"

"You got a better idea?"

"I'll think of one," he snapped.

Lisa held the ice while Jacob wrapped her arm, and then he fashioned a makeshift sling for her. "At least you're right handed," he pointed out.

She started to say something smart but decided against it. He was finally being almost friendly again, and she wasn't about to discourage that. "True. Could be worse."

They called Bill and told him what happened, and he agreed to come on out to the ranch to handle that end of the day. Without the pressing urgency to the afternoon—if Bill was there, McGillis wouldn't get his hackles up—Mary Beth was able to focus on the pregnant mare blowing snot everywhere.

"Man, I just cleaned that bucket," Gary grumbled as the mare sneezed in it.

"Sorry, hon. Now do it again," Mary Beth replied as he rolled his eyes. "Just think, by the end of the day you'll be really good at cleaning buckets."

"Yeah, thanks," he muttered as he pulled the bucket down and took it out to scrub.

"You're good with kids," Jacob said as she slowly examined the mare.

"I've got one nephew and two nieces. Someone's got to be the favorite aunt," she countered. "Well, really, they're more my second cousins, but they call me Aunt M."

"I didn't know you did the James Bond thing," he replied with a chuckle.

The mare didn't look any better, so Mary Beth had Jacob get the high-powered antibiotics. "We may lose the foal. Even if it survives, there's a higher chance of neuromuscular problems down the road," she warned him.

He nodded gravely as she injected the wheezing animal.

The rest of the herd was looking better—even Bell was moving her head a bit easier. "The kids are doing the compresses after they get done with their chores," Jacob explained.

"I'll bring them some chocolate chip cookies the next time I'm out," she offered as Jacob wrapped Jezebel's foot. As she sat on a bench, her arm still numb from the ice she'd finally taken off, she felt a bit too helpless for her own good. She still didn't know how she was going to get back to her truck. Unlike most barns, there weren't any four-wheelers or other trucks around. And Mick wasn't even saddled, for heaven's sake.

Jacob got Jezebel's foot wrapped and the protective boot on. "Come on," he said as he stood up and took her hand, cautiously pulling her up.

"What are we doing?"

"Mick can carry us both. I'll boost you up."

Instantly, he was lifting her up just as he lifted Kip up, like she weighed nothing. He sat her on Mick's wide back and patiently waited as she swung her leg over.

"Jacob—"

But he had already mounted up behind her and was reaching around her waist to grab the reins.

"What are you doing?"

"Taking you home," he replied, his warm voice only inches from her ear. Without another word, he headed Mick back to the ranch at a slow walk as Jezebel did her best to keep up.

"I don't know about this," she muttered as she tried to figure out where to put her hands. His legs were pressed against hers, her back to his chest, his free hand resting on her thigh, his face—his face had to be buried in her hair. She began to sweat.

"You can ride bareback, can't you?" he murmured.

"Do I have a choice?" she snipped.

"That's some mouth you've got there, Mary Beth," he murmured again, his voice warm and honeyed and right against her ear.

"Yes, I know. That's what everyone says, all the time. Well, listen, you," she said as she tried to lean forward, away from his solid chest. "This isn't going anywhere."

"Sure it is. Back to your truck."

"No, *this*," she snapped as she lifted his hand off her leg. "This isn't going anywhere. I got the message loud and clear last time."

"Last time?"

"Don't be dense, Jacob. Look…" she sighed in frustration, "… I'm sorry if you felt I did something

112

wrong. I didn't know where we were and I thought I could help you out. But that's no reason to stop talking to me."

He was silent as he slipped his hand back on her leg.

"Seriously? Are you even listening to me?"

"Mary Beth," he said in that low voice again, "you didn't do anything wrong. It was crummy of me to be a jerk, and I won't do it again."

"I don't think you are listening at all," she snarled as she took his hand off her leg again. "I don't know what your damage is, but I'm not your play toy, ready to swoon just because—because—Jesus, knock it off!"

"What?" he said, all innocent even as he traced the edge of her ear with his stiff leather nose. "I'm not doing anything."

"If I could, I'd punch you right now, Jacob Plenty Holes," she growled as she tried to elbow him in the ribs. That was a bad idea. "Ow!" she yelped as her sore shoulder pulled.

"See, you're only making it worse," he said, but he pulled his hand off her leg.

"I'm making it worse? I've got news for you, buddy, you haven't even seen worse. Wait until I get off this horse…"

"Calm down."

"Give me one good reason," she seethed.

"First, you're going to either hurt yourself or push one of us off this horse."

The tone of his voice—like she was a child that had a little trouble understanding him—made her even madder. "You, I'm hoping."

"Second," he continued as if she hadn't

interrupted, "I'm apologizing for being a jerk, and that rarely happens. You... you got under my skin, I guess. I've never had anyone get under my skin before and I didn't know how to deal with it."

Great, she internally moaned. A new variation on it's not you, it's me, but this was more irritating. "And somehow, the standard seventh-grader response was the right action?"

"Ninth grade," he corrected her.

"The year you met Susan," she guessed, and immediately wished she had a brake or a five-second delay or a censor's beep on her mouth—anything to keep from sticking her foot in it around him.

"Yeah," he said, but instead of the sorrow she expected, he sounded almost silly. "That was the last time I had to try to figure out what to do about a girl."

"Okay, well, in girl world, for future reference," she started, "you don't ignore someone you just slept with for a month. You ask them out on dates or say, 'Let's be friends', but you *don't* ignore them."

"Okay. Mental note made," he responded with a brief hug.

"Why are you apologizing now?" she demanded, pretty sure he was tracing his leather nose over her hair. "It's been a month of ice-cold cowboy, and now you're all warm and snuggly? I'm *not* sleeping with you," she emphatically stated.

She could hear the leather creak. He must be smiling.

"I don't like not talking to you. I've never met anyone like you. You are an amazing woman, Mary Beth, and I want to make it up to you."

Her insides started to go all gooey, but she wasn't

114

about to let him off the hook just yet. "Is there a third?" she asked as he rested his hand back on her leg. "Because that was a good start, but it wasn't the rest of the apology."

He was silent as Mick navigated a small stream. But as soon as they were safely across, he leaned forward and kissed her neck. The hot touch of his lips made her shiver with the promise of what he could do, but she knew he wasn't going to.

"I can't ask you out. You don't date clients," he said simply.

"I don't sleep with them either, and see where that got me," she retorted. "Don't kiss me if you aren't going to ask me out."

"I can't help it. I like kissing you," he replied again, his mouth moving against the skin under her ponytail.

"Jesus, Jacob." She shuddered as his other hand left her leg and circled just under her breasts, pulling her back to his chest. "You are totally cheating right now."

"Try to understand," he whispered into her ear. "It's been almost eight years since I felt anything for a woman—any woman. I'd given up on all of this," he said as he kissed her neck again, "until you came along."

Eight years? For crying out loud, she considered herself in a drought if she'd gone six months without sex. No wonder he was such a grump sometimes. The man had a sex backlog that would kill anyone else.

Slowly, he nuzzled his way up to her ear before he took the lobe in his lips, tugging gently. She couldn't help but turn to meet his mouth, her breath coming in short, hurried pants. Who could think about eight years when he was seducing her right now?

"But you... you taste like strawberries in sunshine, and I still haven't figured out how I can be around you without sweeping you off your feet or ignoring you. I don't know how to find a happy medium. I'm sorry I'm not good at this."

Oh, sweet Lord, she thought as his tongue traced the edges of her ear. *How strong does one woman have to be?*

"Well," she tried as her eyes fluttered from the touch of the hot wetness of his mouth, "let me help you out. Focus on not being a jerk, okay? Right now, you are still being a jerk, because you are turning me on with no intention of doing anything about it."

"Are you turned on?" he asked as he cupped her breast, his thumb already pulling her nipple tight.

"Jesus, Jacob, stop it right now, or I'm going to stab you in the leg." She tried to grab at her knife with her right hand, but the twist pulled at her shoulder again, and she moaned a bit.

"Calm down. I'll stop." His hand left her breast and slowly traveled back down to her leg.

"Okay." She blew hard, trying to get her mind to focus. "Ways Jacob can not be a jerk. One: No seducing without intent to satisfy. Two: Answer questions with more than a grunt. Three: Don't ignore me and don't treat me like your special toy."

"Technically, that was three and four," he corrected as he rested his chin on her shoulder. She could just see the black leather tip of his nose in her peripheral vision.

"Whatever. Can you handle that?"

"I will do my best. I don't want you to be mad at me, although you are pretty funny when you're all worked up."

"Great. Here for your amusement," she scoffed.

Jacob pulled Mick to a halt and quickly slid off, still resting his hand on her leg.

"What are you doing?"

"We're close to the ranch," he replied as his fingers trailed down her the whole length of her leg, a thousand goose bumps in their wake. "I don't think the hands should see us… together."

"This is what you call together?" she shot at him, shaking free from his touch.

"You know what I mean."

"Fine," she huffed. "But don't be a jerk, Jacob."

He looked up at her, his eye dancing as he smiled that good smile, the one that turned her brain to jelly. "I promise, I'll do better."

It was a hard promise to keep. Every day she came out to the ranch, starting when she slid out of the cab of her truck, her boots crunching the frost-covered gravel as she held her left arm close to her side with her mouth already screwed into a challenge, he had to resolve not to be a jerk all over again. Every night as he lay in bed and stared at the mask on the small shelf next to his bed, he wondered how he'd do it again the next day she came out.

It had been a relief to know she still wanted him, but damn if he couldn't shake the feeling that he was a teenager again, hopelessly in puppy love with another woman so far out of his league she was in a different sport.

Not that it hadn't been torture to ignore her. Every wounded look she'd shot him, every smart-ass comment she'd muttered under her breath when she thought he couldn't hear her, every single time she'd tried to smile at him only to have the smile die on her face—it had torn him up.

God, but he hated being a jerk. Wasn't his nature. But keeping his mouth shut was. That was what his grandfather had taught him, and Jacob had always been a good student.

Jacob wondered what his grandfather would do. Samuel Plenty Holes, the respected council elder, had raised Jacob after his parents disappeared back in the early 70s. It was at his grandfather's knee that Jacob had learned how the tribe worked and what his place would be as a tribal leader.

Never a demonstrative man, Samuel had lived the philosophy of his favorite author, Mark Twain. "It is better to keep your mouth closed and be thought a fool than to open it and remove all doubt." The only time Jacob had ever left the state was the year he turned ten, and his grandfather had packed him into the beat-up Ford still parked behind his trailer today and driven him to Hannibal, Missouri, to tour his hero's home.

Jacob still had his leather-bound copy of *Huckleberry Finn* Samuel had gotten him on the trip tucked between his mattress and the thin wall.

Of course, that trip had also taught him what it was to be an Indian in a white man's world. Far removed from the familiar brown sameness of the rez, Jacob clearly remembered the shock and shame that filled him as complete strangers walked up to his grandfather—the leader of the Lakota tribe—and said, "How!" like it was the best joke they'd ever heard.

And all Samuel did was smile kindly, as if the joke was indeed somewhat funny. Better to be thought an ignorant savage than open your mouth and prove some idiot right.

At least the experience had prepared him for college. His grandfather had been one of only a handful of Lakota men with a college degree, and it had never been a question of *if* Jacob would get his as well. He'd gotten his bachelor's in three years, and his MBA a year later. That had finally shut some of those *washitu* up, to have that kind of power in the white world.

It had taken a long time for Jacob to realize his grandfather was a powerful man, but after years of going with him to council meetings, he figured it out. As the tribe struggled through the years, Samuel sat silent through the raucous procedures until everyone else was argued out. Then he'd make his pronouncement of what the tribe should do, and the tribe would do it.

He wasn't always right. Jacob could remember loud arguments—in private, of course—with his best friend, Henry Steele. Samuel felt the tribe had to modernize to avoid extermination and extinction, but Henry had fervently believed that the only thing that could save their people was a return to the old ways.

He still remembered the last thing his grandfather said to him before he died of a heart attack a month before Jacob's vision quest.

"*Thakónala*, what's right and what's honorable aren't always the same. As a Plenty Holes, it falls to you to decide for the tribe."

Jacob had never figured out which kept his

grandfather from telling him what had happened to his parents. Henry had finally told him they'd gotten into drug running and never come back from a trip to Mexico one summer when he was two.

He did his best. Working for Buck wasn't honorable, but keeping a Lakota hand on the land was the right thing to do. He gave his friends—the next generation of Lakota men—good paying jobs as long as they stayed clean and took care of their families. He set up anonymous scholarships for kids who wanted to go to college, and made small loans to people like Ronny. He encouraged the young ones to respect the old ways, even if they chose a different path.

And, while it wasn't honorable, he kept working at his plan to steal back the Lakota land.

The McGillis men had been trying to destroy the tribe for years—rumor had it that Buck's great-grandfather had bribed BIA officials to give him the cows meant for the Lakotas one winter just to starve them off the land, and not much had changed since then. Jacob could still remember how mad his grandfather got every time Buck's father, Clint McGillis, trucked in case after case of beer to the rodeos, making money off the ruination of the Lakota people.

Samuel Plenty Holes hadn't been able to stop the McGillis men. But Jacob was determined. It's what his grandfather would have wanted, and moreover, what he would have expected.

Mary Beth Hofstetter? Another matter entirely. While ignoring Mary Beth may have been the honorable thing, it wasn't the right thing. Not even close.

To fall in love with a white woman? A complete stranger to their ways? He couldn't shake the feeling that his grandfather's spirit *wanagi* was frowning down on him. Sometimes when she shot off that mouth of hers, he could almost hear the old man rumbling in displeasure, just like he used to rumble at Henry.

But for all their arguments, Samuel Plenty Holes had loved Henry Steele as family. The two had been fast friends for more than fifty years, each bringing out the best in the other in good times and bad.

Maybe that was part of it. Everyone else treated Samuel Plenty Holes with respect, but no one got close to him except Henry. His grandfather and Henry had never thought of each other as leaders. They were just brothers.

For too long, people looked at Jacob and saw what they wanted to see. A rancher working for the enemy, a leader who walked away from the council, a man hiding behind a mask.

But not her. When she leveled those gray-blue eyes at him, he couldn't shake the feeling that she saw him in a way that no one but Susan ever had. Not that she didn't wonder about the mask, about the working for the enemy, about his place in the tribe and even about Kip, but somehow, it seemed she could see past that. It was the same when she looked at Kip after school. No one else could get past the silent-albino thing, but Mary Beth seemed to be looking deeper.

And none of it seemed to scare her off. She kept coming back for more.

Some days, when Mary Beth was in fine form, he thought that mouth of hers was the most attractive thing about her. No matter what the situation—breech cows or surly cowboys—she always had some lethally smart-ass comment flying out, half the time before even she knew what she was saying.

If he didn't want her so bad, it would be so much easier. But he couldn't look at her without thinking about red silk bras or the taste of her lips or the way she screamed—actually screamed—in pleasure at his touch. *His* touch.

He'd certainly never done that for Susan, although not for lack of trying. Undoubtedly though, Susan's patient instructions had finally paid off, so many years after he'd given up.

And those were the thoughts that haunted him into the deepest parts of the night. He'd convinced himself that he could live without a woman because his destiny was to keep Kip—and the land—safe. That was what Albert, the old medicine man, had interpreted his made-up vision to mean a dozen or so years ago. Jacob was a guardian, a caretaker of the land and the tribe. And, as that fit with the role his grandfather had prepared him for anyway, Jacob accepted it, grateful that no one had figured out he was faking it.

But now? Now he wasn't so sure. He still had to protect Kip and his people's lands, but he wasn't sure he could do it alone anymore.

He wasn't sure he wanted to.

He could try calling Rebel again. Except that Rebel would probably want him to go to a sweat lodge, and Jacob didn't have time to sit around and sweat just for the hell of it. But Jacob was also pretty sure that Rebel was much smoother with the female sex than Jacob would ever be. Maybe, even if visions weren't involved, Rebel would know what to do about Mary Beth. But any conversation that started with Mary Beth would end with Kip, and that time hadn't come yet, because she wasn't safe yet.

No, he was pretty much on his own about this. And the loneliness never felt keener than it did when he was around her. And every morning she slid out of that truck and shot him a look that said, *What's it gonna be*? Well, it just got that much harder.

He struggled.

He struggled with the urge to touch that skin that he knew was off-limits. He struggled to come up with the right things to say in front of the ranch hands that wouldn't raise their eyebrows but also wouldn't piss her off. He struggled against the comforting silence that he knew would definitely piss her off.

It was a fine line between holding her at arm's length and just holding her.

Thank God, she came with Bill most days, what with her arm still in the sling. With Bill around, there was a constant buffer, a steady stream of patter about Leslie packing, Leslie shipping furniture to the new house their son had picked out for them in Tampa, Leslie buying Christmas presents for the grandkids. With Bill filling any silent void, Jacob didn't feel the pressure to either talk or not to her.

Most days, Jacob could have hugged the older man for saving him from himself.

But she healed. Within a month, she was out there alone again, riding out to check on the newborn foals at his barn or carefully preg-checking the cows.

Jacob had to hand it to her, she made it as easy on him as she could—at least when anyone was around.

She asked him direct questions, her eyebrow only arched a little bit.

But the time came that they headed out on the range alone. The hired hands had already headed out to round up the cattle they'd be working. It was just him and her for about forty minutes of riding.

Jacob panicked so hard he thought he might have to put his head between his legs as he broke out in a cold sweat.

"I'd ask how you're doing, but you look like you're going to pass out," she said simply as they trotted away from the ranch.

He took a deep breath. "I'm working on not being a jerk."

"Good. Good start. That was a whole sentence. Perhaps you should also consider breathing on a more regular basis as well, unless you aren't up to multitasking today," she said as she kept an eye on the trees—and pointedly not him.

"No," he smiled, relieved she was still normal, even if he felt anything but, "you're right. Breathing is good."

"One of my favorites. Good old air. Can't go wrong."

Jacob wasn't sure what to say next, so he kept his mouth shut.

Finally, she tilted her head at him. "Do you need help?"

"Help?"

"With what comes next. That's not your strong suit, that whole talking thing."

"Oh." He blushed, thankful that at least the mask covered half his face. "Um, what do you recommend?"

"Well, most people start with, 'How are you,' and occasionally, 'How are things going.' More advanced conversationalists will remember something from the last meeting and ask about that."

"I'm not very advanced."

"That I can see," she giggled at him, and again, he was back in high school, clueless about girls. "Here, I'll help. So, Jacob," she said, her voice artificially bright, "how are things going out at the barn? I know you were having a problem with bots in some of the horses."

"Um, fine."

"No," she scolded. "The correct answer was, 'Fine. Dave's had Lisa and the boys out doing checks after school. You know, they really liked your chocolate chip cookies.'"

He turned to stare at her. "That was the right answer?"

"Yes," she snipped in mock irritation—at least he hoped it was mock irritation. "You are supposed to remember something nice about me and work it into the conversation."

"Hmm. So, I could say, 'Fine. Alex has a crush on you' and that would be okay?"

She went bright pink. "Alex has a crush on me?"

"You didn't notice? He follows you around like a puppy dog," he grinned. "He's in love."

"Okay, first, not too bad, if a bit of a sudden gear shift and second, Alex isn't the only one."

Jacob's mouth dropped open. "What's that supposed to mean?" he finally stuttered out, sounding more foolish than he cared to.

She pulled Sue—not as steady as Jezebel, but still a good horse—up next to Mick. "Jacob," she whispered, her voice low and confidential and all the sexier. "Just relax. I'm not going to tell anyone, okay? No one will know. No one has to."

Before his brain could stop his hand, he reached over and cupped her face, rubbing her cheek with his thumb. By the time he realized what he'd done, she'd already closed her eyes and leaned into his touch, just like she belonged there.

And he knew he wouldn't be able to stay away from her, not even if he wanted to. Something in her face—the gentle curve of her lips, the way her cheek fit perfectly in his hand, just like the rest of her had—it was something he knew he wouldn't be able to live without. He wouldn't fight it anymore.

"See?" She sighed as he reluctantly pulled away. "That wasn't so bad. Probably only hurt a little bit."

Embarrassed, he barely smiled. "That was okay? Didn't break rule number one?"

"Well, it did come close." She grinned. "But I'll allow it." And she kicked Sue away from him, towards the horses and their bots.

"Right. You'll allow it." Man, this was going to be harder than he thought.

But it wasn't. Mary Beth was so much better at this than he was, and once he relaxed and followed her lead, it got a lot easier. She didn't mind if he was quiet around the hands, but she expected him to talk and flirt when they were alone.

And the more they were alone, the more he couldn't help but touch her. He discovered he liked to ride up to her, trail his hand down her arm or her leg to make her lose all focus as she got that dreamy, lovesick look about her.

He wanted to kiss her again, even if it was just her cheek, but he was pretty sure that would break rule number one. Still, every time she touched him—even the time she slapped his arm to get his attention while she was elbow-deep in a mare—the urge to taste her only got stronger.

"Are you ever going to ask me out?" she asked out of the blue one afternoon as they rode back from the mustangs, a light snow starting to drift past them. He was riding right next to her, occasionally reaching out to graze her shoulder with his gloved hand.

The momentary panic froze him for a second, but she tilted her head to the side, and the teenage part of his brain remembered that when a girl tilted her head like that she wanted you to kiss her. But he wasn't sure, so he stalled. "It's a free country. You could ask me out too, you know."

"Pshht. I wouldn't have the first idea what to do on a date in greater Faith Ridge."

"Not much, especially in the winter," he admitted. "Maybe this spring, after the snows melt, we can go to Rapid City," he casually offered.

"Super," she snipped, "I'll mark my calendar now." But she tilted her chin a little more to the side and looked at his mouth.

Okay, that was it.

Jacob circled Mick back around and pulled up until their legs were touching. Sue shifted nervously at the close contact, but he didn't care either way. He grabbed the reins and hauled her horse over to him, then grabbed a surprised Mary Beth by the coat and kissed her.

It was the sweetest kiss he could ever remember

as she lightly parted her lips for him and leaned into him. Heaven help him, she really did taste like strawberries in the sun.

But then she pulled back, her eyes flashing with a mix of desire and irritation. "Jesus, Jacob," she hissed when he let her go. "You're breaking rule number one."

"Oh, I intend to satisfy," he said with a grin as he spun away from her, reveling in the erotically stunned look on her face. Clearly, the first time hadn't been dumb luck.

"Before spring?" she shouted at his back.

His only response was the faint shrug.

He knew it'd drive her nuts.

Chapter Nine

The first snow came in late October. The meteorologist on the Rapid City station her TV could barely pick up said it was going to snow for three or four days straight.

"Looks like we got a blizzard on our hands, folks." He'd beamed into the camera like an unusually early snowstorm was a fabulous thing.

"Great," she mumbled. "Remind me to thank global warming personally." Bill wasn't about to come out in this kind of weather—he barely made it to the office most days of the week now that her arm had healed—and she was supposed to head up to the ranch tomorrow. "No idea how that's supposed to work," she fumed at the perky anchorwoman listing the advance school closings.

The phone rang, causing her to jump.

"Mary Beth?" an older voice crackled over the line.

"Hey, Bill. I heard we had a blizzard coming."

"Jacob called. He said a few buffalo wandered onto the ranch, but he didn't see why you had to come out tomorrow in this weather. Said everything would keep."

Oh, how nice. Like he couldn't pick up the phone and call me himself. What is wrong with that man sometimes? Silently, she fumed while she tried to sound normal. "So what should I do tomorrow?"

"If you can make it to the office, that's fine. Take a book. Might be a slow day," he chuckled.

"Sure. Can do. You and Leslie stay warm, okay? Tell her I said Tampa's calling her name." Mary Beth smiled.

"Trust me, she hears it," he replied before he hung up.

Slow day at the office. Mary Beth stood in front of the bookshelf, wavering between studying the new buffalo manual and a new romance she'd gotten.

"No contest." She sighed. "Cowboys win every time."

She finished her romance before lunch, with the heavy flakes already piling up outside. Fran left as soon as it started to stick, and Mary Beth was alone. Again.

She inventoried the stockroom, wrote lists of supplies they'd need throughout the winter and browsed the catalogs. She reorganized her desk, and then did it again. Finally, with nothing else to do, she bundled up and grabbed a shovel.

The wind was biting as she tried to clear the steps to the Ram, whipping the snow into her face and back across the walkway. At least her new duster kept her legs warmer than her barn coat would have.

"Well, hell," she muttered as she tried to make it back into the office, the drifts already covering her footprints. By the time she got back inside, it was four.

"Quitting time." She grabbed her pack and trudged back out to the truck.

The café was empty. "Hey, Mary Beth, don't you

know there's a blizzard out there?" Robin said as she got the tea ready.

"I'm going to be stuck in that little house for the next few days. Thought I'd come hang out with you before it got too nasty," she explained.

"Right. No need to get cabin fever on the first day." Robin nodded. "Hey, good news."

"Oh? Gonna stop snowing?"

"Nope." Robin beamed, the light catching the glitter in her eye shadow. "I mailed my applications in."

"You did?"

"Yup. Ronny told me that I had to go, so I wanted to make sure I got on the list for next fall early."

"Ronny!" Mary Beth hollered back to the unusually quiet kitchen.

The big man popped his baseball-cap-covered head out. "Yeah?"

"I love you!"

Ronny was very much a big brother to all his regulars. Even if he hadn't been steadily dating a schoolteacher at the consolidated high school for over a year, Mary Beth was quite certain there still wouldn't have been anything between them.

"Oh, she told you about the college?" He shyly grinned. "She better go, or I'm going to tell Mike Nolan about the time she—"

"Stop right there!" Robin screeched as she raced back to tackle him. "Don't you dare!"

Mary Beth chuckled at the two of them, Robin chasing him around the kitchen with a pair of tongs. "While you're back there, bring me a hamburger!" she yelled over the melee as she flipped on the TV.

Ronny got better reception than she did. The grinning meteorologist looked like a semi-real person instead of a fuzzy ghost on the screen. But the news wasn't good. He was calling for several feet of snow well into next week. "But it should all melt by next Friday," he gushed to the plastic-looking anchorwoman who reacted like he'd given her diamonds instead of storm warnings.

She sighed as she fished the ketchup out from behind the bar. "I hope everything can keep up at the ranch, because I don't have any idea how to get there."

Robin brought out dinner for both of them and plunked down on the stool next to Mary Beth. "Did it snow like this where you're from?"

"Not in multiple feet. We had thirteen inches one December."

"Both Mikey and Ronny have snowmobiles, so if you need to get out, just call."

"Lord," she muttered, knowing full well Robin would be spending her blizzard with Mike Nolan. She'd have someone to chase the cold away. All Mary Beth had was an extra blanket. But rather than get Robin started on the subject of Jacob again, she feigned mild terror. "Snowmobiles? Can't wait."

"Chicken." Robin giggled.

Mary Beth glanced over Robin's poufy bangs. Across the street outside, the door to the schoolhouse was open, and she could just make out the shapes of Mrs. Browne and Kip against the interior light.

"Jacob's going to make it to get Kip, isn't he?"

"He always does." It was hard to understand Robin with her mouth full of fries, but Mary Beth caught the gist. "Why, is she out there?"

Mary Beth nodded as she got up and walked to the door. But by the time she got there, Mrs. Browne and Kip had gone back inside.

"It's just the weather. He'll make it." Robin shrugged as she flipped the channel to *The Simpsons*.

But as the wind buffeted the snow against the small buildings, Mary Beth wasn't so sure.

Fifteen minutes later, the door to the schoolhouse opened again, the only light on the dark street spilling out and being swallowed by the snow.

"Okay, he's not here," she said to Robin as she hurried into her coat.

"He'll be here."

"But he's not here *now*," she said as she shoved the door open against the wind and waded across the river of snow that used to be a street to the school house.

"Mrs. Browne? Is everything all right?" Mary Beth shouted into the wind as she slogged her way through the snow.

"Dr. Hofstetter, is it?" Even in the middle of a blizzard, her voice was crisp and authoritative.

"Yes. It's nice to officially meet you," she replied as she offered a gloved hand to the older woman.

"Have you seen Jacob?" she asked, unmoved as a wind gust blew snow into their faces.

"Not today."

Mrs. Browne looked down the dark street again. "Come in from the cold, dear," she said, although Mary Beth couldn't tell if she was talking to her or Kip.

Mary Beth followed the two of them into the schoolhouse. It was a small building with a row of cubbies lining the entryway. Robin said there were only twenty or thirty students—up to grade eight— Mary Beth recalled as she looked into the single room filled with large and small desks. On the other side of the hall was what appeared to be a cafeteria with the tables pushed against the wall to clear the floor for the basketball hoop in the corner.

The proverbial one-room schoolhouse, Mary Beth marveled. "Do you always stay this late?" she asked.

"I stay with Kip. She needs... extra attention. Jacob has asked me to look after her." As Mary Beth nodded, Mrs. Browne solemnly added, "Jacob is never late."

She led Kip back to a small desk off to one side. "Dear, would you like to read the book again?" Without waiting for an answer, she pulled a creased copy of *Tales of a Fourth Grade Nothing* out from under the seat and opened it to the middle. Kip sat on her hands and stared down at the book.

Mary Beth looked down at the silent, white child. This was as close as she'd been to her, and now, only a few feet away under florescent lighting, she could see that the girl's skin was nearly translucent, especially her eyelids. Her eyes didn't move as she looked at the book.

Something about this child pulled on the very deepest strings of Mary Beth's soul. She crouched down beside the girl and whispered, "Judy Blume is one of my favorites. I named my pet turtle Dribble because of that book."

Kip slowly raised her head, and it sounded like Mrs. Browne gasped. Just as slowly, she turned her head to Mary Beth and blinked, her hand silently reaching out and resting on Mary Beth's face.

Her hand was cold, but Mary Beth reasoned that

it was because she'd just been out in the snow as she studied Kip's face. She had the most unusual eyes Mary Beth had ever seen. They were pale purple around the irises, fading to a pale blue that reminded Mary Beth of her father's eyes.

Kip blinked again, and suddenly Mary Beth couldn't breathe. Kip's eyes were colored like a bruise erupting from an untapped well of unspeakable pain. It hurt to look at her. What had she seen?

Suddenly, like a bolt out of the blue, Mary Beth realized. It—Jacob's mask, the strange, bloodstained house in the woods, the girl who didn't exist before she appeared—all of it didn't just connect back to Kip—it all went *through* Kip.

"They were your parents, weren't they? And you saw..."

For the first time, Mary Beth saw the corners of Kip's mouth pull down—not much, just enough to answer the question. *Everything.* This little girl had seen everything with her bruised eyes. It hadn't just been Jacob's old girlfriend and her husband who'd died on the floor of that house. It'd been Kip's parents.

Maybe that was why she didn't look at anything anymore. It hurt too much.

Mary Beth fell back on her heels, her head reeling and her heart breaking. Life wasn't fair. She knew that—had lived that. But this? This was an injustice of epic proportions. And she didn't think she could let it stand. She *knew* she couldn't.

"Dr. Hofstetter? Are you all right? Oh, let me help you." Suddenly Mary Beth was hoisted onto her feet, strong hands steadying her as she sucked in ragged breaths.

Slowly, Kip turned her blank eyes back to the unread book.

"Kip looked at you. Very odd. Kip never looks at anyone but Jacob," Mrs. Browne went on, politely ignoring Mary Beth's lack of coherent response. "Here, let me get you some water."

As Mrs. Browne disappeared into the other room, Mary Beth shook the last of the sadness from her head. That whispering urge to protect this odd child—a pull on her soul she'd barely been able to contain before—was now a screaming howl. She'd die to keep her safe if that was what it took. She didn't understand this ferocious new power that seemed to course through her veins, but she didn't need to. She'd stood up for her mother, then for herself. The answer was an easy one.

She needed to protect Kip. That was enough.

"Kip," she whispered, but the child didn't move. "I will keep you safe."

Kip raised her head but didn't look up.

Mary Beth swallowed hard as she gently stroked the blinding white hair. "I promise."

She pulled her hand back as Mrs. Browne came back in with a small glass of water.

"You look a bit flushed. Are you sure you're all right?"

"Yes, Mrs. Browne," she replied, feeling more sure than she had in a long time. "I'm certain it will all be fine."

She saw the kind teacher nervously glance at the clock on the wall. "It's getting late. There's already a good six inches out there," Mary Beth offered, knowing full well the older woman wanted to go home.

"Well…" Mrs. Browne hemmed.

"I could take Kip."

"Oh, I'm not sure that's—"

Kip stood up and slipped her small hand into Mary Beth's. It was still cool, like she was a few degrees colder than normal people. Mary Beth smiled as she looked down at the child, although Kip didn't look up and didn't smile back.

"Kip? Dear, are you sure?"

It occurred to Mary Beth that Mrs. Browne was the only other person who Kip could trust, and that perhaps Mrs. Browne didn't relish sharing her special charge. But as Kip stood there silently, her hand resting in Mary Beth's, the older woman shrugged. "I do have to be running along… we could leave Jacob a note on the door…"

"Whatever you think would be best."

Mrs. Browne looked at the clock again. "Yes. Well, let's check for Jacob one more time."

Chapter Ten

Mary Beth shoved open the sticky door with an *oof* before she flipped on the light. "This is where I live, Kip," she explained. Mrs. Browne treated her as if she were sweet but slow, but Mary Beth knew that wasn't the truth.

Kip was smart—smart enough to survive.

"I'll make some dinner. Do you like chicken?"

Kip sat at the table.

"Okay. I make a mean chicken and dumplings. My cousin's recipe. You'll like it. Maybe the next time you come, we can make cookies."

Quickly, the pot was bubbling. Mary Beth kept an eye on the child sitting perfectly still at her table, but Kip was a statue. Maybe she'd been giving Jacob lessons in inscrutability.

"Do you talk to Jacob, Kip?"

There was no response.

"No, I would imagine not. He keeps you safe though."

In the face of overwhelming silence, Mary Beth felt compelled to keep up a one-sided conversation.

"You ride your horse really well. Does Jacob let you ride around after school?" She shrugged, getting more used to the lack of a response. "I rode when I was a little girl. My mom says that she thinks I was born on a horse, next to a cow. By the time I was your age—you're seven, right?—by your age, I was helping wean new calves. Do you help Jacob?"

Suddenly, someone was pounding on the door. "Kip!" a deep voice rumbled.

Mary Beth spun to grab her knife from the counter, and when she turned back around, Kip was gone. She just caught the movement of the curtain that covered her little washer-dryer combo flutter.

"Good girl," she whispered as the pounding continued. The knife at the ready, she growled at the door, "Who is it?"

"Mary Beth? It's Jacob," he said, his voice softening. "Please tell me you have Kip."

She swung the door open, oblivious to the snow piling in and only lowering the knife a bit. Jacob stood there, nearly as white as Kip from the flakes that dusted him completely. His shoulders slumped in relief until he saw the knife. "What are you doing?" he snarled.

Seeing that he was alone, Mary Beth scowled at him as she yanked him into the house. "Where have you been?" she spat at him, stalking back to the kitchen. She slipped the knife back into the sheath and stirred the dumplings. They were almost done.

"I got stuck with the buffalo. Half those men Buck hired didn't show today. Something about a blizzard, I guess." He looked at the clock, smacking himself in the forehead. "Where is she? Is she all right?"

Mary Beth pointed to the curtain that was as still as it could be. "She's fine."

139

Kip was nowhere to be seen. "Kip? Where are you? It's me, Jacob!"

"If I were Kip," she said, realization dawning, "I'd be hiding in the washing machine."

Jacob flipped up the lid and, making an uncharacteristic squeak, plucked the shaking child from the drum. "Good Lord, Kip, you scared me."

He gave her a quick hug, which brought Mary Beth up short. The tenderness—she'd never seen that from Jacob before. This wasn't him awkward or unsure or even surly. This was him looking almost like a regular dad. Except for the mask, of course.

Mary Beth set the steaming bowls of dumplings on the table with a flourish. "Dinner is served. Kip, would you like some milk?"

While Kip didn't talk, she did eat. She ate three bowls of the dumplings with three whole glasses of milk. As Mary Beth marveled at the girl's appetite, she asked, "So, tell me about the buffalo."

Grinning, Jacob shook his head like he was talking about a toddler that got into the candy jar. *So protective of them*, Mary Beth realized. *So protective of us all.*

"This one buffalo bull got wrapped up in some barbed wire."

Oh, heavens, buffalo in barbed wire. "Was it okay?"

Jacob chuckled. "Barbed wire is no match for buffalo fur, but he was plenty pissed at being tangled up. Every time we'd start to get him unwound, he'd spin on us and we'd be right back to square one. You're lucky I didn't call your butt out there."

"You'd have had to come get me, you know."

His eye held hers as his eyebrow moved up. "I know." Something in the way he said it sent her temperature spiking up, but before she could dwell, she saw Kip's head began to nod.

Mary Beth looked outside. The drifts completely covered her porch, already erasing any trace of Jacob's footprints. This was no weather to send a child out into. "Did you bring the paint?"

"Mick? Not in this weather. I rode the snowmobile."

Mary Beth swallowed down the nervous anticipation. Would he go if Kip stayed? "She's already half-asleep, so I guess you'd better leave her here."

"I don't leave her. Not at night."

Mary Beth wasn't sure if she was breathing or not, but she wasn't going to let this opportunity pass her by. "Then I guess you'll need to stay too."

"Guess I will," he casually answered, as if it were the most normal thing in the world.

Jacob pulled the back cushions off the couch while Mary Beth dug out all the extra blankets. Soon, they had Kip snuggly tucked in, almost invisible amongst the piles of comforters.

"Will she be all right here?" Mary Beth whispered, unconsciously slipping her hand into his.

He tightened his fingers around hers. "She sleeps okay. She should be fine." He let go of Mary Beth and knelt beside the resting child. "Good night, Kip," he whispered as he kissed her forehead. Nearly lost in the warm blankets, Kip smiled in her sleep.

Mary Beth felt the part of her heart that had broken earlier in the school stitch itself back together. Whatever had happened to Kip's parents and Jacob's

141

face, he refused to curl up and die. He did everything he could to protect this little girl.

It was a feeling she understood more and more.

"I have to know what's going on," she whispered in his ear. From this angle, she could just see where the mask separated from his face, a few millimeters of space.

"I told you what I know," he replied.

Kip rolled over on the couch, so Mary Beth pulled Jacob into the bedroom. He shot her a snide look, but she defended, "It's either this or the bathroom if you want to talk." Amongst other things.

Without a word, he flopped down on her side of the bed and kicked his boots off.

"What makes her special?" Mary Beth asked as she folded cross-legged onto the far side of the bed.

He shrugged, but she could see him watching her under those heavy lashes.

"And I don't mean special like Mrs. Browne thinks she's special. She's not dumb and she's not autistic."

"What makes you think she's not?" he asked, carefully testing the waters.

"Aside from the fact that she's an albino? Jacob, I can't explain what happened. I knelt beside her and said something about the book Mrs. Browne put in front of her, and she looked at me." Jacob snorted, but she had his full attention.

"She's not blind."

"First off, lots of albinos are. Have you had her vision checked?"

His confident exterior faltered just a bit. "No... do I need to?"

"Albinos have a lot of vision problems. You need to be getting her to regular check-ups," she replied, sounding like a doctor again. This part, she could handle. The rational, known medical reality.

"Oh," he said, his voice unusually soft and vulnerable. For a split second, he actually looked adorable, mask notwithstanding. But as he said, "Second off?" the note of vulnerability disappeared.

The part she couldn't handle. Mary Beth took a deep breath, resting her hand on her chin. "You know damn well she doesn't look at people. I've been watching you get her for months, and she's never once looked at me or anyone else at the café, not even Robin. She looks at the ground. If she can't see people, she thinks they can't see her. She thinks it makes her invisible. And she looked at me."

"You're pretty observant," he dryly remarked.

"I'm a doctor."

"You're a vet," he corrected, leaning forward and kissing her.

Unlike the haul-you-out-of-the-saddle kiss he'd given her on horseback a few weeks ago, this was a tender kiss, like the kiss he'd given Kip's forehead while she lay sleeping.

For just a second, Mary Beth let herself be distracted as she tasted his deep musk, salty and earthy. But then her brain snapped back to attention, and she realized she'd almost fallen for the trap. *Fine. You're going to play dirty, I'm going to play dirty.* Stealthily, she reached up to grab at the strap of his mask.

In less than a heartbeat, he had her hand and was holding her flat against the bed.

"I told you not to do that," he growled as the weight of his body pinned her against the mattress.

"Then stop changing the subject," she quietly snarled back. "If you're going to be a jerk, I'm going to be a jerk, okay?"

"Fine. No jerks allowed." He frowned as he let her go and they both sat up.

Hell, she wasn't sure she believed it either. "Now," she demanded, hopping off the bed to pace around the small room, "tell me why you watch over her, and I don't want to hear any crap about how you used to love her mom. She's special, and I want to know *why*."

Jacob sat there, his shoulders tense as he hid his eye behind his hand.

"Jacob?" she asked, fearful she'd pushed him too far. "What is it?"

"You aren't supposed to know about her," he whispered, his voice dangerously low.

"Apparently, I'm not supposed to know a lot of things," she replied evenly. "And yet here we are."

Jacob threw himself off the bed and walked right up to Mary Beth, grabbing her by the shoulders so tightly she was afraid he would leave marks. "Kip— here's the thing," he said as he leaned into her ear, like he was afraid someone would hear them. "I think—it's possible—she's a holy woman."

"A what?"

"Okay. This all makes sense if you just believe," he whispered, his eye pleading for understanding.

"Believe she's a holy woman?"

"Kip comes from a long line of powerful women. Susan was the daughter of the last holy woman to lead our people, Joy Clear Waters, although Susan didn't get the same gifts."

"You are talking about psychic powers, right?"

"Right." He nodded. "It's more common for those who follow the traditional old ways."

"Yeah. Sure. Of course," she said as she forced a smile. "Makes perfect sense."

"It does if you believe," he replied, finally letting go of her, albeit slowly, trailing his fingers down her arms.

Darned if he didn't give her goose bumps even through the sweatshirt. "Do you believe?"

At that, he seemed to struggle. "I... I believe I'm supposed to keep her safe. That's good enough for me."

He didn't sound convinced—at least, not about the whole holy-woman thing. But she wasn't going to push him on that. She had no room to talk about spirituality or religion or anything. "Okay. Let's say, for argument's sake, that I believe. Stranger things have happened. How does that explain anything?"

"Okay. If you believe, it makes perfect sense," he repeated, although he didn't look like he thought he could convince her. "After Joy Clear Waters died, there was a vacuum in power in the tribe."

"One woman held the tribe together?"

"It's not like that," he scoffed, and Mary Beth resolved to keep her mouth shut. "She kept the tribe rooted in the old ways—our traditions, our culture— what makes us Lakota. And when Susan didn't take her place, a lot of people thought that was a sign that the old ways had died too."

"So when Kip was born—"

"A white child is special." That was something of an understatement—how many albino Indians were there? But the way he said it made it clear that he meant *special* in a different sense. "Susan and Fred knew she had received her grandmother's gifts. But a lot had changed in fifteen years."

"You're saying some people wouldn't want the old ways—which I still don't understand, but that's okay—to come back."

"Buck McGillis sure as hell doesn't," Jacob grumbled.

Lord, am I ever going to be able to keep up with what goes on in this town? She tried not to sound like a smartass. "Why does he matter? He's not Lakota, is he?"

"Rumor is that his grandmother was—a black soul who abandoned her people for the white man."

That doesn't bode well for whatever we've got then. Mary Beth winced as she tried to sympathetically nod.

"And since Joy's death, McGillis has convinced some in the tribe to sell their lands, taken it from others."

"Okay." She knew she was whining, but she couldn't help it. Her head was swimming. "I really don't understand what he wants with the land. I mean, no offense, but when all of us bad white people shoved all you noble Natives onto reservations a hundred years ago, didn't you get the worst land there was and the whites got the good stuff?"

Jacob smiled, bitter and rueful. "That was before."

"Before what?"

"Before uranium."

She froze. "*What*?"

"The reservation sits on huge deposits of uranium. Buck has already started to strip the land on

146

the northern tip of his ranch. He's making millions. He's sitting on millions more. *Hundreds* of millions."

Sweet merciful heavens. This wasn't just about some bad beef or sick horses. Those were small, isolated things. But uranium? She had horrid visions of Chernobyl—a wasteland so complete nothing could live. And the hell of it was, she knew Jacob was right. Uranium wasn't exactly a renewable resource. To find a huge vein of it? Buck could be sitting on closer to billions. With a B. "So he's ripping the Lakotas off?"

"Some. Others, he's paying."

"He's paying you."

"That's not why I do it," he growled.

"Then why?" she pressed. "Robin told me you gave up your own rightful place in the tribe and went to work for that sleaze. How is what you're doing any different than him paying off some other Indian?"

Jacob's eyes flashed with a dangerous anger. "I run a good ranch."

"I know that. Bill said that my first day there."

"I keep the land clean." His voice was rising in righteous anger.

"That's obvious, too."

"I give good jobs to guys like Tommy, guys who need a place." His voice was got louder and louder as he defended himself. "I keep a Lakota hand on the land."

"I know all that," she said calmly, trying to bring his volume back down. "But why do you have to do it for Buck?"

The anger peaked and quickly fizzled. Jacob sighed heavily as he flopped in resignation back onto the bed. "If I let the ranch go, he'd strip the whole thing tomorrow. He'd ruin it forever."

"What's he waiting for? I'd think a guy like Buck would want more money now, not later."

Jacob shrugged. "He wants more land. He knows that as soon as he starts mining no one else will sell him their land, so he's trying to steal everything he can before he starts. I make him enough money that he's content to sit and wait. The tribe sues him every so often, but our lawyers..." he half-shrugged. "That's why I sent Tommy's younger brother, Shawn, to Harvard. Cost me a chunk of change, even after all those minority scholarships he got."

"Wait... you? You sent a guy to Harvard just so you can sue McGillis?"

"The lawyers the tribe has aren't good enough. I'm in this for the long haul, Mary Beth," he said calmly as he patted the bed next to him. "I can wait while Shawn finishes up next year."

"Seriously?" She sat down next to him, and his hand was instantly on her back, fingers splayed out as he gently traced up her spine. *There go the goose bumps again*. She shivered under his touch but forced herself stay on the topic.

"Seriously." He smiled at the repetition. "Not even Robin knows about that. And between you and me," he whispered, "Robin's going to get some help next fall too."

Her mouth was on the bed as she gaped at him. "You fund scholarships?" He nodded. "*You*?"

"Anonymously."

Mary Beth couldn't help but roll her eyes. "Well, duh. But I still don't know what any of that has to do with Kip."

"Try to understand," he muttered in frustration even

as he rubbed her back in slow, sensual circles. "A return to the old ways would cost some people a lot of money. Strip-mining the land isn't a part of the old ways."

"So let me see if I understand this." She hopped up and paced around the room, struggling to understand everything before he tried to distract her again with soft touches. "Kip is a holy woman because she's from a long line of powerful psychic women who kept the tribe rooted in the old ways, whatever those are."

"Right."

"And there are some people, white and Indian, who don't want the old ways to come back because of uranium?"

He sat up and nodded. "Right."

"So her life is in danger because of money?"

"Basically. Susan and Fred decided they couldn't take the chance that someone would come after her, so they ran."

"Okay. I can believe that. It makes sense." Although if she were going to hide, she'd do it in a major metropolitan area with more than one restaurant. Mary Beth sat next to him and he wrapped his arm around her shoulder as she opened her mouth. "So who killed her parents?"

Jacob's confident façade faltered. "I don't know if it was an evil spirit after her powers or something more… mortal after the money."

"The evil spirit thing is still on the table?"

Jacob nodded in all seriousness. "The evil spirit is still on the table. It makes sense."

"If I believe—" Anything else she was going to say was cut off as he nuzzled her head back with his forehead to push her lips up to his.

"Mary Beth," he breathed against her skin.

"Jacob…" She let the sentence trail off, feeling paralyzed by the desire rolling off him.

He tilted his head into hers, the stiff leather nose pushing hers to the side as he kissed her with the perfect blend of tenderness and ferocity. His hand was holding her face, his rough calluses brushing against the fine hairs on her cheek.

As he tentatively traced her lips with his tongue and entwined his fingers in her hair, pulling her in closer, she forgot about the mask. She even forgot about the holy Lakota child sleeping peacefully on the couch. She forgot about the creature, her student loans and the blizzard blowing outside.

All Mary Beth could remember was the last time she'd had sex with Jacob—that frenzied coupling of frantic bodies in desperation to focus on something, *anything*, else.

As she remembered how he effortlessly filled her, easily made her come three times in a matter of minutes, harder than she'd ever come—with or without a man—her body trembled at his touch.

"Do you believe?" he asked, his voice filling her ear as he slipped his hand to the small of her back, pushing her into that broad chest.

"Jacob," she whispered in warning. "Rule number one."

"I fully intend to satisfy, Mary Beth."

All of her sexual frustration ebbed from her into the bed. Satisfaction, after two long months, was near.

He nipped at her ear. Then he dipped his head down to hers again, his tongue searching hers out. When he pulled back, his eye focused on hers.

Then her bra gave beneath her sweatshirt.

"I want you." His hand was up under her sweater, pushing the bra aside as he found her nipple. God, his voice carried right into her body, setting everything on fire.

"Okay," she weakly replied, powerless to do anything but let his thumb roll her nipple against all those calluses.

"I want to make love to you." He cupped the whole of her breast in his hand. "Not like before."

Through the haze of yearning that was clouding her mind, she held onto one of the facts of his past. "Like with Susan."

"Better," he said as he ducked his head down and traced her nipple with his tongue while he moved his hand down beneath the waistband of her pants. "Better."

As he touched her sweet spot, she bucked under his hands, pushing her breast farther up into his mouth. "Don't make me beg again, Jacob."

"I won't."

Quickly, they were naked, curling into each other beneath the mound of blankets. Every part of him was hot to the touch, and Mary Beth touched it all. He hadn't been circumcised, she discovered as she moved his hood up and down, eliciting a low groan that shook his entire body.

"Please," he begged. "Don't. Not yet."

She nodded. She still didn't have any condoms, but she hadn't been with anyone else since last time, and she was willing to bet he hadn't either. Without hesitation, she slipped on top of him. "This?"

He found her clit again. "That."

Like the promise of the kiss, Mary Beth rocked onto

him with the perfect blend of gentle aggressiveness. His eye rolled back into his head as she pressed him against the pillows with the force of her hips.

"God, Jacob," she panted as he flicked his thumb around her clit in perfect time with the crashing of their hips. "Oh, God."

His only response was to grab her bottom, pulling her even farther apart so he could drive in deeper and deeper.

His hand cupping her bottom, his thumb driving her clit, his—Mary Beth gasped as she realized he was slowly rubbing the stiff edge of the leather nose back and forth over her nipple.

"*Oh!*" she quietly screamed through clenched teeth as the climax left her rag-doll limp on top of him.

Without a word, he flipped both of them over, holding her hands over her head as he drove hard and fast. She struggled to break free from his grasp so that she could touch him as he'd touched her, but he held firm, the tip of his mask hovering inches from her nose. The long parts of his hair cascaded down around their faces, closing them off from the rest of the world. In the dark little room of his making, there was only Jacob and Mary Beth and a passion neither could ignore.

With a final crashing thrust, he shuddered as he came deep inside of her. Her whole body shaking with the power of the release, she finally pulled her arms free and held his quaking body to hers.

Eight years since he'd done this. She never would have believed it, not given the way he made her feel— the way he felt *inside* of her. Normally, the feeling of responsibility that would come with that kind of knowledge—that she was the first person he chose to be with beyond his high school sweetheart—would have weighed heavily on her. Mary Beth didn't like to mix this much emotion with her sex. She didn't sleep with virgins and she didn't like to stick around long enough for any man to fall in love with her. Sex was a matter of conveniently relieving her sexual energy. That's the way it had always been.

But as Jacob left her bed and went to get cleaned up in the bathroom, she knew this was different. The first time—that had been different from anything she'd ever experienced. She could have written it off as a one-time-only thing—rough sex against a door.

This time? It should have felt like it always did—but it hadn't. It had been something else. Something different.

She got cleaned up and slid back into his arms. He pulled the blankets up over both of them and held her to his chest. He was warm and solid and real—something she could believe in, even if she couldn't quite grasp everything else. She hugged him and he responded by pressing his lips to her forehead. Something about it made her feel safe. Protected.

"*Thenhíhila*," he whispered in her ear, then his chest rose and fell with even breaths.

As she drifted off to sleep, she wondered what that meant.

That night, Mary Beth had dreams—nightmares, really. She saw the little house with the bloodstained floor, but this time, she saw the bleeding people too. A thing—not quite a man, not quite a bear—moved at the edge of her vision like a shadow, followed by screams. Everything happened out of order—one minute, the dead people were eating dinner, their necks already slit. The next minute, Jacob was bursting in, already wearing the mask. Always, the thing moved where she couldn't see it. And she couldn't see Kip. Where was that girl? God, let her still be safe.

Just a dream, Mary Beth tried to tell herself as the swish of a knife blade passed close to her ears. *Bad dream. Not real. Wake up. Wake up* now.

She shook awake, the remnants of horror still clinging to the edges of her consciousness. Her heart pounding, she rolled over, trying to reorient herself to the here and now—not some shadow of a past she hadn't even been here to experience. Jacob, she thought. Jacob was here and now and maybe a little morning sex was just the thing to chase the rest of that nightmare away from her.

She groped around the bed, reaching farther and farther for his warm, real body.

She came up empty.

Gone. Mary Beth sat up with a start. The sheet fell forward, leaving her bare shoulders freezing. She was alone in bed. Throwing on her robe, she raced out into the living room, only to see the couch was put back together, the blankets neatly folded and stacked in a pile on the floor. The table was empty as well. No one was in the bathroom, and in her mounting panic, she even checked the washer/dryer combo before she saw the note taped to the fridge.

"Took Kip home. Jacob."

She sagged against the table, flooded with relief that everything was normal and yet crushed that he was gone again.

Gone.

Again.

Chapter Eleven

A fter five long days, Ted Yellow Robe managed to get his plow up to the ranch. Six days after he slipped out of Mary Beth's bed without waking her, Jacob stood outside the barn, waiting. He had no idea how much trouble he might be in, but he was pretty sure she'd be pissed at him.

She had every right to be.

The air was already warming in the morning light, and soon there would be nothing but mud as far as the eye could see. But it didn't matter, because she was coming back to the ranch.

She was coming back to him.

Jacob didn't think that she'd appreciate why he'd left without saying goodbye, but his reasons were honorable. He knew that if she woke up in his arms and kissed him with that mouth, made him breakfast and kept on treating Kip, well, like Kip was a normal girl, he might never leave.

When was the last time he'd had a conversation over dinner with someone who was interested in his day and understood his job? For heaven's sake, when was the last time he'd had dinner with someone who *talked*? It felt like normal—like he'd always thought normal would feel. Like normal looked on *Happy*

Days and *The Brady Bunch* and all those shows he'd watched when he snuck over to Ronny's or Tommy's after school as a kid. Like normal had been in the Benge or Yellow Robe households, where he'd been just another kid instead of a future tribal leader.

Sitting at Mary Beth's table, eating the homemade dumplings, talking late into the night and taking the comfort of her bed—well, the whole thing had been profoundly, wonderfully normal. She'd looked at him like he was just a man—not a leader who stepped away from the tribe, not a guy without half his face—just a man. A man she *liked*.

The temptation to stay shut away in her little house, safe from everything but her ferociously sweet mouth, had almost overpowered his better judgment.

But not quite.

Kip liked her. Kip went with her. He had a sickening sense that the safer Kip felt with Mary Beth, the more danger the vet was in.

It was that thought, above all other baser wants and needs, that had propelled him from her bed. The logical part of his brain knew that the more distance between them, the safer she was.

Try and explain that to his dick.

God, but she was good in bed. The way her legs wrapped around him—the way *everything* wrapped around him—it had felt like he'd finally found his place in the world. It wasn't right that the two months between their first and last time had seemed every bit as long, if not longer, than the eight years between his first and last lover. Suddenly, the line between being wanted and needed and wanting and needing was gone, obliterated by a white woman with almost-gray eyes crying out, "*Oh*!" as she took from him what he hadn't believed he still had to offer.

Despite the gusting winds, the mere thought of her body shaking in his arms sent his temperature spiking up a few degrees. There was a long way to go until spring. He wasn't sure when she'd let him back in her bed, but he knew damn good and well it wasn't going to be soon enough.

Here she came. He forced the memory of her warm, bare body curled against his chest as he stroked her hair before dawn broke to the back of his mind. *Don't be a jerk.*

She almost smiled at him as she dug her boot heels into the compacting snow, but he could see he'd guessed right. She was pissed and he had it coming. He couldn't stop his face from going blank. Old habits died hard.

"Jacob," she almost sneered, her eyes narrow slits as she started to stalk past him to the waiting horses.

"Morning, Mary Beth," he replied, trying to remember what he'd practiced. "How are you?"

That pulled her up short. Slowly, she pivoted on her heels, those furious gray-blue eyes looking all the grayer in the early morning light. She smiled a nice smile, but the rest of her face wasn't having any of it. "Fine." She sounded anything but. "How are you?"

He couldn't help but gulp in air as she glared at him. "Good."

"How's Kip?" she asked, her fists jammed into her hips like he was a teenager three hours late for curfew.

"Good," he squeaked out. *Remember the compliment. Gotta give her a compliment.* "Hey,

157

thanks again for dinner. Kip really liked your chicken and dumplings. They were great."

Her eyebrows shot up as she screwed her mouth into a slightly-more-amused-than-pissed smirk. "Oh?"

Jacob was sure he was bright red, but it was too late to turn back now. "There's a good restaurant in Rapid City—Minerva's—I'll take you there this spring to make it up to you." Hopefully, she'll take that the right way, he silently prayed.

Jesus, if looks could kill, he'd have died three minutes ago. "Listen, *ya khara*, if you think I'm—"

Tommy loudly cleared his throat from just inside the barn door. "Hey, Doc. Good to see you back."

Her eyes stabbed through Jacob for just a second more before she turned, all bright and cheery, to one of his oldest friends. Who had probably just figured out Jacob was holding out on him. Damn. Now both Mary Beth and Tommy were probably some degree of pissed.

He sighed. *Can't win for losing.* Then he followed her into the barn.

One day, he'd have to find out what *ya khara* meant. He guessed it wasn't anything good.

Mary Beth knew it was foolish to get her hopes up, but she still roasted a turkey breast and made a pumpkin pie for Thanksgiving, just in case she had company.

She ate alone. Somehow, the phone call from her mom just reinforced how darned depressing her life was. Why else would she be so relieved to hear her mother's voice?

She had to be fair. Jacob had done exactly what she'd told him to. After the blizzard sex, as she thought of it, he'd asked her out, albeit not for another six months. Since then, he'd asked her how she was every morning, usually managing to mention something from a previous conversation. He answered her questions while generally looking at her, although he hadn't touched her again. And when he picked up his dinner at the café before he picked up Kip, he smiled at her, and she saw the man she wanted to know more.

Which was just enough to string her along.

For a month, every night after she sudsed off the smell of manure and sawdust, she hoped that there would be a knock on the door and he'd be there, his black felt hat pulled low over his eye as he slowly looked her up and down. It sent shivers through her body. Every single time.

How ludicrous was it to put on Berry Pink lip gloss before bed? Completely ridiculous, but that didn't stop her. You just never knew when that man would show up.

But after the non-event that was her loneliest Thanksgiving ever, she resigned herself to her fate. Only five months and twenty-two days until May 1. And then she wanted a date. A real date with the masked cowboy.

The second week of December turned bitter cold. Mary Beth couldn't bring herself to trudge down to the café. Why torture herself when the wind chill dipped past minus twenty degrees? Besides, she needed a beef break. A girl could only eat so many hamburgers.

So she stayed home.

Robin was getting more serious with Mikey Nolan anyway, and she wasn't around the café as much since business was so slow. Apparently, Mikey was good for more than just ferrets, but Robin was surprisingly mum about it. Maybe Robin was growing up. She was going to Sinte Gliske University on the rez this coming fall, and realizing that Mikey Nolan— half-Lakota with his own home and business—just might be the kind of guy she needed.

Mary Beth was proud of her surrogate younger sister, even if intense flashes of jealously spiked out of nowhere. Robin seemed to be getting it together and Mary Beth felt stuck in the ninth grade, unable to figure out if the boy she liked really liked her or if he was just playing.

So she channeled her energies into cooking. She made a run to the big Safeway in Rapid City, stocking up for the winter—or at least through the next blizzard. Two hundred and fifty dollars for chocolate chips and Crisco, canned soups and dry beans, tea and cocoa, frozen chicken and frozen veggies—the freezer barely shut. She tweaked Mom's Chicken Masala recipe until it was perfect, honed her cheesy macaroni bake and experimented with homemade lasagna.

One Tuesday night, the temperatures hovering near zero while a pot of chicken gumbo merrily bubbled on the stove, there was a knock on the door. Mary Beth shot out of her chair, knocking *Ferrets, Rabbits, and Rodents: Clinical Medicine and Surgery* onto the floor. A second, more impatient knock followed the first only a millisecond later.

"Jesus, if that's Jacob, I'm going to strangle him for scaring me," she muttered as she grabbed her knife and tucked it in the back of her waistband.

In the middle of the third round of knocking, she flung the door open. "What?" she demanded, dodging Jacob's fist as he tried to hit a door that wasn't there anymore.

"Oh, good, you're home. You haven't been at the café for the last few days."

"It's cold. Or didn't you notice it was December?" she replied before she crouched down to the white figure in the huge puffy coat, the quilted black fabric nearly swallowing her. "Hey, Kip. You staying warm enough? Are you hungry?"

"We've got dinner," Jacob said as he nodded back towards the horses, a curious eye on the stove. "Hey, what are you doing tomorrow night?"

"What?" Mary Beth asked, completely caught off-guard as she remembered she wasn't wearing any lip gloss at all. She licked her lips.

His gaze traveled over her body, sending shivers snaking up her back. "What are you doing tomorrow night? Any plans?"

Is he asking me out? On a date? Mary Beth's brain spun into action. She'd have to shave her legs—time for a new blade on the razor—and wash that pink and green bra and panties set. Maybe Robin could come over and help her get ready. Should she get him a Christmas present? What did you get a masked cowboy? "Well, I guess I'm doing something with you," she cooed.

He looked mildly amused. "Around six?"

"Sounds good." She leaned seductively against the door.

"See you then." He turned back to the waiting horses. Kip wordlessly followed him, a walking black marshmallow.

She shut the door and raced to the window to watch them ride off toward the hills. A date—a real date—with the masked cowboy, and it was still

December. Suddenly, she wasn't in high school anymore, but all grown up. Maybe, after she got into his pants, she could get under that mask.

Although, she mused as she began to dig out her date top, getting into his pants was definitely the priority.

"Ow!" she howled as Robin accidentally brushed her ear with the hot curling iron. "Let's keep the damage to a minimum, okay?"

"Sit still and I will," Robin snipped as she twisted another strand around the iron. "Will this stay up for another few hours? Ronny wasn't all keen on me coming in any later than five, although it's been pretty dead."

Mary Beth debated asking about Mikey Nolan and his many ferrets, but decided that another distraction would only lead to another burn. "It'll stay. You've already put half a can of hairspray on it." Which didn't stop Robin from misting her head again.

"I'll give you credit on the top," she replied, a critical eye assessing Mary Beth's outfit. "He's going to trip over his tongue when he sees you in that."

"Are the sandals okay? Or should I go with the green pumps?"

"Depends." Robin cast a quick glance out at the voluminous clouds that were building. The day had been surprisingly warm, but that wasn't a guarantee there wouldn't be four inches of snow instead of an inch of rain tomorrow morning. "Do you think you're going to get out of the house in that top?"

"Well…" Mary Beth bit her lip, looking to the perfectly clean bedroom. She'd gotten up at four this morning to wash the sheets now crisply folded into hospital corners before she headed to the clinic. If he didn't want to go anywhere, she didn't either.

"Wear the sandals if you can walk in them. Did he tell you who's going to watch Kip?"

Mary Beth nervously began to chew on her finger, and then jerked her newly polished nail out of her mouth. "No, but surely he wouldn't bring her on a date, would he?"

"Don't call me Shirley." Robin giggled.

"Like I've never heard that before." Mary Beth rolled her eyes.

"Almost done." Robin hit her with another flourish of hairspray. "Geez, look at the time. I've got to run, but I want details tomorrow, okay? I want to know how good he is."

Oh, Mary Beth thought as Robin wriggled into her raincoat, *he's plenty good.*

Plenty Holes is plenty good.

With her hair about a foot wide, her nails peppermint red, her strappy sandals strapped on, Mary Beth sat at the kitchen table to wait.

"Only another half hour to go," she muttered, sitting up as straight as possible to keep from wrinkling the silk.

Time crawled. Absolutely crawled. The half hour until six seemed to take about three hours, the second hand refusing to move as the clock mocked her.

She tried to pass the time by imagining all the things she wanted to do to Jacob, and all the things she wanted him to do to her. *It will be nice to take our time tonight. Just me, Jacob and some smoking hot sex. Nowhere to go, no one to see.*

Except Kip, the little voice in the back of her mind said.

"Surely he'll have someone watch her," she tried to reason with herself. "Surely he won't bring her on a date, right?"

Right, the voice giggled, sounding just like Robin. *And don't call me Shirley*.

Finally, an agonizing seven minutes after six, Jacob knocked on the door.

"Coming," she cooed, her voice lilting as she tried to sashay in the unfamiliar heels. She lost her balance, nearly falling in to the door. *Whoa*, she thought. *I'm so out of practice*. But she shook off the klutziness and said again, "I'm coming."

Slowly—and she hoped seductively—she opened the door and leaned against the doorframe. "Hello, Jacob," she said, hoping she sounded husky.

Underneath his sopping wet overcoat, Jacob was wearing a deep-brown suit cut close to his broad chest. Over the white button-up shirt was a turquoise bolo tie. The formality seemed to sit easily on him, although he still had on his scuffed boots. "I'm ready," she added as her gaze fell on the small figure behind him, completely cloaked in a wet poncho.

While she'd sort of expected Kip—Jacob never left her anywhere—she was still disappointed. Hard to have smoking hot sex with a seven-year-old around.

"Uh, hello, Mary Beth," he stuttered, his eye trained on her carefully arranged cleavage. For a second, he looked like smoking hot sex was on his mind as well, but then the stone-faced cowboy glared at her. "Why are you dressed like that?"

"What?"

"You got a date or something?"

This isn't a date, she realized way too late. How ridiculous was she to have assumed that an attractive man asking her if she had any plans automatically meant a date? "Oh, this? This is how I like to unwind after a long day of neutering ferrets," she countered. God bless her mouth. It always covered for her, even when she was embarrassing the hell out of herself.

He stared at her in stony silence for a moment before he said, "Kip, go on in. I'll be back later."

"Yeah. That sounds good." *He'll be back for her? He's not even staying?* Mary Beth's embarrassment flashed into hot anger. Not only was this *not* a date, but he wasn't even going to be here.

She was the babysitter.

The edge of his eye crinkled as if he was smiling at her but his mouth didn't move. He knelt beside Kip and shucked off her slicker.

"Mary Beth will keep you safe, Kip. I promise." He hugged her before she walked in and mechanically sat on the couch. Jacob stood and thrust a ratty looking backpack to Mary Beth. "Here's her bag. It's got her pajamas in there."

"What? Wait, how long are you going to be gone?" Mary Beth was aware she was shouting as he headed back outside into the rain, but she couldn't help it. How in the hell could she have gotten this so wrong?

"Depends on how long the council meeting takes." With that, he turned and sprang lightly onto the back of Mick. As Mary Beth stood there with her mouth open, the rain ruining her hair and running down her cleavage, he clucked to the horse and took off.

165

"*Ya khara*," she muttered as the cowboy melted into the rain. Then the lightning cracked and she realized she was still standing outside. "Jesus." She threw herself back in and she bolted the door behind her.

Kip hadn't moved from the couch, water dripping off the heels of her sneakers as they dangled six inches off the floor. She sat as still as the dead. If Mary Beth weren't pissed, Kip would be freaking her out.

Mary Beth took a deep breath. Just because Jacob was a jerk didn't mean that Kip should suffer. She buried her resentment at the hours spent shaving and primping for nothing and focused on the task at hand.

Kip.

"Hon, you're soaked. Let's get changed, then maybe we can make those cookies I promised."

At least he'd packed Kip's toothbrush. Mary Beth quickly got the girl's face washed and the man-sized T-shirt that was apparently her nightgown over her head without staring at the unmarred ghost-white skin too much. She was surprised to see how thin Kip really was. The few times they'd eaten together, she'd mowed through everything like a growing teenage boy. As Mary Beth wrapped her arms around her and carried her back out to the couch, she wondered at the ribs that poked out.

Maybe she doesn't eat at school? Surely Jacob is feeding her. Robin sends home food every night.

Another unanswered question. Just add it to the list.

Then it was her turn. She stripped off the sodden chemise and tight pants and slipped back into a clean, worn pair of jeans and her college sweatshirt. *I could probably walk around in a chicken suit and Kip wouldn't notice*, she thought as she brushed out the hairspray and pulled her hair back into a low ponytail.

Kip hadn't moved by the time Mary Beth got back into the living room. She looked at the clock. Only 6:15. "You want to make cookies? My cousin's recipe is amazing."

She'd always loved baking with Granny in that cozy little farm kitchen. It often seemed like when the rest of the world went wrong—as it did so many times when she was growing up—there would always be something right happening in that kitchen.

"The secret is to be patient, you know," she said as she dug out the chips and began to preheat the oven. As she assembled the rest of the ingredients, Kip almost glided over to the kitchen table. "You can't eat them right out of the oven. They have to cool. Patience is key."

As the cookies baked, Mary Beth kept talking. She told Kip about the first time Granny let her make the cookies by herself, and how she'd forgotten to put the eggs or sugar in.

"They were terrible." Mary Beth smiled at the memory. "Even the pigs wouldn't eat them."

She told Kip about how she went home to the farm every summer to help her Uncle Hank out. "He taught me how to really work with animals. Uncle Hank showed me how to understand the cows. He's the one who really made me the vet I am."

Finally, the first sheet out of the oven was cool enough. "You want milk, right?" she asked as Kip's hand moved stealthily toward the brimming plate.

Quickly, the cookies were reduced to crumbs.

"Okay, those were good," she agreed with the unspoken compliment as Kip licked a smear of chocolate off her fingers. "We should save some for Jacob though."

They each had one more cookie but by then it was eight o'clock and Mary Beth thought she saw Kip's head begin to nod.

And she had no idea when Jacob was coming back.

Resigned to another slumber party, she quickly got the couch ready. It was raining even harder as lightning streaked across the sky, and Mary Beth wondered if Jacob would just expect to spend the night in her bed again.

Nope, she decided, only a little bitter about the failed date. *That jerk can sleep out here on the floor.*

She dug out her copy of Scott O'Dell's *Island of the Blue Dolphin*. "I'll read it to you. This was one of my favorites when I was a kid."

She slowly spun out the tale of the girl alone, and after a few chapters, Kip's chest rose and fell in even breaths.

Mary Beth looked at the clock. Almost 9:30. *Where the hell is Jacob?*

Jacob sat in the back of the nearly empty meeting room, trying to be invisible. He wasn't doing a great job at it though. Hard to hide in a crowd of seven.

The six people sitting at the half-round table in the front of the room—complete with microphones— were bickering about lawsuits and Buck McGillis. Specifically, half the council wanted to sue McGillis again and the other half didn't see the point. A lone reporter from the *Lakota Times* had struggled out in this God-awful weather and was dutifully taking notes. That was it.

There were more than a few pissed glances from those who didn't see the point, especially as their main argument was that Buck could hire shady-enough lawyers to make another lawsuit a moot point. That, Jacob gathered, was his fault. He was the one who earned Buck his money. He *was* the problem. Didn't much matter to the council if Jacob was also in favor of suing Buck. Anything to slow him down was a good thing, in Jacob's opinion.

He was only half paying attention to the proceedings. His thoughts were on the woman who had greeted him at the door today. As much as he didn't want to admit it, he was developing feelings for Mary Beth Hofstetter. But tonight? Damn. He was feeling *something*, all right, and that something had a lot to do with the way that pretty top had barely covered up her curves and everything to do with the way she'd looked at him, nothing but another night in bed on her mind.

However, the part of his brain that wasn't dedicating itself to finding out what color her bra was this time was a little worried. Okay, a lot worried. Why the hell had she looked so damn good? So he wasn't the most sensitive guy in the world—even he knew that a woman didn't dress like that to watch a little girl. She dressed like that for a date—and her expression when he'd sent Kip inside? He was probably lucky she hadn't stabbed him. He had a horrid feeling that he'd screwed up, but he didn't know how or why.

He had an even worse feeling that he'd find out soon enough.

The door behind him opened, letting in a blast of cold, wet air. The council paused mid-argument. Jacob fought the urge to crane his head all the way around to see who'd come in.

Sheriff Tim Means crossed in front of him and sat down on Jacob's good side. The two men nodded at each other but didn't say anything as the council went back to arguing and the reporter went back to reporting.

Minutes passed. Jacob was aware of the water that was dripping off the ends of Tim's official rain slicker, forming a small pool under his chair. Jacob got the feeling that Tim was waiting for him to start. Well, he could just wait. Jacob had all night.

Finally, the sheriff broke the silence. "Any news?" he asked in a tone too low for anyone else to hear.

"My horses got sick. Strangles."

"What the hell is strangles?"

"Like strep throat."

Tim chewed on that for a moment. "That normal?"

So far, no one else seemed to notice that Tim and Jacob were talking. "No."

"How'd they get sick then?"

Jacob sat on that for a while. If this were a normal conversation—well, hell, if it were normal, they wouldn't be having it. "One of my hands heard something late at night."

"Nobody?"

Yeah, no love lost between those two. "He wouldn't hurt the horses."

Out of the corner of his eye, Jacob saw Tim look doubtful.

"Anything else?"

"No. You?"

"Still waiting on lab reports. The good doctor is giving them hell, but it's going to take time." He was quiet for a moment as the council tried to bring the lawsuit issue to a vote, but they couldn't even agree on voting on it. The bickering continued. "Did you ever find the field?"

Damn it. He was supposed to have found the field—until a storm and Mary Beth drove him way, way off. But he didn't want to admit he'd failed so spectacularly. "Rained out."

"Shit." Jacob nodded in agreement. "When the lab results come back, the big boys will take over."

Jacob understood. Once the BIA and possibly even the FBI got involved, Tim—and anyone who understood anything about the tribe or the rez—would be locked out. If they wanted to catch the person—or persons—responsible, they needed to do it sooner, rather than later.

The council attempted to call a vote again, and this time they succeeded in voting three to three. Then someone else argued that they couldn't vote without the seventh council member, who was probably busy trying to keep his trailer from flooding.

Jesus, Jacob hated this crap. How his grandfather had sat on this council for several decades without committing manslaughter was beyond him. The whole lot of them were no better than kindergartners arguing over who had the cooler crayons. Meanwhile, nothing important got done.

"Have you talked to Rebel Runs Fast? He's usually at the clinic."

That was the second time someone had asked Jacob that question. Maybe the medicine man knew something he didn't. Maybe it was time he looked the man up, although why a medicine man hung out at a clinic was a bit beyond his grasp. Seemed to Jacob that doctors and nurses might not see eye to eye with someone who told people to go into sweat lodges and pray for a cure.

Then he remembered something Mary Beth had said—he should get Kip's eyes checked. If Rebel was at the clinic, Jacob would have a good excuse for trekking all the way across the rez. Two birds with one stone, such as it was. He could placate Mary Beth, get Kip checked out and maybe find out something about whatever the hell was going on. Maybe Rebel could tell him what to do about Kip. "I'll look him up."

"If you hear anything…" Tim stood, scattering water droplets everywhere.

Jacob answered with a nod as Tim walked past him.

The meeting fell apart after that. Nothing had been accomplished. For the first time in a great while, Jacob missed his grandfather. Hell, he even missed Henry Steele. They would have whipped this crew into shape. They could be doing something—anything— instead of just jockeying for position and power.

Disgusted, Jacob slipped out before the reporter got it into her head to start asking him questions. The rain was still coming down. Mick looked less like a horse and more like an upright puddle at this point. Nights like this always made Jacob think about buying a truck. But trucks could be traced and followed and bugged. Horses could come and go and no one would be the wiser. So, resigned to being soaked to the bone, Jacob mounted up and pointed Mick toward Faith Ridge.

He wanted to be excited about Mary Beth and that top and the bed in a room with a door that shut and locked.

He had a feeling that wasn't what was waiting for him.

Chapter Twelve

A slow knock on the door jolted Mary Beth awake. Which was odd. She didn't remember going to sleep. Another knock—not the hard, scary knocking that had her grabbing for her knife. It was quiet, like he knew Kip was asleep.

Mary Beth looked down at the small girl whose head was resting on her lap. Oh. Yeah. Kip *was* asleep. Mary Beth must have dozed off. There was more knocking, growing louder. Still slightly befuddled, she reached down and picked up her knife. As she headed towards the door, she glanced at the clock. 11:45.

"Who is it?" she demanded.

"Jacob, Mary Beth. Open up. I'm soaked."

She opened the door at a languid pace. She knew she was supposed to be mad at him for leaving Kip without telling her his plans, but her mind still seemed to be operating under water. "I'm not sleeping with you, just so you know."

A pair of saddlebags thrown over his shoulders, water was cascading down off the brim of his hat as he looked at her through the small waterfall. "Does that mean I can't come in?" he asked with a sideways smirk.

"Oh!" Mary Beth snapped fully awake. *Wait*, she

thought as she took the saddlebags while he peeled off the soaked top layer. *Did I say that out loud? Oh, hell.*

"Where were you?" she whispered, remembering that she was mad at him.

He smirked again as he kicked off his boots. Slowly, he set the hat on top of the boots. Then the suit jacket came off, followed by the so-wet-it-was-transparent button-up shirt.

Okay, I wasn't *going to sleep with you.* She gawked at the *Flashdance*-style strip tease he was putting on right in her living room. Then he undid his belt and then the pants button. *I may have to reconsider my earlier statement.*

But Jacob paused and took the saddlebags from her. "Excuse me," he said as he walked on the balls of his feet back to the bathroom.

Mary Beth collapsed against the door. *Jeez. Can you be mad at someone while you're shagging them?*

Jacob padded back out, still shirtless but now wearing a pair of black sweatpants. Mary Beth marveled at how differently he seemed to walk without his boots on. He moved silently across the room, scooping up his wet things and returning to the bathroom, no doubt to hang them out to dry.

He planned on staying, she realized. He planned on it all along and hadn't told her. *That's it!* Her anger rose. *Definitely not sleeping with him, and that's final.*

Before the thought faded, Jacob was back, kneeling next to the couch and kissing Kip on the forehead.

God, her mind rushed with the contradictions. A stone-faced cowboy with the soul of a playful Lakota. A seemingly heartless man who tenderly guarded a little girl. A maimed man who didn't want you to look at him unless he *wanted* you to look at him. A righteous Native who worked for the white bully. A man who practically ignored her unless he was sleeping with her.

Jacob lightly ruffled Kip's hair with a smile before he stood up and closed in on Mary Beth. "She really likes chocolate chip cookies," he whispered in her ear and the hot air rushed down her neck as his chest lightly grazed her crossed arms.

Mary Beth's eyes fluttered, but she shook the surging desire out of her head. Not *sleeping with him*, she reminded herself. *Not.*

"We saved you some," she replied, trying to sound cool. "I'll give them to you if you tell me where you were for five hours."

He leaned in even closer, the stiff leather of his nose rubbing the edge of her ear. "I don't want the cookies," he growled as he put one arm around her waist.

"Tough shit, because that is the only offer on the table," she snarled, stepping out of his grasp. Kip rolled over in her sleep. *Damn it*, Mary Beth thought. *I can't yell at him out here without waking her up. Now I've got to take him back to the bedroom.*

Sighing in resignation, she grabbed the plate of cookies and headed back to her room. Chuckling, Jacob followed her, shutting the door behind them without a sound.

"If the cookies are on the bed, does that mean they're off the table?" he asked as he took her side of the bed again.

"Okay, that's it." She tossed the plate at him. He

176

caught it without losing a single cookie, still chuckling. His unflappable ease only made Mary Beth madder. "You listen to me, you... you ass. You are a complete jerk. You can't say, 'Hey, Mary Beth, what are you doing around six tomorrow night?' And not expect me to think that it's a date. Just because we— well, you know—doesn't mean you get to just dump that sweet girl on me without any notice, any explanation, for five freaking hours and then act like I'm just going to swoon at the sight of your perfect body and that's going to make everything okay."

Jacob snorted in amusement as he ate a cookie.

Mary Beth saw red. "If it weren't for the fact that she's asleep out there, I'd kick your sorry ass outside in this weather and keep all your clothes. You didn't ask if you could spend the night and you aren't spending it in my bed, that's for damn sure."

"The cookies are good," was his only response.

"Hey!" she yelped as she raced around the bed and tried to grab the plate from him. He grabbed her hand. "Go to hell," she all but yelled out as she tried to smack him.

He caught her other hand and held her fast. *Damn it.* First-hand knowledge told her she wouldn't be able to get out of his hold unless he was darned good and ready to let her go.

Jacob pulled his legs out of the way and sat her down on the bed. While he still had a death-grip on her, he wasn't hurting her. But he wasn't letting go either. Mary Beth tried to turn away from him, but she couldn't get very far.

"Mary Beth," he began after a painfully long moment, "I'm sorry. That was uncalled for."

177

"You don't own me, Jacob. I'm not a play thing—not yours, not Buck's, not anyone's."

With a steady, unforgiving tug, he pulled her up to his bare chest and kissed her. With her blood already pumping, just the touch of his lips was enough to break her resolve, but she wasn't about to give it up just for a kiss.

A long, wet, sloppy kiss.

When he finally let her go she was more breathless than she cared to admit. But she couldn't let him win, not with something as underhanded as a stupid, wonderful kiss.

"Stop doing that. Just because you are good in bed doesn't mean you get to end any argument with sex." She scowled at him.

"I wasn't ending it with sex. You already said you weren't going to sleep with me tonight." He let go of her hands, and Mary Beth shivered where the cool air touched the flushed skin he'd been holding tight. "Unless you've changed your mind."

"Not a shot in hell," she snipped.

He kissed her again, this time with enough force to bend her backwards. "I have never owned you, but I possess the part of your soul you've already given me. I'm a part of you now, no matter how mad you get," he whispered as he rested his forehead on hers before he kissed that as well.

Not sleeping with him, she chanted over and over. *Not. Sleeping. With. Him.* No matter how beautifully romantic and wonderful and delicious and—

She scooted away from him. One more kiss like that and she was a goner. "Where were you tonight?"

"None of your business."

"Like hell it's not. You show up, dump her on me and expect me to be all panting smiles when you come back? Spill it."

He chuckled again, and Mary Beth thought about trying to smack him for the second time in less than five minutes.

"I went to the council meeting on the reservation. I haven't been in three years."

Robin's stories floated back up. *A Plenty Holes has run this tribe for a long time. Jacob is the first to step away from the council.* And the whole thing with Kip had happened three years ago.

No, not a coincidence, she knew. He'd already said he didn't leave her at night.

"What made tonight so special, hmm?"

He reached over and she tensed against the expected touch. But instead, he grabbed another cookie. *Oh, I'm going to kill him.*

"The tribe wants to sue McGillis to stop his latest land grab. He claims Elmer Tall Hat's will leaves him a huge chunk off the edge of the White Sandy, but that's a load of BS."

"Elmer didn't own it?"

"None of us own anything, Mary Beth. We are merely occupiers. The tribe manages the land for our children. That is how it has always been, and that is how it will be, if I have anything to say about it," he replied matter-of-factly, like it was common knowledge. "Besides," he continued, eating another cookie, "I knew Kip would be safe with you."

Mary Beth opened her mouth to rip him a new one but nothing came out, so she shut it again. She couldn't tell if it was a compliment that he thought

179

enough of her to leave Kip, or if she should still be insulted that she was little more than a combination babysitter and bed buddy.

"And anyway, this almost counts as a date."

"Jesus, Jacob, you are dense, aren't you? This isn't a date. This is a fight that I'm winning, because I'm right and you're wrong."

He looked her up and down, and despite her anger, Mary Beth wished she still had on that slinky little top.

"Oh, I don't know. I like you better like this anyway. You look like you, not some creation of Robin's."

"Great. Well, the next time you ask me if I'm free for the evening, I'll be sure to keep on the shitkickers. I didn't know that was such a turn-on for cowboys."

He leaned back, his eye laughing as his mouth curled up into a knowing grin. "Not like red bras and panties are."

"Get your mind out of the gutter!" she yelped, more to herself than to him as the sensations of their wild rutting during another pounding rainstorm flooded her system.

"You started it. Red panties and shitkickers? On you, that's a wet dream waiting to happen," he goaded her, kicking her thigh with his foot.

She almost went ballistic, but as his eye grazed her chest, she froze. *I'm in charge here.* The realization made her feel wicked—but probably not the kind of wicked Jacob had in mind.

"It's just too bad you won't get to see what color they are tonight," she purred with aggression. "I had a nice set all picked out for you, but you blew that chance out of the water, didn't you?"

The Rancher

He frowned as he shifted, grabbing a pillow from the other side of the bed and pulling it over his waist.

Yup, Mary Beth almost crowed. *I'm the boss.*

"I'll make it up to you, I promise," he started. It almost sounded like he was begging. *Good.*

"I doubt it. You've still got to pay me for babysitting and cookies. This requires far more than a nice restaurant in Rapid City."

"I'm good for it."

"Well, you're good for something." He squirmed again and Mary Beth smiled. She leaned way over, her ponytail brushing against his arm. He stiffened as he watched, waiting for her to kiss him, no doubt.

But Mary Beth kept going and picked up her clock. "12:40. Let's call it a night, shall we?" She sprang up off the bed, not bothering to shut the bedroom door behind her as she went into the bathroom.

She jumped back from the made-up woman who greeted her in the mirror before she remembered how much glitter Robin had slathered on. Quickly, she washed up, brushed her teeth and changed for bed, trying to focus on anything but what had been under that pillow. God, he made her so mad and so horny at the same time. An enigma wrapped in a riddle inside a mystery—that was Jacob Plenty Holes.

Something about him was completely, compellingly irresistible. Maybe it was the mask or that chest or the way he looked right into her. But that other part—that inscrutable part of him drove her bananas. Unless he was naked, or close to it, she couldn't tell what he was thinking about her, Kip or anything in this screwy little town.

"Not going to sleep with him," she reminded her

181

reflection before she headed back out to make sure he wasn't still in her bed. She opened the door and purposefully strode out into the dark hall.

And right into his bare chest.

"Eep!" she squeaked as she bounced backward. As if he'd been doing it his whole life, he caught her before she fell, effortlessly pulling her back onto her feet—and into his arms.

He practically carried her back into the bedroom. "I'm sorry I bailed on you tonight. It was a crummy thing to do to you, especially when you looked so nice."

Jesus, this just gets worse. Mary Beth cringed. Not *sleeping with him.*

"I won't do that again, and I will make it up to you."

"There's always a condition, isn't there, Jacob? You'll work for Buck on the condition that you can screw him over like he screws everyone else over. You'll sleep with me if it's what you want, when you want it. You'll tell me what's going on when it's convenient for you. Well, it's not convenient for me. As sweet as Kip is, this isn't convenient for me. You aren't convenient."

His mouth screwed into a knot as his eye narrowed. She could almost see the leather nostrils flaring, but she was sure that was her imagination.

"That's how it is with you?" His voice was clipped and low. "Convenience first, heart second? Is that what you told all the others when you walked away from them?"

This time, he didn't catch her hand as she slapped his cheek. He stood there and took the hit, almost daring her to do it again.

"Nothing about you is convenient, *thenhíhila*, and you're just going to have to get used to that," he growled as he stared her down. She thought about slapping him again but decided it wouldn't have much impact.

"There are bigger stakes at play here," he went on, leaning toward her as his eye flashed. "Wanting you, falling for you—that's not my idea of convenient. Everything was going according to plan before you showed up."

Whoa! Her brain screamed. *Did he just say*—?

"I've got too much invested here to throw it all away on someone who just wants convenient. I'm sorry I brought Kip here. I clearly misjudged you."

As Mary Beth sucked in a pained breath, he turned, his hand on the knob as he took a deep breath. "It's one thing to push me away but don't do it to Kip. We're all she has in this crummy world."

Mary Beth staggered under the weight of his words. He was falling for her, but he was willing to walk unless she put the same faith in him that he apparently had in her. And Kip needed them both.

Mary Beth sat down, dumbfounded. Finally, her mouth moved. "Well then, there you go."

"Yup. There I go." He stood and grabbed the comforter off her bed, careful to miss her entirely. "Goodnight, Mary Beth." And he was gone, the door shutting silently behind him.

"Yeah," she muttered to herself. "Goodnight."

Somehow, she didn't think they'd be there when she woke up.

And they weren't. He didn't even leave a note this time.

Gone.

Again.

Only five months and one day until May 1st.

Then she might get a date.

Chapter Thirteen

This time, when Mary Beth rolled up at the ranch, Jacob was ready for her. Or thought he was anyway. He was ready for her to be pissed and mad and probably a few other kinds of angry with him. She'd mouth off and try to kill him with a look.

Unfortunately, that's not what he got. When she got out of her truck, she seemed... quiet. He'd never seen her quiet before. All of that sparking energy that he found so attractive was sort of drained from her. Hell, she didn't even look at him.

He decided he liked this much less than her calling him names in Arabic. In fact, he didn't like it at all. "Morning."

Her back tensed, but she didn't respond. She just kept organizing her saddlebags of medical supplies.

Shit. This was bad. Getting worse by the second. All of his smooth talk at asking her out on something that might have past for a date abandoned him in his panic. "I got Kip a doctor's appointment," he blurted out, knowing it was his only shot in hell of getting her to acknowledge him.

"Did you now?" She still didn't look at him, but at least she was talking. Quietly.

"It's at the clinic on the rez. The appointment is Friday afternoon. Tomorrow."

This wasn't coming out the way he wanted it to, not even close. He wanted to say, real smooth-like, "and we could get some dinner afterwards. A little night out. An almost-date."

"That's good." Boy, she was giving him nothing to go on. Not even hope.

"I—" *I want you to come with me.* The words were right there, but his tongue got mixed up with his teeth and nothing came out.

She sighed, a weary thing that only made her look more tired. "What do you want from me, Jacob?"

You. That was what he wanted to say. Hell, it was probably what he should say. He'd wanted her last night and screwed it up. Every time she got under his skin, he stuck his foot so far in his mouth that he about choked on his ankle.

At least he was consistent.

"Because last night," she went on when he couldn't come up with anything brilliant to say, "you seemed to make your position pretty clear."

It didn't come out right. I messed up. That's what he should say—what he needed to say—but he couldn't. His mouth, in a state of panic, had completely shut down on him.

"I..." Mary Beth's shoulders sagged, "... I'm not trying to screw up your plans. Hell, I don't even know what's going on."

His mouth didn't have a freaking clue what it was supposed to be saying right now. But the rest of him had a better idea.

He closed the distance between them in seconds, roughly pulling her into his arms and kissing her. Hard. Her teeth clipped his lip, but he didn't care. This was what he needed, more than anything else. *Her*. He didn't care if anyone saw them. What mattered more was that she knew the truth, even if he couldn't tell her what it was in so many words. He'd always been a man of action anyway.

She was all steel in his arms for a terrifying few seconds, but then she melted into him, tasting of sun-ripened strawberries. The taste of forgiveness.

She pulled away from him, her eyes closed. "You confuse the hell out of me."

He kissed her again—not as hard, but this time, she let her tongue tangle with his. "I don't know how to be around you. Every time I try, I mess it up." She nodded in complete agreement. For some reason, it made him want to smile. So he did. "I do trust you, Mary Beth. Kip trusts you—and that's saying something. I wasn't wrong in that. I was wrong in getting my feelings for you mixed up with... everything else that's going on. They're not the same, and I'm going to do a hell of a lot better remembering that from here on out."

She didn't say anything for a moment, but it didn't matter. He took the chance to kiss her sweet lips again.

Eventually, she pushed him back. "That was a pretty damn good apology, for you."

"Been practicing that whole apology thing recently."

That got him a smart-ass look. "So we're even then."

"Even," he agreed, relieved as hell to see the corners of her mouth curve up into a small, kissable smile. "Come to the clinic with me. With us. I'll buy you dinner on the way home."

She arched an eyebrow at him. "And after?"

His temperature spiked. What color was her bra today? But, even though Jacob didn't always know what to say, he did have an idea that asking would be the wrong thing. "I leave that up to you." He'd prefer to take the comfort of her bed again—perhaps several times—but she'd made it blisteringly clear that one of his many screw-ups last night had been to assume that she'd want to sleep with him. So this was him, assuming nothing.

"We'll see," was all she said.

Damn, she was going to leave him hanging—again.

He deserved nothing less.

On the way back to the ranch after a day's worth of tagging, they made arrangements. Kip's appointment was at four, the last appointment of the day. Since Friday was her day in the clinic and Mike Nolan hadn't scheduled any ferret appointments, Mary Beth could leave early and pick Kip up from school. Jacob would meet them at her house. They'd drive to the White Sandy Clinic, talk to a medical professional and then swing up to the highway north of the rez and hit a restaurant in Wall, South Dakota, for dinner.

Something about the plan felt... cozy. Like something normal people did every day. Mary Beth snorted to herself. Assuming, of course, that normal people had albino children or wore a mask. Hell, she was the most normal one in the bunch—and that wasn't saying much.

"Is it okay if we take your truck?" he asked.

She shot him a scolding look that he couldn't see.

She was on the wrong side, dang it. "I don't know where we're going."

"I can drive."

Mary Beth shot him a doubtful look.

"No, really, I can." He pulled Mick to a stop and fished his wallet out of his back pocket. She snatched his license out of his hand, hoping that it had a pre-mask picture, but no such luck. Just Jacob's normal unreadable scowl. The image could have been a mug shot, more or less a license picture. "I passed the driver's test two years ago. I'm street legal."

"I've never seen you behind a wheel. That's a brand-newish truck. You crash it, you buy me a new one."

Jacob stuck out his hand and Mary Beth shook it. Then, because the man did not fight fair, he kept his grip on her and hauled her halfway out of her saddle to give her one of those searing, possessive kisses that tended to end whatever conversation they'd been having.

"Decided what we're doing after dinner yet?" he asked when he finally let go of her.

Mary unceremoniously plopped back in her saddle, causing Sue to skitter sideways. "I'm still weighing my options."

That got a lopsided grin out of him. "I'll plan for any contingency then."

So last night had been a bust. So he wasn't convenient. So nothing about this was normal.

That didn't make it bad.

Mary Beth picked Kip up at 2:30, which allowed her to see the rest of the children Mrs. Browne taught. A mix of kids—including Lisa, Alex and Gary—paused whatever they were working on to stare at her as she gathered Kip's things. Mrs. Browne was overjoyed that Jacob was finally taking Kip to a doctor. It was the most excited that Mary Beth had seen the stern woman. "And be sure to ask about that school in Rapid City," was Mrs. Browne's parting order.

"Will do," Mary Beth called over her shoulder.

She walked Kip home and wrapped up a couple of cookies for the drive. Jacob showed up a little before three, and they bundled into the truck.

"I still don't like this," Mary Beth grumbled as Jacob pumped the brakes and gas a little too enthusiastically.

"You can drive on the way home," he said, not bothered by her doubt in the least. "We'll cut straight up to the highway. I don't do so good in the dark anyway."

"Is that supposed to be comforting?" she asked through gritted teeth as he took a corner at an unnecessarily high rate of speed. "Jesus, Jacob! Are you sure you can drive this thing?" She clung to the oh-shit bar for dear life. "I mean, not to criticize or anything, but she's supposed to be in a car seat for when you kill us all by driving off the edge of the bluffs."

"Really?" Jacob asked, completely at ease as the truck whipped around another tight curve.

"Yes," Mary Beth snapped through gritted teeth. "Children up to sixty-five pounds need to be in a booster seat and she's not there yet."

"Oh," he said. Mary Beth couldn't tell which part of that quiet little *oh* she liked better—the part that said she was right, or the part that made him sound all vulnerable.

"How do you know all this stuff?" he asked as the tires squealed onto Beech.

"I've got two nieces and one nephew, all under ten. I do this amazing thing—you should try it sometime—called paying attention. Works great."

"Thanks for the tip."

"Honey, does he always drive like this? No wonder you all ride horses instead," she asked the small white figure in back. No response.

"Sorry," he said, sounding anything but. "I'd forgotten how much I like driving."

"Wonderful. Just try not to kill us all, okay?"

"Decided what we're doing after dinner yet?"

She wanted to punch him in the shoulder, but she also didn't want to crash and burn. "Depends on if we make it to dinner, doesn't it?"

Instantly, the speed of the truck dropped down to reasonable levels. Of course, that could have had something to do with the fact that they were suddenly on gravel roads that appeared to veer south into prairie. "Trust me, I'm not going to do anything to jeopardize dinner."

"One thing at a time. Just drive, Jacob."

So he drove.

The ride was eye-opening. Mary Beth realized she'd only ever been on the edges of the reservation, on open range and at barns. But Jacob was driving past houses that were little more than shacks, with rusted-out cars scattered around them. It didn't look like America. It looked like a third-world country, only thirty miles from where she lived.

"*This* is the rez?" she asked in awe.

"A little different from Faith Ridge, isn't it?" He snuck a sideways glance at her. "You really haven't come in this far?"

Ashamed of her ignorance, Mary Beth shook her head.

"I thought Robin might have brought you."

A small child without pants on darted in front of the truck. Jacob slammed on the brakes as both he and Mary Beth threw their arms out to brace each other.

"*Wahtéšni šíne,*" Jacob muttered. "You okay?"

Mary Beth was already checking on Kip. If possible, she didn't look like the jolting stop had moved even a hair. "What?" Mary Beth asked.

"Kid," Jacob explained. "Just a kid."

"Without pants? It's the middle of winter!"

"Mary Beth," he scolded her, "this is the rez. The kid may not have any pants."

Shame flooded her again. "It's really that bad here?"

He turned to look her in the face. "Worse." He slowed as they drove past a hovel of a trailer with a blanket for a door and plywood over the windows. The roof was curled up, looking like one strong puff would pull it free of its moorings. "That? That's where Tommy lives."

"But you pay him!"

"And he gives most of his money to his girlfriend so she can buy food for her kids," Jacob patiently explained. "On the cold nights, he stays with her. She's got a nice cob house, but there's at least ten of them living there."

"I had no idea," was all Mary Beth could say. She just couldn't reconcile Tommy with a hovel like that.

"They haven't gotten rid of us yet," Jacob said, almost to himself, "but they have tried."

They. Mary Beth knew who *they* were. And she was one of them.

191

"Jacob—"

"We have a nicer trailer," he blurted out, his cheek fire-engine red. "All the doors, all the windows, heat in the winter."

A nicer trailer? Compared to Tommy's scrap heap? Anything had to be nicer than that, but that left a lot of room in shack territory. Mary Beth shuddered at the thought of Kip not being warm enough, but she knew that pity would be misplaced. "Oh," she finally choked out. "That's good."

"I'm working on it," he continued as the Ram picked up speed. "We're almost there. You ready?"

"As ready as I'll ever be," she muttered, but suddenly she didn't feel ready at all. It was like she'd studied for a history test only to find herself in an algebra final, the entire semester resting on this one event that she was completely unprepared for.

The truck crested a low hill. At the bottom sat an ugly building, but at least it appeared to have windows and an intact roof.

"That's the clinic," Jacob said.

"You been here before?"

"Once." The way he said it—like it hurt—caught her attention.

She looked at him, at the hard lines on his face. He stared straight ahead, parking the truck without comment. Had he been here the night of the attack? "Jacob…"

He shook her off. "It's time for her appointment." He got out of the truck, not giving her a chance to ask.

Fine. Be that way. As she unbuckled Kip, the door to the clinic opened and out came a huge man wearing medical scrubs.

The man whistled. "Jacob? That you?"

"Hiya, Clarence." He pointed to the side of the clinic that looked like it was half built. "You expanding?"

Whoa, what had happened to Jacob's voice? Suddenly, his accent was twenty times stronger. And sexier, dang it.

She went to lift Kip up and was surprised when the girl's arms went around her neck. "It's okay, honey," Mary Beth said in a soothing tone. "You know Jacob will keep you safe. Me too." But Kip's arms stayed around her neck, so Mary Beth hefted her up.

"The new doc decided we needed a day care. Building it with her own money. Think her sister's supposed to come out and run it or something." He shrugged. "I can't keep up with the plans. All I know is, she's a hell of a good doc, and it's best not to piss her off on a regular basis."

"Good to know."

The big man—Clarence—was staring at Jacob's face. "Nice mask." It could have come out as mocking, but he sounded sincere. "I thought they saved your nose?"

Mary Beth could see the tension rippling across Jacob's shoulders. Kip's grip tightened, just a little. "They did."

So he *did* have a nose under that mask? But if he did, why did he wear it? And how did this guy know about it when no one else did?

Clarence noticed her—or, more specifically, the girl in her arms. "Is that Kip?"

Mary Beth could tell that this whole conversation was exceedingly painful for Jacob. Actually, she was surprised he was even talking.

193

"Yes."

Clarence took a step toward Kip. Jacob took a corresponding step backward, keeping his body between the big man and the small girl in Mary Beth's arms. "Man, I was so worried about her. When they wouldn't let her in the ambulance with you? *Man.*" He let out another long, low whistle that told Mary Beth more than any words could. "I held onto her for as long as I could, but Tim said it was a matter for the law. Broke my heart when social services took her. But you got her back."

"As soon as I got out of the hospital." Each word sounded like a knife in Jacob's mouth, cutting its way free.

"That's good." Clarence looked like he wanted to pat Kip's head, but Jacob's body language made it clear that would be a very bad idea. Then, for the first time, the big man seemed to notice Mary Beth. "Oh, hey."

"Hi." Mary Beth couldn't offer to shake his hand without dropping Kip, so she sort of waved. "Mary Beth Hofstetter, the new vet in Faith Ridge."

Clarence's mouth quirked up into a smile as his gaze darted from Mary Beth to Jacob. "That so? Well, welcome to the rez, Doc."

"Thanks." What else was she supposed to say? She was afraid if she opened her mouth any further, she'd accidentally wind up grilling this guy on everything he knew about Jacob and Kip and the night of the attack, and if she did that, it was a hell of a long walk back to Faith Ridge.

Because one thing was pretty clear. Jacob and Kip had wound up here at the clinic the night of the attack, and this man had played a big part in saving Jacob's life.

"Man," Clarence said, turning his attention back to Jacob, "you should count yourself lucky the new doc wasn't here when that all went down. She'd have hunted your ass down if you hadn't shown up for your follow-up appointment."

Jacob didn't say anything. Not that it stopped Clarence. He grinned and shook his head. "You be careful in there. Even nobody's afraid of her."

Two things happened at the same time. Mary Beth thought, *Nobody*? And Jacob's face moved for the first time since the clinic had come into view. He looked positively shocked. "That a fact?"

"That's a fact. She don't like to take no for an answer."

Jacob seemed to mull over this new information while Mary Beth's mind kept going, *Nobody? Who the hell was nobody*?

"I'll keep to the straight and narrow then." He held out his hand. "Good seeing you, Clarence."

"Good luck, man. And nice meeting you, Doc."

"Likewise." She managed another half wave in Clarence's general direction. After the big man had gotten into his car and driven off, Mary Beth turned to Jacob. "What—"

"We're going to be late," he cut her off again. She scowled at him but decided not to push it right now. They had a long drive home—and she'd be behind the wheel.

The waiting room was empty. A tall, dark and unusually handsome man sat behind a desk, clearly waiting for them. Jacob pushed Kip back into Mary

Beth as he stepped forward to the man and extended his hand. "Rebel."

"Jacob." They shook. Briefly.

Wait, what? Maybe she was hearing things, but it had almost sounded like Jacob said—

"Mary Beth, this is Rebel Runs Fast. Rebel, this is Dr. Mary Beth Hofstetter."

No, she'd heard him right the first time. This man's name was Rebel. Why not? Apparently there was someone named Nobody running around here. And to think, she'd once thought a name like Yellow Robe was weird. "Hello," she said, trying to set Kip down so she could shake his hand. But Kip wasn't having any of it. She hung on with far more strength than Mary Beth would have given her credit for.

So, again, she settled for waving at Rebel. And trying not to look at his long hair. Really long hair. Damn, this man was *gorgeous*.

She immediately came to an important conclusion. While Jacob and Rebel had many things in common, such as their black hair, strong jaws and Lakota heritage, that was pretty much where the similarities ended. Everything that was stony and silent about Jacob was warm and humorous about Rebel. He grinned broadly at her, his whole face lighting up. "A pleasure to meet the new vet. I've been hearing good things about your work. Top-notch."

Whoa. Mary Beth knew she was blushing, but boy, that compliment had just flowed out of his mouth. She shot a look at Jacob, hoping he was taking notes on this. He looked... pissed. At least he'd noticed. "Thank you."

"*Lé winhínala kin hé é he?*" Rebel took a step

196

closer to Kip. This time though, Jacob didn't block his path. Kip seemed to lean into Mary Beth a little more.

Jacob noncommittally shrugged.

"*Thakóna, anhíphe-he ló,*" Rebel said. He didn't pretend she was a grown up and hold out a hand, nor did he go for the condescending pat on the head. He just stood there, waiting.

Mary Beth felt Kip's body tense. Did the little girl speak Lakota? She knew Jacob did—but it had never occurred to her that Kip spoke Lakota. Heck, she didn't even technically speak English. She just didn't speak.

"Oh, for heaven's sake." A woman—a white woman in a lab coat—appeared behind Rebel. Her curly blonde hair was barely contained by a bun. "How many times—" She pulled up short when she saw them. "Oh." Her hands flew to her hair, smoothing it back as she glanced from the cowboy in the mask to the woman holding an albino child. She made eye contact with Mary Beth and managed a small, nervous smile before her hands dropped to her sides. "Hello. I'm Dr. Madeline Mitchell."

"Dr. Mary Beth Hofstetter, large animal vet. I'd shake but…"

Dr. Mitchell smiled with understanding.

"And this is Jacob Plenty Holes." If anything, Rebel seemed amused at Dr. Mitchell's confusion. "My *thenhíhila*, Madeline."

"Wait—what does that mean?" Mary Beth asked Rebel, but she looked at Jacob. He'd said that to her, a couple of times now.

"My love," Rebel said, with a long, lingering look at Dr. Mitchell. "I love you."

Jacob didn't move. She wasn't sure he was

breathing. She knew she wasn't. Was that was he was saying to her? Was that what he really *meant*?

Dr. Mitchell cleared her throat. A bit of color came to her cheeks but otherwise, she showed no other sign of being embarrassed by this announcement. Instead, she was staring at Jacob.

Mary Beth could tell Jacob was not a big fan of this new development. If she didn't know any better, she'd think that Jacob had taken Clarence's warning about somebody—Nobody?—being afraid of the new doctor to heart. "Ma'am," he got out, sounding like Dr. Mitchell had made straight for his incisors with a hack saw.

Still grinning, Rebel carried on with his introductions. "And this is Kip—is it Two Elks or Plenty Holes now?"

Anything pained about Jacob was gone in an instant, buried beneath a glare so dangerous that a lesser man would have had the good sense to take cover—or at least protect his nuts.

Mary Beth looked down at Kip, whose eyes were shut. But her grip on Mary Beth was too tight for her to be asleep. Two Elks? Was that her last name?

"This is Kip," Rebel finally said into the agonizing silence. "She has an appointment."

"Come on back," Dr. Mitchell said. "What brings you in today?"

Mary Beth waited for Jacob to say something, but he had apparently decided he was done talking for the time being. So she took over. "I don't think she's had a checkup in three years and I'm worried about her eyes."

Dr. Mitchell nodded. "Look up, sweetie."

Kip didn't move.

Mary Beth felt stupid, which translated into her glaring at Jacob. "Oh, and I doubt she's spoken a word in three years. Her teacher thinks she's severely autistic."

Dr. Mitchell's mouth curved into a frown, but she didn't miss a beat. "I see. That rules out the vision chart then." Moving slowly, she tilted Kip's head back. "I'm just going to shine a light in your eyes, okay, sweetie? Nothing bad. Just a little bright light."

The exam continued. Dr. Mitchell asked questions, Mary Beth did her best to answer them on behalf of Jacob. Which was to say, she had almost no answers. What the hell was wrong with that man?

"And you?" Dr. Mitchell turned to Jacob, clearly not intimidated by his best intimidation.

For a man with only one eye, he packed a lot of punch into that glare.

Dr. Mitchell stuck her hands on her hips and met Jacob's glare with a look that Mary Beth could only call a sneer. "I'm going to assume you haven't followed up on your injury either. Are you having any problems, either with vision or breathing?"

Rebel had the nerve to chuckle, but Mary Beth could see why anyone would be afraid of the doctor. "Easy, Madeline." He turned to Jacob. "This is usually the part where she tells you that you should be seeing a therapist and have Kip enrolled in a special school and all that stuff."

Dr. Mitchell huffed at him. "And this is usually the part where you tell everyone to go to a sweat lodge."

They seemed to be having an argument—a

familiar argument—but underneath, Mary Beth could sense an affectionate current.

Rebel turned back to Kip. "Three years, huh?"

Jacob nodded. At least, Mary Beth thought he did. Hell, at this point, she couldn't even be sure he was breathing.

Rebel crouched down in front of Kip and looked her in the eyes. Everything seemed to slow down as the two of them stared at each other. At some point, Mary Beth noticed that Rebel's eyes had gone surprisingly blank and he seemed to be wavering where he stood. His wife noticed too, and steadied him.

What the hell? It was as if the man had slipped into a catatonic state or something.

Unexpectedly, Rebel shook back awake. In the process, he lost his balance and wound up on his butt on the floor. He drew his knees up and stuck his head between them as Dr. Mitchell rubbed his back. "It'll pass in a minute," she reassured them. "It always does."

Kip didn't move, didn't even blink, but Mary Beth got the feeling she was... nervous about this whole thing. She scooted up on the table next to the girl and looped her arm around Kip's thin shoulders. "It's okay, honey," she said in a quiet tone, but she couldn't tell if she was reassuring Kip or herself.

Finally—although it probably only was a minute—Rebel sat up and moved into a cross-legged pose. "Nothing."

"Nothing?" It was the first thing Jacob had said in close to half an hour.

"Nothing. Either she's buried everything deeper than I can see it or..."

"*Or?*"

"Or she doesn't have the gift."

This pronouncement settled over the clinic. Then, without warning, Jacob exploded. "*Doesn't have the gift?* Are you kidding me? But if she doesn't have the gift—if it's just not *there*—then why the hell would anyone have come after her and her parents? Why the hell would they have done—" He was in such a state that all he could do was wave at his mask. "*Why?*"

Rebel remained calm. "For the same reason that you protect her, Jacob. She doesn't have to be holy to be special." He reached up and patted Kip's foot. "It will be all right, little one."

That shut Jacob up. Dr. Mitchell looked at Mary Beth, the only person in the room to realize how confused she was. "Rebel can see," she said, as if that explained everything. "If you can believe it."

If you believe. Jacob had told her that once. Looked like now was as good a time as any to start believing.

Then a voice spoke from near the waiting room. "So." A massive man seemed to have appeared out of nowhere.

Muscles was all Mary Beth could think, followed closely by *scars. Lots of scars.* The man was, hands down, the scariest person she'd seen in the flesh in a long time—and that was including Buck McGillis. Instinctively, she threw her arm around Kip's shoulders and leaned forward, trying to shield the little girl with her body.

No one else in the room moved. Hell, no one else even seemed disturbed by this brute of a guy. If anything, she thought Jacob might be… smiling?

The guy looked around the room without actually looking at her. She braced herself for the worst—would he pull a gun or what?

He didn't. He just said, "You called."

Chapter Fourteen

Jacob sat in a chair in the waiting room. Mary Beth was in the chair next to him and Kip was spread out over both of their laps, fast asleep. Rebel was sitting cross-legged on the floor, leaning back against his wife's legs. She'd pulled the desk chair around to the side but she kept a hand on the desk, fingers drumming.

Nobody was, for lack of a better term, mopping the clinic. Jacob watched him. It wasn't the first time he'd cleaned the place, that much was obvious. Didn't make any sense.

"After Albert died," Rebel explained, "Nobody helped out."

"He did a good job staying on top of things during the outbreak," Madeline added.

Jacob snuck a look at Mary Beth, who did not look mollified by these ringing endorsements. When he'd introduced Mary Beth to Nobody, they'd both managed a polite nod. Jacob could see Mary Beth trying to form the words. God only knew what she'd come up with. So far though—nothing. Odd as that was.

Rebel was telling him everything he knew about the rancher. "I went out with Nobody the second time, but by the time we got there, wasn't much but the stink and some stains. I took some samples—"

"And I got them processed," Madeline added, fingers still tapping. At first, Jacob thought it was because she was nervous, but nothing about her said she was uncomfortable. Instead, he got the feeling that she was sitting in judgment of him.

Damn, no wonder Clarence had tried to warn him about Dr. Mitchell. For a second, he'd expected her take the mask off herself and start examining him. No wonder Nobody seemed cowed by her—as cowed as Nobody ever got anyway.

He asked the question he didn't want to ask—but that's why they were all here, wasn't it? "Have you seen anything?" Anything beyond Kip not inheriting her grandmother's gifts. Jacob still couldn't get his head around it. He'd assumed that between being Joy Clear Water's granddaughter and the whole albino thing, Kip had to be a holy woman. Clearly, Susan had assumed the same thing. As had whoever had come after her.

And they'd all be wrong.

Jacob looked at the little girl whose feet were in his lap. Mary Beth was stroking her hair with one hand and had her other one looped around the girl's waist, holding her on their laps. *Still special*, he thought. That was what he had to remember.

Rebel looked lost in thought, making Jacob wonder if he was about to slip off into another vision thing. But then Rebel sighed. "I have seen something. Understand the past, understand the future."

Beside him, Mary Beth startled—not enough to be rude, but enough that he could feel it. "Is that like 'those who do not know the past are doomed to repeat it'?"

Rebel favored her with a kind smile, which made Jacob want to punch him in the teeth. "Do you know what the Sun Dance is?"

"A what?"

Madeline cut in. "They erect a pole, tie a rope to the top and attach bear claws or bones to the other end. Then the medicine man—" she looked at Rebel, "—will pierce a young warrior's skin and thread the claw or bone through it. The warrior then dances around the pole until he pulls the claw or bone free."

"We do it for a good reason," Rebel said quietly.

"It's not my favorite thing," Madeline said, more to Mary Beth than to her husband. "Messy to suture. Big scars."

"Scars are a thing to be proud of," Rebel insisted, a little louder.

"You're… you're serious? You rip holes in your chest?" She looked at Rebel's shirt. "Seriously?"

"It symbolizes a warrior's sacrifice to their family and their tribe." Then Rebel's tone changed, slipping more back into an argumentative tone. "And I haven't done it. I only performed the ceremony once, at a warrior's request before he shipped out to Afghanistan."

"Still messy to suture," Madeline grumbled.

"The vision," Jacob prodded them. He could feel Mary Beth's eyes on his chest as well. "I haven't done it either," he added under his breath.

"Right. In the vision, a warrior is tethered to the pole and he dances. He is tired and he wants to fall down—to pull free and accept his scars for his tribe—but there is a shadow. A *shadow*," he repeated in a quiet tone, like he hadn't figured that part out yet. "And this shadow, it won't let him fall. It blocks out

205

the light, hiding the warrior. The warrior, he dances and dances but he can't break free as long as the shadow is watching. He cannot finish."

The weight of these words settled over the room. Even Nobody stopped cleaning and came to stand in the doorway that separated the waiting room from the rest of the building.

Accept his scars for his tribe. Jacob felt gut-punched by these words. How much longer would he wear the mask? Hide the girl? Be alone? He knew the answer, of course. There wasn't any doubt about it.

For as long as it took. That was that. That was all it had ever been.

Mary Beth reached over and took Jacob's hand in hers. It was light, warm—real. She was really here. Kip was here. Hell, *he* was here and that was something. Rebel's little vision was just that—a vision. Nothing he could touch with his hands. Nothing he could measure or plan for or work with. Nothing he could make sense of. None of it.

But then he looked down at Kip, still sleeping. He'd seen what killed her parents, what carved him up—well, he'd sort of seen it, but it had been real. And he still hadn't been able to plan for it. He still couldn't make a damn bit of sense about the whole thing.

Rebel seemed to sense his confusion. "Understanding the past can be complicated. These things are always open to interpretation." Jacob followed his gaze to Nobody. The silent man stood, apparently unmoved by Rebel's story, but Jacob saw the scars that covered Nobody's arms and remembered the gunshot wound healing on his shoulder.

"Okay." Mary Beth exhaled loudly, breaking the

tension in the room. "Let's say, for argument's sake, that I believe everything you've said tonight—about Kip being special but not that *kind* of special, about seeing and visions and whatever the hell a Sun Dance is. Stranger things have happened, sure. But the question remains—how does that explain anything *now*?"

Her hand was still in his, resting on top of Kip's rising and falling tummy. All he could think was, *she's got a hell of a mouth on her*. And she was here with him.

"That," Rebel said with a sheepish grin, "is the tricky part. But this vision has come to me twice now. These things don't usually happen in repeats. It means something."

"But *what*?"

Jacob squeezed her hand. It was a damn fine question, but she had a particular way of asking it that he liked. Hell, there wasn't much about her he didn't like.

"I think it means that the shadow is still out there. But what that shadow is—a rancher doing something in the fields or whatever took her parents—" he motioned to Kip, "I don't know. I don't know if it's the same person, as much as some people might like it to be." Rebel pointedly looked at Jacob. "All I can say at this point is, keep her safe."

"I do."

"Not enough." When Nobody spoke, Mary Beth about cleared her chair, causing Kip to curl into a tighter ball, her eyes squeezed shut.

"What?" Jacob demanded.

"It's not safe enough, your place. One way in, one way out. No phone, no way to call for backup." By any objective measure, that was a lot of talking for

Nobody. "Someone lights a fire, drives you out, picks you off. Easy." He made a popping noise with his mouth that made Mary Beth jump again.

"I can protect her."

Nobody stared down at Jacob, who suddenly realized he'd left his gun at Mary Beth's house.

"I've seen tracks."

"*What*?" Jacob shot out of his seat, causing Mary Beth to have to scramble to keep Kip from falling to the floor. "What do you mean, you've seen tracks?"

Nobody didn't flinch. "Been checking."

Rebel was up now, positioning himself between the two of them. "Easy, boys."

"*Fuck* easy," Jacob said as he shoved Rebel. "What the hell do you think you're doing, stalking around my trailer?"

"Watching your back." Nobody's words were tight. Angry. *Dangerous*.

"You stay the hell away, you freak." At this, Nobody took a step forward, his arms down low. Jacob knew he wouldn't win, but he'd be damn sure he went down with a fight on this one.

"That's enough!" The lady doctor's ice-cold voice sliced through the air, bringing everyone up short. She stood and glared at Nobody, who took that step back and dropped his eyes. "You—stop stalking people without their express written permission. And *you*." She turned to Jacob, her mouth twisted into something that was more horrific than mean. Against his will, he shrank back. "Accept that you're not in this alone. Both of you, shut up. You're scaring the girl. I swear, I won't stitch either of you back together."

Jacob spun to see Kip curled up into an

impossibly small ball on Mary Beth's lap, her eyes wide open, staring at the window at the last gasp of the sunset. Shit. He'd woken her up.

Plus, Mary Beth was trying her damnedest to kill him with her eyes. "For crying out loud," she muttered, rubbing Kip's back. "Are you two done yet, or should we come back later?"

He wanted to apologize to her and to Kip—especially to Kip, poor kid—but not in front of Nobody.

Ever the diplomatic one, Rebel asked, "What kind of tracks?"

"Don't know. Couple of human tracks one night—maybe size twelve, men's—but then..." he shrugged. "Don't know what those other things were. Bigger. Pointed."

Flashes of the thing that had cut him passed before Jacob's eye. Big—bigger than a man and not quite human. "Hooves?"

"Or something someone wanted to be a hoof," Nobody agreed.

A tiny noise, barely audible, came from behind him. Then Mary Beth gasped. "Did you hear that?" she demanded in as quiet a voice as she could.

"Was that you?"

"It was Kip."

In an instant, Jacob, Rebel and Madeline were all crouched around the small girl. Even Nobody had come closer, looming over everyone.

No one spoke. Instead, they all stared at Kip, who, if anything, had curled into an even smaller ball. Eventually, her eyes closed, but not in sleep. Instead, her forehead creased with the effort. She looked like she was in pain.

It was still out there, whatever *it* was. And Rebel had spoken the truth—maybe it was tied to the rancher or Buck, maybe it wasn't. That didn't change things. He still had a duty to keep Kip safe. He owed it to her, to her parents and to himself.

"Nobody's right," Rebel said after another silent moment had passed. "Your trailer isn't safe enough."

"Where are we supposed to go?" Kip did best with her routine. She was already so scared...

"You'll stay with me, of course." Mary Beth's tone made it clear she wouldn't take no for an answer. "I have a land line, a smart phone and a back door. The porch is crumbling, but it's an exit. And if anyone tries to smoke us out, we can open a window and yell for Robin and Ronny. Problem solved."

Jacob felt everyone else in the room relax—everyone except him. If he started crashing at Mary Beth's house, people would notice. People would *talk*.

For some crazy reason, that made him almost as nervous as knowing something had been stalking him to his trailer.

"Jacob," she said, her voice dropping down several notches until it bordered on sultry. "Trust me on this."

Hell.

After Mary Beth and Madeline had exchanged office numbers, home numbers, cell phone numbers and email addresses, she and Jacob loaded Kip up into the truck. Night had well and truly fallen, the dark sky endless over the grasslands of the rez.

"Dinner?" he offered. He'd promised, after all.

He remembered. She smiled at him, but it felt a

210

little shaky on her face. "I think…" She looked up at the night sky, interrupted only by the light of the clinic. "I think I'd like to go home now."

Jacob looked at her with his one eye. She couldn't tell what he was thinking. Hell, she didn't know what to think anymore. This world she'd stumbled into? If she believed. The problem was, she didn't know *what* to believe anymore.

Jacob nodded. The only talking was him giving her directions up to the highway.

Finally, after a long forty-five minutes, they hit the Faith Ridge exit. Mary Beth took the corners a little faster than she normally would have, but she couldn't help it. The night seemed extra scary.

She tried to tell herself that she was being ridiculous, that that they were in no immediate danger, that even if something—besides a very scary man named Nobody, that was—was stalking them, it'd take everyone a few days to realize that Jacob and Kip were staying with her, but all those true things didn't stop Jacob from flinging open the truck doors, grabbing Kip and racing into the safety of the house with her hot on his heels. It wasn't until the doors were safely bolted and the table safely shoved behind it that Mary Beth realized that Kip was out like a light.

"She fell asleep, even after that nap earlier?" Mary Beth whispered in surprise.

"She always liked the movement, even as a baby." Jacob carried her back to the bed. When he came back out, he continued, "Freddie always used to ride her around on this old gelding he had when she was fussy. Worked every time." His smile grew as he kicked off his boots. "You should have seen them.

Fred was this big guy—made Ronny look tiny—up on this old horse with this little white baby over his shoulder. That's what he was doing the day I found them."

It was unusual for him to talk about Kip's family, but then, what part of tonight had been normal? "How long had you been looking?" she carefully asked as she slipped off her jacket and curled up next to him.

"Three weeks. And it's not what you were thinking," he defended.

"What? I didn't say anything. What was I thinking?"

"I didn't go looking for Susan. Freddie won her fair and square. I loved them both." His eye grew misty as he ran a hand through his hair. "After my grandfather died, I didn't have any other family except for the Benges and the Yellow Robes and Fred and Susan—you know. The tribe was my family."

Mary Beth nodded. One big extended family, linked by blood. Once, they'd taken care of him, and now he returned the favor as best he could.

"But by the time I finished college—well, I only had Fred and Susan. Ronny was back from Iraq, but he wasn't *back* from Iraq, and Tommy—well, he had it rough for a while, and I didn't have anyone else."

She'd never asked, partly because she'd never thought it was any of her business. But he was making it her business, even after he'd told her he didn't have anything else to give. *One of these days*, she thought as he leaned his head against hers, *I'm going to figure you out. It's just not going to be today.*

"I didn't want them to just go away. I didn't want to feel so... alone," he whispered.

She fought the urge to tell him if he stayed with her, he'd never be alone again. "So you tracked them down."

"Freddie was plenty mad at me at first. They didn't want to be found, and they figured that if I found them, others would too, but Susan... she was smart. You would have liked her a lot." He smiled at the memory, and Mary Beth was sure she would have.

Once, Susan had loved him. Mary Beth couldn't help but wonder what had changed that. Maybe it hadn't been her destiny. Sometimes, fate had a funny sense of humor.

"She cooked up the idea that I would say I'd heard from them in Pierre and stuff," he continued.

"You became the decoy."

"And the pack mule." He snorted. "You can't just go off the grid with a three-month-old, you know. You need stuff."

Mary Beth smiled. "I can just see you buying Pampers and formula." Strangely enough, she could. He wouldn't be terribly good at it, like he wasn't any good at dressing Kip, but he'd do it without blinking an eye. One eye.

"Yeah, something like that," he said with that half-shrug. "I went out every week or so, stealing a day from studying. Made sure to take a different route every time. Never the same way twice."

The *until* hung in the air as his face darkened and stilled into the stone-faced cowboy again. "Jacob," she said quietly, "I'm sorry they died. I really am."

"Yeah." He picked up her hand and laced his fingers between hers. "It just doesn't make any sense why this is happening." He looked around, coolly assessing the defenses. "Only the porch door in the bedroom and that one window?"

She nodded.

"Tomorrow, we'll move the bookcase in front of the window. She can sleep with you, and I'll guard from the couch."

The horrifying image of a shadow—a thing with big hooved feet chasing a dancing warrior around—floated up in her mind again. "What about tonight?"

"Tonight?"

Mary Beth stood and faced him. Her smart mouth deserted her and she felt small and insignificant in the face of something she couldn't even begin to understand. "Jacob, please, I don't want to be alone tonight. Please."

He wrapped those strong arms around her and kissed her forehead. "Yeah. Neither do I." He turned and pulled the sweatpants out from behind the TV.

"You left those here?" She almost laughed.

"I was planning on coming back," he sheepishly explained as he began to undress.

But this wasn't a show. This was life or death hanging in the balance, and sex was not part of the equation, not tonight. So she turned away and went to change in the bedroom.

As she slipped her old Garfield nightshirt over her head, Jacob silently padded in. They worked in unspoken unison as they slid the dresser in front of the door. While Jacob took the shade off the lava lamp and set it under the window, Mary Beth scooted Kip off the covers and climbed in bed.

She wrapped her arms around Kip, and seconds later, Jacob was behind her, his arms circling her waist as his stiff leather nose poked through her hair.

She half-rolled over. "Do you always sleep with the mask on?"

"No," he whispered, looking ashamed.

With her free hand, she reached up and traced the edge where leather met skin. "I won't look. I promise."

As she rolled back over, she heard three small snaps before his arm was back around her.

"You are an amazing woman, Mary Beth Hofstetter," he whispered, his mouth against her ear as he molded his body against hers. His breath rushed against her hair at a different angle, bathing her in his warm musk.

Safe in his strong embrace, with Kip tucked into hers, Mary Beth fell asleep.

And slept dreamlessly.

Snap.

Huh? Mary Beth thought. *What time is it*?

Snap. Snap.

Oh. Right. The mask. She opened her eyes and found herself face to face with Kip, her purple eyes only inches from Mary Beth's.

"Morning, honey," she whispered. "Do you get to see Jacob without his mask on? He won't show me."

"I can hear you, you know." He chuckled behind her. "I'll be right back." Jacob shoved the dresser out of the way. The bathroom door clicked a few seconds later.

"You okay, honey? I hope Jacob and that Nobody didn't upset you too much last night."

Mary Beth wasn't expecting an answer, but she was surprised when Kip reached up and rested her hand on Mary Beth's cheek. Even for being wrapped in blankets and against Mary Beth, her skin was still cool to the touch.

"Yeah. Okay. Just have to remember that patience is the key." The bathroom door clicked again as Mary Beth stretched out. "It's Saturday. I've got cereal, toast and eggs. You want breakfast?"

After they mowed through the last of the eggs, Mary Beth asked, "You want me to walk with you two?"

"People would notice." Jacob shrugged.

"Yeah. Okay. No need to set the gossips off."

"You stay with her until tonight. I'll run by the trailer after I check on my horses and grab some stuff before I come down."

Mary Beth brushed her hand over Kip's hair. "It's just you and me, honey." She was on call today. Hopefully, there wouldn't be any calls, though.

Jacob kissed her forehead. "See you tonight. And be safe."

Despite the weirdness of the situation, Mary Beth couldn't help but float as she dressed.

He hadn't been gone when she woke up.

He was coming back tonight.

She'd never been so happy at the thought of having a man to come home to in her whole life.

Kip polished off the spaghetti and buttered bread, and then Mary Beth gave her a bath before Jacob tucked her in. Mary Beth read two more chapters of *Island of the Blue Dolphin* before Kip's little body settled into sleep.

Out in the living room, Jacob was sitting cross-legged on the couch wearing nothing but his sweatpants again, an open book on his lap and a Colt .45 beside him.

"Man, and I thought everyone had knives," Mary Beth muttered as she sat next to him.

Grinning, he wrapped his arm around her shoulders as she picked up the book.

"*The Ecology and Management of Grazing Systems*? Sounds like fun."

"Always."

"You really have an MBA?"

"University of South Dakota, class of 2010. *Summa cum laude*."

"I am impressed, you know."

"White people usually are." He snorted.

"What's that supposed to mean?"

He sighed heavily, his eye apologizing. "It's just that it takes a lot of work to walk in both the white and Lakota worlds, and few people appreciate that."

"So the Lakota don't think much of the MBA?"

He snorted again. "Which ones? The ones that think I've sold out the tribe, or the ones who treat me like an endangered species? These days, the only person who really gets it is Shawn—and he's still at Harvard."

She threw up her hands, dropping the textbook back in his lap with a thud. He winced. "I'm *trying* over here. I don't speak the language. I talk with medicine men. I have an albino asleep on my bed. And you are about the best damned businessman I've ever seen."

His eyebrow shot up as he carefully turned the page. "Businessman? Not what I was hoping for."

"You're impossible!" She sighed as she collapsed on his bare shoulder.

Lightly chuckling, he wrapped his arm around her, snuggling her in tight as he turned another page filled with charts and graphs.

Mary Beth sat and listened to him breathe for a few moments, but the question that had been bothering her all day refused to go unanswered any longer. "Jacob?"

"Hmm?" he asked, turning the page.

"What happens next?"

"What do you mean?"

"Okay. Let's just assume, for argument's sake, that we defeat the shadow thing and save Kip and earn our superhero tights. Then what? What happens next?"

He cocked his head in that way that Mary Beth knew meant she had his undivided attention. "I'm still not sure I know what you're talking about."

"You do realize that she's just a little girl who misses her mom and dad? She's only seven. She's not ready to lead the free world or the tribe or do much but run around and ride horses. You'd do her a big favor if you just treated her like a real girl, okay? She just wants to feel normal."

"She's not normal," he patiently explained. "Even if she's not a holy woman like her grandmother, she's not normal."

"I *know*." He was being intentionally obtuse, damn him. "That doesn't change the question. What happens next? Will she ever be normal?"

He thought about that for a while. "She used to be pretty normal, for a four-year-old. Giggled at squirrels chasing each other, laughed when I stuck straws up my nose and snorted milk—"

"Geez, you are a boy, aren't you? Garth Courland used to do that all the time in school."

He hugged her tighter. "I've got some money set aside for her. Then, when she's around thirteen, she'll go to Bear Butte for her vision quest. After that—well,

218

it depends on what she sees. The elders—and that does include Rebel—will interpret her vision. No matter what happens, I'll take care of her for as long as she needs me to."

Mary Beth looked at him next to her, the proud Lakota warrior. "You're a good man, Jacob Plenty Holes."

He kissed her forehead with a smile. "You make me better."

She blushed under the weight of that compliment. It was a damn good one, made all the better by the fact that he'd given it in such a casual way. He could turn on the charm when he wanted to. "Great." She rolled her eyes. "When puberty hits. Can't wait to see what raging hormones do to her. Looking forward to it."

"You know," he leaned forward, his lips hovering just beyond hers, "you've got some mouth on you. I like it."

As he kissed her, Mary Beth let herself get lost in the sheer manliness that was Jacob Plenty Holes. His strong arms around her, his firm lips pressing against hers, his tongue caressing hers—it was almost too much to bear. She broke away from him before she completely lost what was left of her mind.

He ran his fingers along her jaw, lifting her face to his. "You are an amazing woman, Mary Beth Hofstetter. I keep waiting for you to run screaming."

"I couldn't leave her. She needs me."

"Yeah," he agreed as he feathered kisses down her neck. "She's not the only one."

The next kiss was anything but light. Mary Beth curled into him as she wrapped her arm around that fine bare chest. Her cowboy hero, sworn to protect the weak and helpless, just like in romance novels. *Maybe one day*, she thought, *we'll ride off into the sunset together*.

But then an old memory bubbled up to the surface, and she could almost hear her Granny saying, "Romance is a tragedy that happens to someone else," which was what she said every time Mom did something stupid, like take Skeevy Greevy back because he'd done something that was almost romantic.

And this tragedy wasn't finished playing out. So she pulled back from his warm arms and warmer lips, and he let her.

"No, wait." She sighed, forcing herself to push him away. "We aren't done yet."

"Fine," he grumbled, pulling her back up. "What part of this did you want to talk about?"

"Assuming that everything turns out okay, and she's safe and all that good stuff, what happens with us?" She ran her hand down his bare chest. "What happens with this and us?"

He froze. "What do you mean?"

Something in his eye was a warning, but it was too late to stop her mouth. "I mean, what do we do? At this exact moment in time, you are sort of living with me. Are you two just going to stay? Do we finally start dating? Are we something more? What happens to us?"

Immediately, the playful Indian was replaced with the stone-faced cowboy sitting beside her as all that lovely sexual tension fell like a rock from the room.

"What?" she cried as he scooted farther away from her. *Warning*, her brain shouted. *Danger!* But her mouth was on a collision course, and there was no stopping it. "I didn't mean it like *that*. It wasn't an ultimatum, really."

"Then why did you ask?" he said, his voice low and cautious.

"Because I—I don't know. Because I like you, a lot. You're smart and kind and sexy as all hell, and I can never figure out what you're thinking unless you're naked, and I don't know where I stand with you," she babbled as her brain kept yelling, *Shut up! You sound like a fool!*

But she ignored her better judgment. "Some days I think you like me too, and some days I think all you see in me is a roll in the hay, and some days I feel like I'm your babysitter, and some days I don't know whether to strangle you or kiss you."

Shut up, her brain screamed. *Stop talking. He's just a man. Walk away!*

But she couldn't listen to the voice that had always told her to walk.

For the first time in her life, Mary Beth realized she didn't want to walk.

She wanted to stay, and she wanted him to stay with her.

And he sat there, his eye unreadable, his nose pointed toward the door, his lips nearly invisible they were pressed so tightly together.

"I'm—I'm sorry, Jacob. I didn't mean that," she sniffed, knowing that crying was only making things worse. "I won't ask again. Forget I said anything."

He took a deep breath, his eye darting over to her as she wiped her nose on her sleeve before he stared at the door again, like the door was easier to look at than the mess she was devolving into.

But then he reached back over and pulled her onto his lap, resting her head on his chest as he stroked her hair.

"I lost the first love of my life to that thing," he said, sounding surprisingly unsure of himself. "I can't afford to let that happen again."

A small sob broke free from Mary Beth's throat.

"I'm sorry," he whispered, his voice choked with sorrow, "I really am, but I can't give you anything more than what I already have. I've already given too much."

Unable to speak, she nodded as her tears fell on his bronzed chest. He was so close to her, so warm and strong, the murmur of his blood rushing steadily in her ear, but he was so far from her that she knew she'd never know him, never really possess the one thing she really needed.

His heart.

She tried to pull away from him, tried to walk—at least as far as the bathroom, the one place left in her house where she could sob in private, but he held her tight as she cried.

"I'm sorry, hon," he murmured over and over as he stroked her hair. "I'm really sorry."

Get a grip, her brain whispered in a mocking tone. *Stop being such a girl!*

Finally, her mouth clicked on. "That's too bad," she whimpered, trying to sound like something other than a heartbroken teenager. "The couch is a lonely place to be."

"It doesn't have to be," he whispered, spreading his hand flat against her back. "You can come visit. Anytime."

Now that she had herself under a modicum of control, she shoved herself off his lap. "Jacob," she began as she walked away, "a smart fellow like you ought to know the first rule of holes. When you're in one, quit digging."

And she shut the bedroom door.

Chapter Fifteen

Mary Beth lay in bed, one hand resting on Kip's stomach as the girl slept peacefully.

But sleep eluded Mary Beth.

Jacob had cared for so few people in this world, but nearly all of them had been wiped away by some shadow thing with a knife. And whether he wanted to admit it or not, he clearly cared for her too.

She couldn't blame him for denying it. If he didn't love her, maybe he wouldn't lose her. She'd driven away—how many men? Six?—for more or less the same reason, after all.

If she didn't love them, it wouldn't hurt to lose them. And now she was in love with Jacob. And it would hurt.

Time is short, she realized, *and I want Jacob.*

As she slipped out of bed, she tried to convince herself this was not love, because she knew she wasn't going to get that in return.

No, not love. Really great, really convenient sex. Some deranged shadow demon could come for my soul tomorrow, and if I'm going, I want one last night with Jacob Plenty Holes to tide me over through eternity.

As quietly as possible, she cracked open the bedroom door. He was still sitting on the couch in just his sweatpants, his feet stretched out before him, another huge textbook on his lap, and the loaded .45 by his side. But his head was leaned back against the couch and his eye was closed.

Mary Beth stood there, unsure if she was doing the right thing. She didn't want to wake him, but...

As she stood at his feet, wondering what she should do next, Jacob spoke.

"First rule of holes is to stop digging," he sleepily murmured, his eye still closed.

"Yeah, about that." She sighed as she straddled his outstretched legs. "Sometimes you need to dig a hole. Wells and stuff, you know."

He slowly grinned, sleep still heavy on him as he pulled the textbook out of the way. "Plants too. Gotta dig holes for trees and plants."

As she sat down on his lap, her Garfield nightshirt bunching up around her bare thighs, he wrapped his arms around her and pulled her to his chest.

"I was thinking," she began.

"Always an interesting experience with you, babe," he murmured as he rubbed her back.

"I was thinking that we could all die in a tornado or a car accident tomorrow, and the only thing I would regret was that I didn't get this—" she traced her fingertips down his sides to his waistband "—one more time. I'd miss *this*."

He was silent for a moment as she ran her hands behind his back, holding him as tightly as he was holding her.

"You making fun of my driving again?" he finally mumbled.

"Jacob, I don't want to be alone any more than you do." She nuzzled into his neck. "Let's not be alone together."

He swallowed hard, his Adam's apple bobbing dangerously close to her nose. "Mary Beth, I can't make you any promises."

"I'm not asking for what you can't give me," she said as she put her hand on his heart. "I won't ask that of you. I don't own you, you don't own me."

His pulse was strong and steady under her hand. Finally, he lifted his head up and opened his eye. "You just want the part you already possess."

"I just want the part you've already given me, Jacob. You're a part of me now, and I'm a part of you, no matter what happens tomorrow or the next day," she said, turning his logic back on him.

"I did say that, didn't I?" he muttered, but now he was fully awake.

She kissed him. "And I know you're a man of your word."

In one quick movement, he peeled Garfield off of her. "I was hoping for the red bra," he whispered as he pushed her breast up to his waiting mouth.

"I have other colors, you know," she managed to gasp out as he scraped his teeth over the sides of her soft flesh before he gently clamped down on her erect nipple. She wrapped her fingers in his hair, holding him to her as his other hand slipped down her hip and reached between her legs.

"Mmm. Partial to red," he growled as he found her waiting clit.

At his touch, Mary Beth bucked on his lap. "Jesus, Jacob," she hissed as she bore down on him, giving him better access.

"That's not the right sound," he mused. As his thumb began to circle the sweet spot, first one finger, then two slipped inside, quickly finding an even sweeter spot that he rubbed in short, urgent strokes.

"*Oh!*" She gasped, praying they wouldn't wake up Kip. "Oh, Jesus, Jacob!"

"That's better." He sighed in contentment as he kissed her.

As her body twitched uncontrollably, she shuddered down on him, grinding her hips into his. "I. Need. More," she begged. "Please, please. More."

Sliding free of her wet embrace, he lifted her up and shimmied his sweatpants down before he set her on his waiting erection.

"God," he groaned, his eye rolling back in his head as she enveloped his every throbbing inch. She grabbed his hair and leaned his head back against the couch. Mary Beth ran her tongue up his throat as she pulled his hands away from her hips and pinned them back against the couch.

"Don't talk, Jacob," she ordered as she slowly rose and fell on him. She nipped at his ear and then his neck, relishing the way his muscles twitched to her every touch. "Just come with me."

His eye still closed, he nodded almost imperceptibly as she ground into him, almost pulled free and slammed back down.

He tried to pull his hands away from hers, but she bit him on the shoulder as she held fast. With each slam of her hips, she was getting closer again, closer to that shuddering release that left her shaken and breathless in his arms. "Come... come with me," she gasped in his ear. "Now. *Oh!*"

He obeyed as his body went stiff with tension before he relaxed beneath her final quake.

Aside from the quick rise and fall of his chest, he looked very much like he had when she'd first come out. His head was back, his eye was closed and his legs were out straight in front of him. Mary Beth leaned into his chest, listening to the blood rush through his heart.

No matter what happens, at least I had this, she thought as he wrapped his arms around her and hugged her tight. *I'll always have this*.

But she couldn't start that conversation again, so her brain scrambled to think of something that wouldn't sound like an ultimatum and wouldn't sound sniveling. As she traced the snaps on his mask, she said, "Can I ask you a question?"

"No, you can't take the mask off," he replied, already sounding drowsy again.

"I don't care about that." His eyebrow shot up as she continued, "Why didn't you ever sleep with Robin? You know she wanted you."

"This passes for post-sex pillow talk with you?" he scoffed as he lifted her off and handed her Garfield back again.

"I'm just asking." She slipped the old tee over her head. "She told me you kissed her for her birthday once, and she would have given it up to you right in the middle of the party."

"Yeah, I did that when she turned sixteen," he mused as he pulled his pants back up without opening his eye.

"So why didn't you?"

The silence stretched, and Mary Beth began to

wonder if he'd fallen asleep. But then he said, "I thought about it, I won't lie. She was pretty and sweet and I did like her. I thought about it a lot after Susan married Fred."

She curled into his waiting arm, warm with the afterglow. "But you didn't."

"I—don't make fun of me."

"I asked, remember."

"I couldn't do it. I didn't love her, and I didn't want to just use her, no matter how much she wanted to be used."

"You loved her enough not to do it." *And you love me enough to do it.*

As if he read her mind, he said, "That doesn't make this love. This isn't love."

"That's right. This is convenient."

"Right. Convenient. World-is-ending, no-regrets convenient."

"Right," she whispered. She could feel the tears moving up, even though that was exactly what she'd told herself before she came to him tonight. But she promised herself she wouldn't cry until she got back into her room.

"Right," he whispered back, his voice quivering. For a moment, he held her tight, and with her eyes closed, she could pretend that the conversation hadn't just happened. But then he cleared his throat. "You should go to bed now, Mary Beth Hofstetter."

"Going," she said, hoping the tremble in her voice wouldn't give her away before she got the door closed.

And she was gone.

The world didn't end on Tuesday, although Jacob couldn't tell if that was encouraging or not.

He hated leaving Mick in Mary Beth's garage overnight, but the horse didn't seem to mind it too much. Any other option just announced that they were shacking up.

Not that people weren't already suspecting things. Tommy was waiting for him when he rode up to the ranch, his tapping toe the only sign that betrayed his anxiety. "Everything okay?" he asked as Jacob dismounted.

Jacob glared at him. So much for people not knowing they were shacking up. He'd known this was coming, but it didn't make it any easier.

"So there is something going on. Be careful, Jake." It was almost a warning, although Tommy looked calm.

"I'm always careful, Tommy," he finally managed to say.

"So you're saying she hasn't threatened to castrate you yet?" He chuckled.

"Tommy," he snarled as he threw the door to his office open.

Tommy shook his head in amusement as he looked out the window and the fight was over before it began. "She's coming."

"Let me know if Buck leaves the house."

Tommy's eyebrow shot up, but clearly he'd already anticipated this. "Cole's watching now."

Jacob nodded with approval. Cole was the best tracker Jacob had ever seen. He had a sense of smell that was almost inhuman. Nothing would get passed him.

Tommy turned to walk out, but not before he repeated, "Be careful, Jake."

Jacob glared at his back again before he went out to meet her.

And this time, she wasn't pissed at him. She smiled warmly at him as she acted like nothing had happened, having the same morning conversation they always had. But the moment they were between the horses, she stealthily reached out and traced a single finger down his face before she spun and threw herself onto Jezebel.

Man, he thought as he mounted up, his skin still burning with the memory of her touch, *I could get used to this*.

The feeling only got stronger that night as she opened the door with the same smile, even if she did have her knife drawn. She had dinner simmering— smelled like stew maybe.

"Hey, hon." She beamed as he slid up behind her and kissed her cheek.

"I've been waiting to do this for hours," he replied as his mouth covered hers. He could feel the corners of her lips curving up under his. "Hours."

"I'd ask how your day was, but I was there for most of it."

"You missed the part where Tommy figured us out."

"Tommy figured us out? I haven't even figured us out, and Tommy has?" she wailed, waving a stew-covered spoon dangerously near him.

Grinning, he sat down next to Kip and kissed her cheek. "How about you, Kip? How was your day? Think we'll have a quiet night?"

Even Mary Beth turned to see if there would be an answer, but they both knew they wouldn't get one. Instead, Mary Beth said, "Mrs. Browne said she was fine. Did you know there's a school for autistic children in Rapid City?"

"Man, she's started that with you? Kip's not autistic."

"I know. But she means well. I told her that the doctor visit went well and the doctor's going to do get me a list of recommendations."

"I don't remember that being part of the conversation."

"Hon," she said as she smiled, sending a thrill through him, "you've got to realize that little old ladies want, more than anything, to be listened to. So I tell her I will check it out, and she gets to feel important. No harm, no foul."

"You sound like an expert in little old ladies." He started to set the table. When was the last time he'd set a table? Years, maybe.

"My Granny died when she was eighty-two." Suddenly, she sounded like a much younger girl. "I didn't always have the smoothest childhood, shall we say. But Granny was this tough old farmer's wife, one of those rocks that holds a family together."

Which made it pretty clear that the family had fallen apart at some point. "I would have liked to have met her."

"She would have liked to have met you too," she finally answered. "She taught me to cook."

"I knew there was something about her I liked." He smiled as she scooped up the stew. "Woman after my own heart."

He washed the dishes while she gave Kip a bath. She was so good with Kip that Jacob was beginning to think that maybe Susan wouldn't mind. Certainly, in the three years he'd cared for Kip, he'd tried to do his best with her, but he knew he could never replace Susan and Fred.

But Mary Beth looked at her like she was normal, and talked to her like she was normal and treated her like she was normal. It was beginning to feel normal, all three of them living in the cramped, cozy house.

As she read a book he'd never heard of to Kip, he debated what to do. She'd essentially told him he could stay if he wanted, but then he'd told her he couldn't, just couldn't. Not with the shadow out there.

But last night… last night was enough to change a man's mind.

His mind.

He worked quickly, smoothing his blanket out on the floor before he hastily washed up. He was sure she'd be back out. The heat of her finger trailing down his face said she would be.

Twenty minutes later, the bedroom door quietly whooshed open and then shut and her soft feet padded out into the living room.

He wanted to pretend that he was asleep, just to keep her guessing, but the thought of her tiptoeing around in that old nightshirt—she had to have had it for at least fifteen or twenty years—was too much for him. She probably didn't realize it was nearly transparent, the darkness of her nipples and hair neatly framing poor, clueless Garfield. When he opened his eye, she was already before him, her bare legs next to him as she carefully avoided standing on the blanket.

"No tornadoes today," he said as his hand snaked out all by itself and began to run up and down her calf.

"No major traffic accidents either," she replied, stepping onto the blanket.

He sat up and kissed her thigh. "Who knows what tomorrow will bring."

"We could all die in a flash flood." She ran her hands through his hair as his kisses moved up her leg.

"Right. Wouldn't want to miss this." He sighed in contentment as he pulled her down.

"No." She sank to her knees. "I wouldn't want to miss this."

Without the hurried frenzy that had marked their previous couplings, Jacob was satisfied to move his lips slowly over her body, lolling over her nipples, lapping at her neck, grinning with every faint *oh* he elicited from her. And she made it a lot. Could it really be that she'd never oh-ed for anyone else?

"Have I told you how much I love it when you make that little noise?" he asked as he sucked on her pinkie finger while stroking her clit.

"Jesus, Jacob," she gasped as he slowly climbed between her legs, his finger still rubbing.

"That works too, but the other noise is better." He grinned as he dove in.

It didn't seem possible that this—she—was better every time, but she was. Her every move, no matter how small, grabbed him anew, tightening the web she'd cast around him until the bonds were unbreakable.

Patiently, he brought her up to the edge of collapse several times with his long strokes, only to alter his rhythm ever so slightly and cool her intensity.

Finally, unable to hold anything back in her shivering embrace, he arched his back and came quietly.

"Not… fair…" She panted as he curled up beside her.

"Huh?"

"You don't make any noise," she muttered. "It's not fair. How do I know if I'm as good as you are?"

"Mmm," he hummed in her ear as she rested on his arm, his other hand wrapped around her breast. She fit in his embrace perfectly. Like she belonged there. "I could tell you that you're an amazing woman."

"You already say that," she scolded.

"I could tell you you're the best I've ever had."

"Your selection has been limited," she parried.

God, he loved that fearless mouth of hers. Somehow, it made him want to be stronger. "How about I tell you that I never thought I'd find a woman as perfect as you are?"

"Too general," she groused with a smile. "And a bold-faced lie. I'm so far from perfect it's not even in the same zip code."

He thought for a moment, struggling to come up with the right thing—something enough, but not too much. Not yet. "Mary Beth, if I had *this*—" he said as he ran his hand down her thigh and back up to her breast "—to look forward to every night for the rest of my life, I would be a contented man."

For a moment, she was speechless. She didn't get speechless often, and he didn't want to get her hopes up, but he meant it, every single word. If even Tommy could see it, there was no sense in denying it any more.

If it wasn't for that damn whatever was out there… Maybe one day.

235

Finally, her mouth recovered. "That's not too bad," she said, her voice cracking.

"Good," he chuckled, relieved to have finally said the right thing, "because that's the best I've got."

"Are you ever going to show me what you look like without your mask?" she asked, her voice still a bit jittery.

"Why should I?"

"Jacob." She rolled over, looking him in the eye. "Don't you ever get tired of hiding? You spend all day hiding behind that mask and all night hiding Kip. One day, she's not going to need to hide any more. What about you?"

He sighed as he stroked her hair, moving his fingers easily through the soft waves. "I guess I'll know when the day comes."

"Today isn't the day," she nodded as she kissed his homemade nose.

"What about you?"

"I'm not hiding."

He smirked at her. "Sure you are. You've got to have a reason why you're here, and why you've stayed. Most women would have left about ten minutes after Buck threatened them the first time, but you? You take it in stride. Why are you here?"

Now it was Mary Beth's turn to sigh. "I'm not hiding."

"Not with that mouth anyway," he snickered as he stole a quick kiss.

"I don't know." She shrugged as she shot him a cross look. "I loved summers on the farm. Loved it. The times we lived in an apartment, I couldn't wait to get back to the farm when I was a kid."

Jacob propped up on his elbow and looked down at her. When she lived in an apartment? He thought she was a born-and-bred farm girl. She'd told him once it was complicated. Maybe he hadn't heard what she was really saying.

"But I'm the fifth generation of the same family to live in that house—and Annie's kids are at least the sixth to live on the land," she continued. "Some days, it just felt—I don't know—crowded, like you couldn't turn around without running into a ghost or something."

That didn't make any sense—his people had been on this land for thousands of years—but he wanted to understand, so he carefully asked, "You left because too many people slept in your bed?"

"No." She sighed in frustration before she tried again. "I just felt like so many other people had laid claim to the farm that it wasn't my place. Annie's husband—John—he's farming his family's land and ours together with my Uncle Hank. The farm didn't need me anymore, not after Granny died."

"You miss her." He curled into her arm.

"I miss them all. I just thought that—" she took a deep breath, trying not to tear up. "I just thought that when I got here, I'd find the place where I belonged."

Jacob nodded against her shoulder. He'd always known he belonged here, even when it wasn't clear what he wanted. But he remembered when Ronny came back from Iraq. It had taken him a long, long time to find where he belonged. But he didn't want to worry about any of that right now. He wanted to be with Mary Beth.

All he wanted was to be with Mary Beth.

Maybe he belonged with her. And maybe she really did belong here with him. But he didn't want her to cry again, so he changed the subject. "Did that vision include shag carpeting?"

She giggled as she looked over at the high pile. "Bill set me up, remember?"

"I remember."

They fell silent for a moment. "Jacob?" she murmured.

"Yes, babe?" It came so easily now.

She beamed at the *babe*. "How long will you and Kip stay? Not an ultimatum, just a question."

"As long as we need to," he replied with a yawn.

"Stay as long as you like." And with another kiss, she pulled free of his heavy arms and slipped Garfield back over her head. "I'll be here. I promise."

"Goodnight," he sleepily replied as he reached up and grabbed the revolver and carefully placed it next to his head.

She folded the blanket back over his body and kissed his forehead. "Goodnight, Jacob."

And the door shut silently behind her.

Chapter Sixteen

Wednesday at the ranch was normal to the point of dull. They tagged and vaccinated new calves, and she checked on a few young mustangs that were being broken in. All in all, a remarkably unremarkable day.

But that didn't quiet the pit of impending doom that took up residence in Mary Beth's gut and refused to budge.

"Are you okay?" Jacob asked for the four hundredth time that day.

"I just feel odd, that's all. Have you checked on Kip yet?" she replied again.

"Relax, Mary Beth, please," he said as he rubbed her shoulder. "You're making me nervous. I called twenty minutes ago, and everything was fine."

"Well, unless you've got something else you need me to look at, I'm going to go get her."

"Fine with me. I'll be home around 5:30 or so, okay?"

Despite the butterflies in her belly, Mary Beth beamed at him. "I'll have dinner started. You like turkey chili?"

He made a face as they hefted her packs into the truck that made her giggle. But as she was climbing into the cab, a shout cut across the lots.

"Jacob! Mary Beth! Come quick!"

Mary Beth stepped back out of the Ram to see Nobody riding hard across the lots, a look of terror on his face.

In a heartbeat, Jacob was out of the barn and on Mick. Mary Beth grabbed the vet pack she'd just tossed into the truck bed and threw it back on poor Jezebel, who had already started cropping grass.

"What?" Jacob demanded as they waited for Mary Beth to mount up.

"Cattle," Nobody panted. "Something cut them up."

"What?" they gasped in unison.

"Something attacked some cattle. I was trying to find a horse that went missing—and I found cattle." Mary Beth realized that the big man was terrified, his eyes darting back and forth as his head constantly checked their surroundings. "I found Tommy first. Sent him out with your hands. Told him I'd get you."

Without another word, Jacob slid down and sprinted back into the barn. When he came flying back out, he had a rifle in his hand and his Colt belted on.

"How bad?" he asked as they kicked the horses to the hills.

"Bad," Nobody said. "At least three are dead, and it seems like the rest had their hamstrings cut."

"Sonofabitch," Jacob muttered, kicking Mick on.

"Rustlers?" Mary Beth shouted.

"No," Nobody shouted back. "Rustlers don't maim."

As Mary Beth urged Jezebel on behind them, she stared at Jacob's back, his body crouched and ready for a fight.

She knew what maimed with a knife, and so did he.

The shadow thing was out there and it wanted their undivided attention.

It took fifteen minutes to get to the field filled with bleating, screaming cattle. Tommy and the other cowboys were herding the remaining animals away, but some animals were standing near their downed companions, lowing in sorrow.

Jacob flung himself off Mick and threw the rifle to Tommy in one smooth motion. "Perimeter check. Go with Nobody. Shoot anything that isn't a cow or a cowboy."

"Done." And he was gone.

"Jacob, we didn't see anything," Paul shouted as he rode back to herd the remaining walking cattle away. "We swear, we wouldn't have let anyone do this to them."

The scene was horrific. A revolting smell of rotting sage and blood mingled with the fresh scent of fear and blood. Ten cattle were scattered around the trees. Some were nearly decapitated, their heads being held on by a few tendons or skin. A few were still alive, their back legs pitifully splayed out behind them, the flesh flayed to the bone. They had no chance. The thing had left them for dead.

"Can any of them be saved?" Jacob asked as Mary Beth slowly walked around with her mouth open, unable to comprehend the senseless destruction of animals.

"Jesus Christ, Jacob."

"Mary Beth!" he snapped. "Look at me! Can any of them be saved? Focus!"

"Um, let me—um," she stuttered. A sad bleat caught her ear, and she looked over to see a small calf hobble out of the woods, blood running down its side. "This one's still up. If it can't stand, I can't save it," she said, her medical brain finally clicking on.

Jacob whipped his .45 out from the holster, and seconds later the pop of bullets putting animals out of their misery echoed through the timber.

The screaming of cattle got louder as the pain and panic passed through the ones still clinging to life. The calf began to snort in panic, but she held the tiny thing to her as she inspected the wound. Though the cut was three inches long, the blade had only gone in an inch. *Maybe Nobody had interrupted before the thing had been able to finish this one*, she thought as she packed the wound with ointment and hastily began stitching the hide shut.

"Not permanent," she soothed the terrified calf when it whined in pain as the needle passed through its flesh. "I'll make it better later, okay? You are still alive, little guy."

"Holy *shit*!" Jacob screamed behind her.

"What? What is it?" she yelled as the calf burst free from her hands. Tommy and Nobody came flying back out of the forest.

"Jacob! What?"

Jacob was standing over a dead cow, its throat cut back to the spine, its belly flayed open to the ribcage. It looked like a cow on a slaughter line, but there was something different.

The cow had no nose, and one eye had been cut out.

It looked a hell of a lot like Jacob.

242

He stood there and shook like a child. "Holy shit," he cried again, stuck in a personal hell.

Now it was Mary Beth's turn. "Jacob! Look at me!"

"It's a message, Mary Beth. It's a message!" He finally got his eye focused on her face, and at the same time, they realized what the message was.

"Kip," she whispered.

"Go!" he urged as he threw himself onto Mick. "Tommy, finish! Get the calf and finish! Nobody— Rebel!" he shouted as he and Mary Beth raced to the town below. Nobody took off in the opposite direction. Normally, she might be scared of the dangerous man, but not today. Today, she was glad that he was on her side.

Mary Beth tried not to focus on the sickening nausea that wanted to overpower her as they raced past trees and cut through forest, taking the direct route to town. The thing—shadow or man or demon, she didn't know and didn't care—had set the trap and they'd ridden right into it.

God, she nearly sobbed as the guilt washed over her, *if only I'd gone to get Kip earlier. Please, God or the ancestors or whoever is listening, please let her be okay. Please don't let it be that thing.*

But as much as she wanted to curl up and hide from the horror, she knew that Kip needed her. She had to keep it together if she wanted to keep Kip alive.

Cutting across the land, it took less than ten minutes to get to the valley, and immediately, Mary Beth knew they were too late.

The main drag was filled with people carrying buckets up from the river as the lone fire truck in the county hosed down the flaming remains of the schoolhouse.

Jacob got Mick as close to the schoolhouse as he could before he launched himself into the flames.

"Jacob, no!" Ronny called from his position at the head of the bucket brigade. "You'll get burnt!"

"He's got to get Kip, he's got to get Kip," Mary Beth prayed. "He's *got* to get Kip. Please, God, let him get Kip."

Seconds passed to minutes as the townsfolk pulled buckets from the river and the three volunteer firefighters all worked to douse the flames.

"Please, God," Mary Beth prayed as Jezebel panted beneath her, "Please, God. Let him get Kip."

"There he is!" Ronny shouted as he threw a bucket of water in the doorway. The flames died down just enough for Jacob to run through them, his ankles smoking as he gasped for air. He threw the body he carried on the ground.

It wasn't Kip.

"Mrs. Browne?" Ronny screamed at her. "Are you okay?"

"She's dead. It cut her throat," Jacob sputtered as Ronny threw a bucket of water over his head. Jacob sizzled as the water evaporated from the heat of his clothes.

"What?" Ronny took a step back, paling. "*It*? It *who* cut her throat?"

For a split second, Jacob dripped with sorrow as the water ran off his hair. But the look vanished, replaced with a cold, calculating fury. "Ronny," he growled, "lock everything down. It's got Kip."

"It *who*?" Ronny demanded again. "Jacob, this shit isn't funny, it—"

Jacob threw himself back onto Mick. "Shoot to kill, Ronny. I'm going to get her back."

"Where are we going?" Mary Beth shouted as they headed back out of the valley, leaving the fire and the dead teacher behind them at a full gallop. Storm clouds billowed up out of nowhere, darkening the sky in seconds.

"Shit." He slowed. "It's got her and I don't even know—"

The sky flashed with lightning like a bolt of inspiration. The scene of the crime—a dark house with dark stains on the floor. Whatever this thing was, it'd want to finish *what* it started, *where* it started it. Mary Beth grabbed Jacob's arm. "Her house," she said. "It took her to her old house."

Jacob nodded and urged Mick back up to a dead run.

"How long?" she shouted over the wind rushing up with the surprise storm.

"Thirty, forty minutes," he called back. "It had maybe a twenty, thirty-minute head start."

"Go faster," Mary Beth whispered to Jezebel. "Go faster."

The land flew by as the horses raced against the clock. Tree limbs reached out, smacking her in the face and arms, but she paid no heed to the cuts. A few times, Jezebel started to stumble, but Mary Beth counter-shifted her weight, keeping the horse up by sheer will alone. The clouds burst open, making the darkening night even harder to see through, but the lightning that scored the sky was just enough that she could keep track of Jacob urging Mick on ahead of her.

Mary Beth wasn't sure where they were, but when they splashed through the swelling creek bed, she knew they were close.

The house was just over the next ridge.

Jacob pulled the wheezing Mick into a slow walk, his gun drawn, his ears listening as they approached the silent and dark house.

Mary Beth looked up at the wet, ink-black sky, the lightning jumping from cloud to cloud, and the earth shook from the thunder.

There was a sound off to the right from deeper in the woods. In the blink of an eye, Jacob was on the ground, racing toward it, gun and knife drawn, looking for all the world like a true Lakota warrior.

And Mary Beth was alone on Jezebel, the tired animal's sides still heaving at the effort. The lightning cracked again. Kip had to be here—didn't she? And if she was here, she'd be inside.

Mary Beth tucked her knife in the back of her waistband and slowly walked toward the house, her heart pounding so loudly in her ears she couldn't hear anything else.

The unlocked door swung open, and there was Kip, nearly glowing white in the dark room as she sat silent and still.

"Jesus, Kip—" she rushed up to the little girl sitting motionless on the bed, "—are you all right?"

As her words hung in the air, the taste—rotting sage and flesh and unwashed fur—filled her mouth, gagging her.

No, she thought as the door slammed shut behind her. As an evil laugh filled the room, she knew it was too late.

The shadow had her right where it wanted her.

Mary Beth spun, but she couldn't see anything but a huge black shape moving across the room, a flash of lightning catching on the polished blade.

"Show yourself," she screeched. "You're no bear. Bears don't have knives, and bears don't laugh."

"I am the *Waka Sica*," the thing rumbled, "and I have come for your soul."

She barely had time to think, *What the hell is a* Waka Sika? before it flipped on the light. Mary Beth recoiled in sheer horror. Before her, a foot-long knife poised at the ready, was a seven-foot tall creature with the head and fur of a buffalo. The buffalo face was distorted, with the nose pushed to one side and what looked a hell of a lot like canine teeth jutting out from the lower lip.

Mary Beth tripped backwards over the chairs, nearly sitting on the immobile Kip.

"Kip, get up," she said, her tone urgent. "Get up and get behind me."

"She cannot save you now," the *Waka Sica* said with a sneer. "She will be mine. When I possess the holy woman, I will *know*."

"When she's yours? Jesus Christ, don't you dare touch her!" Mary Beth screamed.

The *Waka Sica* laughed, slicing the air with its knife in preparation, like it was showing off.

"You lay one single hoof or claw or whatever the hell it is you have on her, and I'll kill you a thousand times over," she squawked, sounding anything but brave.

The *Waka Sica* laughed again, but this time it did something else.

With its free hand or claw or whatever that was, it grabbed at its waist like it was hitching up its pants, slowly rubbing its fur up and down over what might have been its crotch.

Mary Beth blinked and then blinked again. She'd seen that gesture before. Only one man hitched up his pants like that.

Buck McGillis.

"Buck?" she whispered, unable to believe that it might just be a man—an insane man, sure—but just a man under that hideous hide.

The thing froze.

"Buck McGillis? What the hell are you doing? Have you lost your mind? You are terrorizing this little girl!"

The deformed hoof-claw thing flipped the hood of the mask off, and it really was Buck standing there, his knife still flashing as his eyes bugged out of his head.

"I'm going to kill you slowly, you nosy bitch," he growled. "I'm going to kill you right in front of her, and then I'm going to make her drink your blood."

"Are you fucking insane?" Clearly the answer was yes. "What is wrong with you?"

"I will own the Lakota," he snarled, taking a menacing step toward her, the knife poised higher to strike.

For a second, Mary Beth was sixteen again, trapped beneath Skeevy Brian Greevy while he pawed at her. *Paralyzed.* Even though she'd crushed his nuts when he'd let go of her to try and undo his pants, the thing that she'd always hated—*always*—had been that she'd let him pin her in the first place. She hadn't fought back immediately—just like the last time Buck had tried to assault her. Her mistake both times had been to try and make nice, to talk her way out of it. It hadn't worked with Skeevy Greevy and it hadn't worked with Buck. In fact, if it hadn't been for Jacob and his horse, she would have been in deep shit.

Just like she was right now.

Well, fuck it. She wasn't about to try and make nice, not when it was both her and Kip's lives on the line.

For only the second time since Mary Beth had known her, Kip squeaked behind her. It was a noise of pure terror.

Not happening, sweetie. He's not going to get you.

Mary Beth slipped her hand behind her back and felt where she'd jammed her Bowie knife into her waistband.

The touch of the handle brought Mary Beth back to the here and now. She shook off the helplessness of a child—Kip's helplessness as much as hers—and grabbed the knife.

Wait for him to get closer. That's what she needed to do—wait for her opening and then take it.

But Mary Beth couldn't just stand there and wait. No, her mouth began to motor as she poured out all of her fury at the position this man had put her in. This man was demented. Demented and armed.

"Seriously, Buck, you are bringing new meaning to the term criminally insane, and your impression of Andre the Giant leaves a lot to be desired. I mean, have you even seen *The Princess Bride*?"

"You talk now, but wait until I cut your throat, you wench," he growled. "Then you won't even be able to scream."

"If you think hurting her is going to help you take over the world, you've got another think coming," she mocked as Buck's face twisted with rage, making him barely recognizable. "You think she's some mystic or something, but she's just a little girl, and when I drag your sick ass back to town, they're going to lynch you for what you tried to do, what you did to Mrs. Browne."

"I am the *Waka Sica*!" he screamed, his voice so loud it shook the thin curtains over the bed. "My father was the *Waka Sica* before me, and his father before him. It is my destiny to destroy her! We have stolen souls for generations, waiting and watching for the chance to destroy the Lakota!"

Do villains really do this, this exposition thing? Mary Beth wondered as he shouted at her. *I thought that was just in the movies.*

"We knew when the white child came, we would finally be able to wipe out this miserable people and take what was ours!" The words ended in a roar so powerful that Mary Beth had to fight the urge to cover her ears.

She couldn't let go of the knife handle.

Where was Jacob? She had to keep talking, keep him distracted until Jacob could get there. "She's no mystic and you're nothing but a bully. And you know what, Buck? All bullies have one thing in common. Tiny dicks."

That did it. Buck lunged at her, but she effortlessly stepped to the side, pulling Kip with her. Now their backs were facing the door, and Buck was pushing them towards it. Nobody would be proud of her. She'd pointed herself to the one and only exit.

So she didn't know what the hell a *Waka Sica* was. All she had to do was believe that she could get

250

them out of this. "I believe," Mary Beth muttered, a sense of calm radiating through her at the words. "I believe."

"You better believe," Buck snarled, misunderstanding her. "She will bear my child, the next *Waka Sica* who will rule this world."

"No way, you freak," she replied, unnaturally calm despite the revulsion that coursed through her stomach. "She's seven. She's only seven!"

"I can be patient. I have waited so long, a few more years won't hurt anything." He laughed again, evil and haughty. Abruptly, his laugh died, and a perverted look that might have been desire flashed in his eyes as he looked Mary Beth up and down. "But you—I don't have to wait for you. Yes," he nodded, pleased with his new idea, "I think I'll show Kip what I'm going to do to her when I do it to you first." Mary Beth's stomach tried to turn, but she was in this weird zen state.

Because she believed. Suddenly, Buck looked more like Buck than he had all night.

"Nobody says no to Buck McGillis."

Mary Beth saw the regular bully who, somewhere along the line, had mutated into a sociopath serial killer.

"N-O spells no—didn't your mom ever teach you that?" she sang.

"My father took her soul as soon as I was free of her!" he roared, morphing back into that not-quite-human thing again.

"So what you're saying is you've got mother issues," she taunted, wondering how much closer he needed to be as he quickly covered the two remaining paces between them.

But she didn't worry. She believed.

Buck's knife flashed toward her face. Her instincts were to duck forward, but she knew that'd leave Kip exposed, so she leaned back. Mary Beth heard his knife slice the air so close to her ear that it burned, but she didn't care. Kip was safe behind her as they took another small step back toward the door. *Where the hell is Jacob?* she thought again as Buck swung his blade back. It passed less than an inch from her nose.

Mary Beth didn't panic. All of her energy was focused on getting her knife out of the waistband and in front of her. Buck's last pass left his right arm fully extended, leaving his chest wide open. Mary Beth lurched forward and drove her knife deep into his chest as she fell on top of him.

Air rushed out of Buck's nose and chest. *Punctured a lung*, her brain coolly assessed as she scrambled to get off of him and away from that horrid smell that permeated him.

But he wasn't dead. His knife still in his right hand, he grabbed the back of her hair with his left and, grunting in pain, stood. "You can't kill me. I'm the—"

"Yeah, I got it, you sicko. You're the *Waka Sica*." She tried to twist out of his hand. It didn't work—her feet were a good six inches from the ground. She knew she should be terrified, but there was no fear, only the rebellious smart mouth that had gotten her this far in life. "You shouldn't have drunk the Kool-Aid, Buck. You've gone completely round the bend."

Buck grinned demonically at her, his mouth filled with blood. "Say goodbye to that albino" he sprayed into her face, "because she's the last thing you're going to see."

"Gee, and miss your pretty mug? What a disappointment, Buck. I would have given you a whole thirty-five cents for that mask. A definite improvement over what you've got going on here." A strange humming surrounded her. Her hair—the pieces he wasn't holding—felt like it was standing on end. *This must be it*, she thought, although the idea didn't seem to bother her as much as it should. She was distracting him. Jacob would come—he *had* to. Jacob would save Kip. That's what mattered.

Mary Beth had never seen a face as contorted as Buck's was as he went apoplectic with rage. "I'm going to eat your liver for—"

The door to the small house flew open, and there stood Jacob, his weapons drawn. *Oh, thank God.*

Buck barely hesitated a second before he spun, holding his knife against Mary Beth's throat. The pressure of the blade hurt, but the rest of her skin seemed to be crackling.

"Good. Excellent," Buck said with a sneer. "You're just in time to see me kill her, and then I'm going to take your other eye, and your lips, and your ears, Plenty Holes. I'm going to leave you so many holes, they're going to have to come up with a new name for you."

Jacob looked frozen somewhere between terror and fury. His eyes flicked down to the bloodstains, over to Kip and back to Mary Beth's face. He took a step back and away from the door. "No," he whispered, his eyes wide with fear.

"Oh, yes." Buck laughed. "That's right, just like last time when I cut that bitch Susan's throat. Remember? The blood sprayed all over you and you

253

screamed like a girl. You couldn't save her then and you can't save them now. Not this time, No Nose. This time, I win."

"Let her go and you can have me," he demanded, strong and weak at the same time.

"I'll take you both," Buck replied as he began to draw the blade slowly across Mary Beth's throat.

As she felt the blood gush down her neck, Mary Beth tried to scream. Nothing came out before she saw white.

Then the darkness took her.

Chapter Seventeen

Good. Excellent." Buck was completely unafraid of the gun Jacob had drawn. And why should he be? He had Mary Beth by the throat, a huge knife digging into her skin. "You're just in time to see me kill her, and then I'm going to take your other eye, and your lips, and your ears, Plenty Holes. I'm going to leave you so many holes, they're going to have to come up with a new name for you."

No. *No.* This was not happening, not again. His eye flicked down to the bloodstains, over to Kip and back to Mary Beth's face. "No." His voice wasn't working right. He sounded scared, even to his own ears.

Maybe because he was. He'd thought the last time had been a nightmare? This was worse. A hundred times worse.

"Oh, yes." Buck laughed. "That's right, just like last time when I cut that bitch Susan's throat. Remember? The blood sprayed all over you and you screamed like a girl. You couldn't save her then and you can't save them now. Not this time, No Nose. This time, I win."

"Let her go and you can have me." Anything to save them. He couldn't lose Mary Beth. He'd given her a piece of him that was too big. Without her, he'd never be whole again.

"I'll take you both." Buck drew the blade across Mary Beth's throat, sending a stream of blood onto the floor.

In that instant, Jacob didn't think, because thinking was a death sentence. Before he could make sense of the movement, he leveled his gun at Buck's face and pulled the trigger. The room shook with the sound of the explosion.

What was left of Buck staggered back and collapsed on the floor, pulling Mary Beth with him. Her blood spurted across the room as she fell onto Buck in a heap. *So much blood.* The unreal déjà vu of the whole thing had him paralyzed. How could this be happening again?

Then Kip let out an ear-piercing scream that broke through Jacob's dumbstruck horror.

No, this wasn't the same. He'd shot Buck, by God—if he could, he'd shoot him again. Although, given the way his face had collapsed into a red pulp, Jacob doubted he'd need to pull the trigger a second time.

His feet spun out from under him as he scrambled down to Mary Beth. Jesus, so much blood. Then he heard the sweetest sound—she sucked in a breath. It was wet and sloppy and half-strangled sounding, but it was a breath and she was breathing.

He had to stop the bleeding.

"Jesus," was all he could say as he held her throat together, only vaguely aware that he was sobbing. Blood gushed out from between his fingers. He needed something else to try and stop the bleeding.

The vet packs. She'd thrown them back on Jezebel before they'd ridden hell for leather. "Kip!"

The little girl let out an agonizing scream again, but he didn't have time for the mother of all flashbacks. "Kip, get over here. Hold her neck!"

The girl looked at Buck—that was something—but the horror in her eyes wasn't helping anyone. "Honey, don't look at him. Look at me. Now *move!*"

That got through to her. She skittered around Buck, his own pool of blood spreading out from where his head used to be. "Hold her head like this, honey. Real tight. Whatever you do, don't let go. Okay?"

He thought she whimpered, but he didn't have time to wonder at that. He struggled to his feet with Mary Beth in his arms, moving slow enough that Kip could keep up with him—could keep her head from doing things he didn't even want to think about.

The three of them straggled out of the house. Jacob didn't see the horses—the gunshot must have scattered them. Damn it. He let out a long whistle, which made Mary Beth jerk a little in his arms. "Hold on," he told both her and Kip as the horses came walking up.

He laid Mary Beth down on the ground as Kip held her neck. "Hold on," he repeated, almost like it was a mantra. *Holding*, he thought as he let her go. *Keep holding.*

He ripped the packs off Jezebel and began frantically digging for the gauze and the suture pack.

"Dear God in Heaven," he prayed, his voice raw with pain, "please." *Please let her live. Please let this work. Please don't take her from me—from us. Please.*

Hastily, he wrapped her neck in at least twenty layers of gauze and bandages. Finally, he took a layer of bandages and wrapped her head to her chest.

Underneath the gauze, she moaned. God, he hoped he hadn't screwed that up. "Don't you dare give up on me," he told her as he hefted her up again. "Not going down without a fight, babe."

Now he had to get her out of here. "Kip, up," was all he said as he lifted the little girl onto Jezebel. Shit, what was the best way to do this? He didn't think Kip could help hold Mary Beth up for the ride back and he didn't think he could hold Mary Beth still while he tied her to the saddle by himself, and he damn sure didn't want to flop her over Mick's haunches like she'd already died. That'd put too much stress on her neck. What the fuck was he supposed to do?

Then he heard it—hoof beats coming in fast from the south. "Jacob?" a voice shouted. "Where are you?"

Rebel—and with him, Nobody. "Here!" he shouted, his voice growing hoarse. "Here! She's hurt. He cut her throat!"

The two men rode out of the shadows, dismounting before their horses had stopped.

"Buck—all along," he said.

"Where?" Nobody's voice was a thing of pure hate.

"Dead. Shot him in the face. When he cut her." Jacob lifted Mary Beth, just a little. "We need help." His throat caught and he was, once again, aware that he was crying.

Rebel pulled—was that a walkie-talkie? Yes, it was. He pushed a button. "Madeline, neck wound. Serious. We'll be there in half an hour."

"Who?" Dr. Mitchell's voice crackled on the other end.

"Mary Beth." Without waiting for a response, he

shoved the walkie-talkie back into his pocket. "Give her to me. Get up behind the saddle. I'll hand her up to you, we'll tie her on, and I'll ride back with Kip. Nobody, give me a hand."

Nobody nodded. Jacob climbed up behind Mick's saddle, then Rebel and Nobody got Mary Beth's legs over the horn and up into Jacob's arms. They lashed her feet to the stirrups. "Hold her tight," Rebel said.

Like he wouldn't. Jacob tucked her head down so it wouldn't bounce. Rebel swooped Kip off of Jezebel and onto his horse, and then he and Jacob were gone.

They couldn't go fast enough.

Mary Beth saw the little house with the bloodstained floor and the bleeding people. Everything happened out of order—one minute, Jacob was bursting in, already wearing the mask. The next minute, the dead people were eating dinner, their necks already slit. Except this time, Mary Beth was sitting at the table with them. *Where's Kip?* she tried to ask the dead people, but her throat wasn't working. She reached up to touch it and felt the huge slit. *Crap, am I dead too? Where is Kip? God, let her still be safe.*

Wait—I've had this dream before. Just a dream, Mary Beth tried to tell herself as the swish of a knife blade passed close to her ears. *Bad dream. Not real. Wake up. Wake up* now.

But she didn't. Instead, Kip appeared inside the dream—floated really. She seemed older—different. *Smiling*, Mary Beth realized. Looking around. Looking normal.

Okay, this has *to be a dream. Time to wake up.*

That direct order to her brain had usually worked in the past, but something wasn't right about this particular dream. No matter how hard Mary Beth tried to move or talk or do something that would startle her awake, nothing happened.

Kip floated over to her. At some point, the table and the dead people eating dinner and the little house full of bloodstains disappeared and it was just Mary Beth and Kip, who was looking almost unearthly.

Smiling a serene smile, Kip reached up and put her hand on Mary Beth's throat. The flesh under her fingertips began to burn and itch.

What are you doing? Her mouth still wasn't working, but she thought it all the same. She tried to rip the fingers away, but Kip held tight. *Stop! Stop, please!*

The heat burned away the itch, leaving only a shining pain that cut clear across her throat and radiated up to her eyeballs and down to her lungs.

Stop, please stop, she begged, clawing at the hand.

Standing on her tiptoes, Kip kissed her forehead and was gone.

"Stop, please stop," she begged, but the words wouldn't form.

"Mary Beth, you calm down this instant, or you're going to get another sedative," Mom warned.

Mom? The momentary confusion distracted her from the pain.

"I think she heard you," another female voice— maybe Madeline, the doctor on the rez? Mary Beth wasn't sure. "Her heart rate's dropped back down a bit."

"Mary Beth, pumpkin, you're okay. You are still alive, okay? You just need to rest. You are still alive."

Mary Beth began to relax, and the pain eased. Mom was here. Mom would make everything better, and she was still alive. The thought was comforting and familiar.

She was still alive.

At least she wasn't still at that table with all the dead people, but Mary Beth wasn't anywhere, as far as she could tell. And it was getting on her nerves.

Lost without an anchor to any firm reality, Mary Beth began to doubt that she'd really heard Mom. Perhaps she'd just hallucinated Mom out of desperation for something comforting.

Just when she thought she was going to finally go completely mad, a voice cut through the space. "Mrs. Hofstetter, is it? How is she?" The nowhere got farther away, leaving her in a hazy darkness. She could almost feel her body—but not quite.

That sounded like Jacob, except that the voice seemed worried. The combination sounded off— almost foreign. Mary Beth tried to open her eyes, or blink, or do something, but nothing happened and the effort tired her.

"She's still alive." Mom again. And she was still alive. Mary Beth tried to sigh in relief, but nothing happened. "And you are?"

"Jacob Plenty Holes."

"I see," Mom replied. Mary Beth tried to smile at how unconvinced she sounded, but again, nothing moved. "And who is this lovely young lady you have with you?"

"This is Kip. Kip Two Elks," Jacob answered. Oh, thank God. Kip was alive. Surely this wasn't a hallucination.

Mom spoke again. "How do you know Mary Beth?" Oh, she sounded pissed, but Mom was a firm reality Mary Beth could hold onto.

"Uh…"

Mary Beth tried to hold her breath as she waited to hear how Jacob would describe their relationship.

"I manage the McGillis ranch. She's our vet."

A wave of disappointment washed over her. If she could have cried, she would have. He'd saved her but he didn't love her. He didn't want her. Even though the world hadn't ended, it wasn't convenient any more.

He was breaking her heart. No one had ever had the chance to break her heart—not since her father had died when she was a little girl. But she'd gone and fallen in love with a masked Indian cowboy. And now her oldest fear was coming to light.

She would be alone. Again.

"I see. Will more of her clients be stopping by?" Mom's voice was cutting, and for the first time, Mary Beth thought Mom sounded just like her, smart-ass and all. She couldn't help but silently shout, *Go, Mom!* Which, of course, meant that she didn't even gurgle.

"No," he answered calmly. "I don't think any other clients know her outside of work."

"I see." Mary Beth could almost see Mom, one eyebrow arched almost up to her hairline, giving him her patented cut-the-crap look. Mary Beth would have given her right foot to see Jacob in the overwhelming face of Mom-logic.

262

He folded a little. "She's—um, she's an amazing woman, Mrs. Hofstetter."

"I know, Mr. Plenty Holes. Oh, yes, dear? Would you like to see her?"

The bed sagged slightly and then a cool hand slipped into hers. Kip.

Kip Two Elks. Jacob had never said her full name before.

She was no longer hiding.

The overwhelming joy blotted out the pain in her heart. Kip was still live. Mary Beth was still alive. This was great progress, really.

Then lips brushed over her forehead—not cool, small lips, but rough lips—lips she knew. Lips she'd kissed. "Don't you dare give up on me, babe," Jacob whispered, and Mary Beth felt him trace his fingers over her cheek. "You're still alive. Keep it that way."

Still alive, she thought back, wanting to talk to him more than she'd ever wanted to talk in her entire life. Nothing worked though.

Didn't matter. She wasn't going to give up on him either. Even if he didn't know it yet.

Being alive was harder than Mary Beth thought it would be. For five weeks, she suffered from crushing claustrophobia from having her head bolted into a Frankenstein-style brace. The whole time, Mom answered for her for everything from what kind of gelatin she wanted with dinner to how she was feeling today. It drove Mary Beth nuts.

Not that Jacob made her less nuts. He made the smallest of small talk during regular evening visits, which left her all kinds of confused about him again.

Maybe it was the presence of her mother that had him all clammed up again, but whatever it was, Mary Beth didn't like it. She did like it, however, when he brought Kip in on the weekends. The small girl was starting to talk again, hesitantly mispronouncing words in a way that was both cute and heart-breaking sad.

Rebel came and sat with her at odd times. He'd just show up, shoot the breeze and head back out again. Once—only once—did he do anything that was even vaguely medicine-man-ly. He brought in a sage bundle and burned it—or tried to, until a nurse got after him. That was it.

At several points during Mary Beth's five-week incarceration, as she came to think of it, Sheriff Tim Means stopped in. He was the one who filled her in on what had happened after the thing with Buck. Nobody had come to fetch him that night, but by the time the two of them had made it back to the hidden house, the whole thing had gone up in flames. Some investigators had come in from the FBI and found enough of Buck's body to make a positive I.D. They'd taken possession of the McGillis ranch, but Jacob was still running it, for the time being. There was talk of selling it off after the feds got done going through Buck's estate, which was going to take a while.

Mary Beth got the feeling that Nobody had set the fire, but it was one of those things that couldn't be proved.

But, hands down, the hardest part of the five weeks was feeling that her throat was the huge, blinking, neon sign in the room that everyone stared at. Sure, everyone was polite about it, but Mary Beth couldn't stand it. She felt like a freak of the first-class order.

She was raring to go home. Sure, Mom would still be there, but it had to be better than the hospital. At least Mary Beth hoped and prayed it would be better than the hospital. If she never set foot in this place again, it would be too damn soon.

The brace finally gone, Mary Beth sucked it up and headed for the bathroom, Mom steadying her from behind. She hadn't wanted to look while she was still in the brace, but now she didn't have a good excuse not to see what she'd survived. After all, she was going to have one of those foam braces that whiplash victims wore—and she was under strict orders not to wear it all the time. The tendons Buck had cut may have healed, but they needed the practice. The more she wore the foam brace, the longer the recovery would take.

Okay, she reminded herself, eyes still closed as she tried to figure out if she was holding her head up straight. *You can do this. You are still alive.* But what she saw took her breath away.

"Only three and a half inches long," Mom said in a voice that was probably supposed to be soothing as she rubbed Mary Beth's back. "It healed nicely."

Nicely? As the tears spilled over, Mary Beth couldn't see a damn thing nice about it. Three and a half inches looked to be half a mile long, and a quarter-mile wide on her skin. And the holes—dear God, the holes! A set of holes marched in lockstep alongside her near-death experience.

Hideous. Like a radioactive centipede had taken up residence on her body and wasn't going anywhere.

"Pumpkin, it's really not that bad," Mom said, slipping one arm around her waist. Holding her up, holding her close—same thing.

265

"The hell it's not, Mom," she replied, snatching the scratchiest four-dollar tissue known to mankind from the box and exfoliating her face with it.

Mom sighed, resigned to losing this battle. "Well, the foam brace will cover it, and if you keep your hair long… It will fade, pumpkin."

But not within the hour. Not by the time Jacob and Kip showed up to drive her and Mom back to the little time-warp house on Beech.

Jacob would see it. And once he did, there'd be no chance of getting back to convenient. There was nothing convenient about that scar. Nothing.

"Hello? Mary Beth? Mrs. Hofstetter? We're here!"

Shit. Jacob would see it *right now*. Not only was she hideous, but the red eyes and a running nose completed the look. *Super*, she thought as Mom went out to get her brace and greet their ride home. *Can this get any worse?*

"Wow, you look beautiful."

Apparently, the answer to that question was *yes*. Jacob appeared in the doorway, brace in hand. She froze, wishing she could get the scar covered or that he'd disappear or that the building would catch fire—anything to get his eye off of her. Anything. But nothing moved.

"You want some help with this?" he asked, his voice soft and quiet, like she was a forest creature who easily startled. One black lock of his hair fell forward over his mask, but he couldn't see it.

Jesus Christ, does he get better looking all the time?

Which was quickly followed by the realization that she must be healed if she was ready to begin the dance around the bed—and the couch, not to mention the floor—with him again.

If he kept his mask on, could she wear the brace? *Mom! And Kip! Like three feet away!*

The rush of desire and confusion and mortification threatened to swamp her as she started to sweat. Unable to stop herself from coming apart at her brand-new seam, she closed her eyes. It was all she could do.

He stepped in behind her and lowered the brace around her neck like it was a freaking diamond necklace. "Move your hair," he gently ordered, his lips brushing against her lobe. "I won't look. Not if you don't want me to."

Feeling helpless as her blood pounded up to her cheeks and down to points lower, she did as she was told. The moment the Velcro scratched shut, Mary Beth felt a little better. She couldn't see the scar anymore—and that meant neither could Jacob.

"There. Beautiful," he murmured, tracing his hands down her back and around her waist as he kissed her ear. He pulled her back against his hard, lean body, squeezing all the air out of her lungs as he lightly nipped at her shoulder.

Where the hell are Mom and Kip? He can't kiss me like this—what if they walk in on us?

She opened her mouth, but by then, he'd already worked his way around to her front and kissed her. Not too hard, so he wasn't pushing on her head, but not anything like those little pecks he'd been giving her.

A real kiss. The kind lovers gave each other.

All of the passion flowed easily from him back to her, nearly knocking her off her feet with the suddenness.

267

"Wait," she whimpered, "Mom—Kip—"

"They're probably halfway to the mall in Rapid City by now," he replied, lowering his lips to hers again.

Finally, finally, her mouth kicked on as she wrenched out of his grasp, tripped and landed on the hospital bed with a dull thud. Her head felt like a pumpkin on a toothpick, just waiting to start rolling. She physically grabbed it just to make sure the darned thing stayed attached. "Wait, what? They left us?"

"Well, yeah. They were going shopping."

"Jacob, what's going on?" she demanded as her temperature spiked higher. "No one told me about this."

"I'm taking you home." He smiled, looking far more confident than Mary Beth was suddenly feeling. "Kind of like a date."

"Well, thank you very much for asking me out on this date," she snipped, unable to stop her mouth now that it was on. "All girls enjoy being kept in the dark when it comes to, you know, plans and dates and stuff. Did Mom know about this?"

"Mary Beth, calm down," he replied, crouching in front of her. "This was your mother's idea."

"You're taking dating tips from *my mother*?" she yelled. Her neck began to ache. She knew she needed to relax. But just when she'd begun to feel like she might have some control over something—even something as simple as a damned car ride home—she was right back to being helpless again. "Jesus, Jacob, how hard up are you?"

He smiled, but his eye didn't move. "She wanted to spend a little more time with Kip before she left, and she thought we might want some time alone." Mary Beth snorted, which sent shock waves down her neck.

"Hey, I like your mother, I do, but it sounded good to me. I've really missed you."

"Well, for future reference, this was a lousy way to get a date." Her whole head was starting to throb, and simply breathing didn't seem to be doing any good. For a second, she thought maybe they'd let her out of that God-awful contraption too soon. Nothing in the neck or head region seemed to be working—brain included. "Did it ever occur to you that I might want to know what's going on?"

"I'm here to take you home. That's what's going on," he replied, sounding more than just a little frustrated. "That was always the plan."

His plan, sure. But her plan? Just like she had since Mary Beth had woken up, Mom had made the decision for her. Irritating enough when it came to which kind of gelatin Mary Beth wanted for dessert— but what passed for her love life? Beyond the pale.

And Jacob had just gone along with it. "You don't have to get clearance from my mother, Jacob. You could have just asked me. I mean, *seriously*. You knew I would say yes."

He froze, an uncharacteristically huge grin on his face. "Yeah, I know you'd say yes."

Her blood began to boil. "You are being a jerk right now, Jacob, and I don't even know why. God, you make me nuts sometimes."

Taking her hands in his, he rolled forward from the crouch until he was on his knees. *Jesus*, her brain screamed, *he's not going to ask* that, *is he*?

269

Weddings—in a church and then in front of a tipi—flashed before her eyes. The kind of wedding Robin was planning, but it wasn't Robin standing next to Mikey. It was her standing next to Jacob, with Kip off to the side.

Isn't this what she wanted? Because she was in love with him?

Wasn't she?

"Mary Beth," he said in all seriousness and her heart just about stopped. "Will you go on a date with me?"

How ridiculous was she? Of course he wasn't going to ask her to marry him. What a normal girl would have seen as a romantic surprise just pissed her off. They couldn't even have a normal date without him reducing her to a confused, furious mess.

And she was hopelessly in love with him.

She opened her mouth, but the darned thing short-circuited at the near miss and silently shut again as she unconsciously covered her neck with her hands.

Hopeless. She was hopeless. This relationship was hopeless, and she couldn't shake the feeling that it was her fault. She was too screwed up—too scarred—to be a part of something that had briefly bordered on normal.

He sat before her, patiently waiting for her response as she blinked the tears out of her eyes. And all she could do was weakly glare at him.

"Interesting," he mused as he leaned forward and kissed her cheek. "That's the second time you've been speechless. Come on." He stood and gingerly pulled her to her feet. "Let's go home."

Chapter Eighteen

Oh, Mary Beth was pissed, that much was clear. But this was a different kind of pissed. Usually, when she was mad at him, she tore into him, but she hadn't said word one since Jacob had started the truck. She wouldn't even look at him. No cutting commentary, no snide remarks, no bitter musings muttered under her breath.

Nothing.

This wasn't part of the plan to sweep her off her feet. Suddenly, he found himself wondering if she really was going to say yes or not.

He and Lily—after a week, Mrs. Hofstetter had insisted on Lily—had been planning this for weeks. The ring had come in the mail last Tuesday.

Her Granny's ring.

When he'd told Lily he wanted to marry Mary Beth one night after she'd fallen asleep, Lily had given him that hard look—the one she'd been wearing when he first met her in Mary Beth's hospital room—for about a second before her eyes had started watering. She'd hugged him, and then hugged Kip, and then called Mary Beth's uncle. Jacob had asked him for permission as well, but before he'd gotten much of an answer, Lily had snatched the phone back and began demanding her brother dig out their mother's wedding ring and mail it immediately.

"She always wanted Mary Beth to have it," she'd explained in a hushed whisper as the shift nurse had glared at them.

"Well?" Jacob had asked Kip.

"She'll shay yesh." Kip had smiled before she frowned at getting the S sounds wrong again. "But where are we gonna all live?"

It was a good question. As fond as they were of the little house on Beech, Kip couldn't sleep on the couch forever. And there was no way the three of them could fit into the tin can of a trailer he'd lived in his whole life. Heck, now that Kip was reading and talking—moving in general—doing everything but sitting silently until she fell asleep, there was barely enough room for the two of them in there.

That night, when he looked at the trailer with a calculating eye, he'd seen what Mary Beth would see—ratty upholstery from the 60s with stuffing poking through the threadbare parts, a kitchen that consisted of a hot plate and a coffee maker, and a miniscule bed crammed behind the bathroom that didn't have a real door. No way she'd want to live there.

It was no place for a wife. No place for a family.

So he'd bought a doublewide trailer—"Manufactured home," the salesman in Rapid City had corrected him, but still—and had it delivered a few weeks ago.

The trailer had the best kitchen he could get, a full-sized bathroom, a roomy living/dining room—"a Great Room," the salesman had crowed—and two bedrooms, one for Kip, and one for them. On opposite ends of the trailer.

"A good starter home," the salesman had promised. And it was. There was enough room for the three of them, and maybe a baby—if she wanted one. God knows, she was so good with Kip...

But that would come later. First, Mary Beth had to say yes. And right now, she wasn't talking to him.

The truck left pavement behind as he headed up the new gravel road to the trailer. It skirted the edge of the valley where the wild buffalo roamed the untouched prairie. He'd thought she might like to see that again, but now he wasn't sure. Her face was as close to blank as it had ever been, with just a hint of surprise widening her gray-blue eyes. Not excitement. Just surprise. *Oh, hell*, he moaned inside, *she's not going to ignore me for two months, is she?*

He scrambled to think of something to say that would get her talking again. "You remember? That was our first almost date," he finally got out as the road curved near the ridge.

Slowly, she swung her head around as her mouth screwed down into an invisible knot. And she said nothing.

"I, um, I was trying to flirt, but you know I'm not really good at it. But I, uh, thought you might have liked me," he stuttered as her eyes narrowed into slits.

Suddenly, the anger bled into something sadder as she turned her whole body away from him. He knew if she could have gotten out of the car, she would have. And fast.

No wonder she was so mad at me, he realized. *This silent treatment thing sucks, and she's only been doing it for an hour.* Somehow, it didn't seem like they were going to make it to the sandwiches, much less the chilled champagne he'd thought she'd like. "Mary Beth?"

"All we have is almost dates, Jacob," she said, her voice already cracking. "Almost dates. Nothing more."

Even in his confusion, he could tell she was on the edge of a breakdown. She'd gotten close a few times while she was still in that awful brace, but that had been the brace.

This was his fault.

"Hon," he whispered, reaching over to stroke her hair, "we've got a lot more than that."

She recoiled from his touch. "Kip doesn't count."

"I'm sorry I didn't tell you about this, but I don't understand why you're so upset. It was just a surprise." The moment the words left his mouth, he knew he'd stuck his foot in it.

She snorted in anger, but at least she didn't look like she was about to start crying. "Just a surprise. My whole life has been a surprise since I showed up here. And not very many of them have been good."

That hurt. "This isn't a good surprise?"

"Jacob, after all we've been through, I don't want another surprise as long as I live," she muttered, her hands hovering near the foam brace. "Everyone seems to know what's going to happen to me before I do, and I'm tired of it. I don't feel like I'm in control of my own life anymore."

Oh, if she was tired of surprises, how was she going to take the trailer? "I should probably tell you that you've got one more coming today."

"Now what?" she moaned, the panic rising up. "Every guy I've ever dated waiting to gawk at the scar?"

The scar. He'd caught a quick glance of it in the bathroom. And then she'd gotten all nuts on him. *It's the scar.* The light bulb finally went off.

He, of all people, should be able to understand how a scar messed with your mind and he'd completely overlooked it because it simply didn't matter to him. She'd survived more intact than he had, and in his relief, he'd forgotten to consider how she felt. If she could love him with a mask, he could love her with a long, red scar. And he did love her, scar and all.

Maybe she couldn't see that. Maybe she needed him to show her. "I want to show you something I got for you. And you can do whatever you want about it."

"No ex-boyfriends?"

He smiled, hoping she'd smile back, but it didn't work. "It's a good surprise. But you can't be mad if I tell you Kip helped. Kip counts, you know."

She closed her eyes and took a deep breath, then another. "Yeah, I know. This better be good."

One more surprise. As the truck climbed headed south, away from the valley she thought of as her own, Mary Beth tried to calm herself down. He was trying to be romantic, and here she was, screwing it up by being a first-class bitch.

So what if this wasn't a candle-lit dinner in Rapid City? So what if, like usual, Jacob missed the finer points of dating interactions? So what if he'd seen the scar?

He still wanted to be with her—or did, before she had seen red and blue all at the same time. Shouldn't that be what she focused on?

But somehow, she couldn't shake the feeling that Mom—and Kip—had done more than just *help* today. Her life was beyond her control—again. The confusion threw her right back into a tailspin. She'd always been in control, always been in charge before, but now she was the last to know about everything. Or so it felt.

She just needed to be in charge of something. What control she had of her neck still felt very temporary. Mom had decided what she'd eat, what they'd watch and what books Mary Beth would like. The only thing she had left was sex.

And Jacob wasn't getting any, no matter how pitiful he looked.

After about fifteen minutes, Jacob turned east as the road that wound back up a gully. When they got to the top, she saw a junk trailer, the kind hippies might have lived in back in the sixties, off to one side. Then, up a hundred feet or so, backed against a stand of pines, there was a brand-new doublewide trailer with a stable peeking out from the back.

They sat there for a moment. Mary Beth half-expected some angry homeowner to come busting out, waving a shotgun and shouting at them to get off his land, but then Jacob hopped out like he owned the place.

"Where are we?" she finally asked as he lifted her out of the passenger seat.

"Home," he replied, taking her hand and leading her up to the steps.

We have a nicer trailer, he'd said months ago. At the time, she'd wondered. This was barely a trailer at all—this was a gleaming house on blocks. "You? You live here?"

His face was inscrutable again. "I do now."

"Now? Where did you live before?"

He nodded back to the junk trailer. "Kip needs more... space now. So I got a bigger house."

The two of them had been living in that piece of rust? *Good lord*, she thought as she tried—and failed—to shake her head. Poor Kip. Better than Tommy's old heap, but still not a real home. "Jacob, is this the surprise? I don't understand—"

"I want to show you around," he cut her off. "Come inside."

The door swung easily open, the whole house still smelling of newness. The furniture was sparse—just a beat-up loveseat that looked like it belonged in the old trailer and a card table and chairs off the kitchen.

Something was wrong. Sure, the odd juxtaposition of the ratty furnishing with the freshly painted walls and sparkling clean kitchen didn't help, but how was Jacob's new trailer a surprise for her? "Jacob—"

"I'll show you Kip's room," he interrupted again, a nervous smile on his face. "She said I could."

Kip's room looked more like a real room. A twin bed with a soft green coverlet embroidered with pink and purple butterflies and a matching pink butterfly pillow on top was tucked under the window with gauzy green curtains. In one corner, a white dresser stood with a framed picture of Kip and two people who could only be her parents on it. Next to her bed was a small white bookshelf with a lamp that had a feathered green shade on it. It was very much a girl's room. Not a holy woman's room but a little girl's room, just like it should be.

"She went a little overboard at J.C. Penney," Jacob said with that shy half smile again, "but I did tell her she could get whatever she wanted."

"Wow. More green than I expected," Mary Beth whispered. "Are you sure she said I could look?"

"Positive." He took her hand and led her to the kitchen. The new countertops shone as the filtered sun floated down past the towering pines just outside the window over the kitchen sink. It was bright and airy, with maybe enough room for one of those islands in it. *A beautiful kitchen without an avocado green appliance in sight*, she thought.

"I got the one with the nicer Whirlpool stuff," Jacob said.

"And a card table? Your furniture is worse than mine," she stiffly commented he pulled her down the other hall. Something was off and she couldn't put her finger on what it was. Even though there was practically nothing in here, Mary Beth suddenly felt like it was too crowded.

"I was going to talk to you about that." He opened the door to a second bedroom. "I'm not much of a decorator."

"Clearly not your strong suit," she said as she hesitantly peeked into the good-sized room that held a crisply made queen mattress on the floor and not much else.

Trying not to smile, he headed back out to the living room. "I was hoping you could pick out what you wanted."

Her mouth flopped open, bouncing off the brace so that she almost bit her tongue. "What I wanted?"

Jacob stopped in the middle of the living room, catching both her hands in his. "Yup."

She could actively see the walls marching in on her now, one determined inch at a time. "Jacob, I don't live here."

He reached into his pocket and pulled out a small handkerchief with the ends knotted together. Carefully, he untied it, revealing a ring. "I was hoping you might want to."

This time her heart definitely stopped, at least for a moment as he got down on his knees again. "Mary Beth, will you marry me?"

It was one of those old-fashioned rings with the diamond set deep in white gold, surrounded by delicate... little... flowers. Her mouth gaping, she snatched it out of his hand and flipped it over. And there it was.

Rose My Love Always Billy

She squeaked a tight little noise as she veered dangerously toward hysteria. "This... this is my Granny's ring!" she finally choked out, caught somewhere between hopeless and out of control again.

"I know. Your mom had your uncle mail it to me."

Heart pounding, her head began to swirl. "My mom knows?" she demanded, her voice shaking as much as her hands.

He nodded, looking a little panicked himself.

The walls moved again, giving her panic no place to go. It turned back on her, wrapping itself around her neck with a brutal efficiency. This was all wrong.

Normally, this would have been a fight—a fight she would have won, because she was right. But her mouth wasn't operating like normal anymore—nothing was.

She wasn't the same woman she'd been—the three-and-a-half-inch radioactive centipede she'd have for the rest of her live proved it. The old Mary Beth really had died on the floor of that little shack and she realized that there was no way Jacob could love the leftovers.

Everyone knew leftovers were never as good as the original. Even Kip had to know that.

"Did Kip tell you I was going to say yes?" she asked, feeling like a boa constrictor was just seconds from eating her. His wounded look said that she had, and Mary Beth officially lost it. He didn't really want her—this sure as hell wasn't convenient—but the tag-team of Kip and Mom was more than even Jacob could withstand. "You—you—you—" She couldn't even talk. The boa constrictor was too tight, cutting off her air. Which was just as well, because the walls were so close that there wasn't any air to be had.

"You think that the only reason I'm asking you is because Kip told me I had to?" he coolly replied, seemingly unconcerned that the walls in this place were squishing him flat. "You think that the fact that I actually love you has nothing to do with it? The fact that I want to spend my life with you because you make me happy—damn it, actually happy—has nothing to do with it?"

He loved the old, convenient Mary Beth. That woman made him happy—content. She knew that just as soon as he figured out that woman was dead and gone, he wouldn't even be able to look at her, much less love her. The scar felt like it was trying to fight back against the boa constrictor, pushing out when everything else was pushing in. The pain was searing.

The light flooding the living room began to pop in little flashbulbs of blue and green as her throat turned to solid stone and took her lungs down with it. Not a boa constrictor, her medical brain realized, but the brace. Gotta get the brace off. Only chance to breathe.

All the blue and green lights began to merge into suffocating black.

Jacob caught her as she collapsed, easing her down to the ground until her head was comfortably resting in his lap. "I'm sorry, babe, I'm sorry. Come on, Mary Beth, breathe," he begged, kicking himself for pushing her over the edge. What the hell was he doing? She'd just gotten out of the hospital. He should have known she wouldn't be strong enough for an engagement ring, much less a trailer. This was all his fault and it was up to him to make it right. "In through the nose, out through the mouth."

She made a gurgling noise as her eyes rolled back in her head.

Shit, what was he supposed to do? She'd just crumpled like he'd hit her, but he hadn't touched her. Somewhere from the back of his mind, he remembered that maybe he was supposed to loosen her clothes. "I'm going to take the brace off, okay?"

"N-n-n," she tried to choke out, pulling his hands away from her throat.

Okay, that was a good sign. She hadn't had a complete nervous breakdown. "Are you gonna breathe?"

281

Her eyes shut tight, she winced as she gave a faint nod.

God, he hoped her throat was okay. *Please, let her be okay*, he prayed as he said, "That's good, babe. Just breathe. I'm right here."

The patches of light coming through the windows without curtains moved across the floor as they sat there. Jacob gently stroked her hair, willing her to calm down with everything he had. Finally, her chest rose and fell evenly as her neck relaxed. A few minutes later, she opened her eyes slowly, and he flinched at the regret that spilled out.

"Jacob," she whispered, the tears running down the side of her face.

"I'm sorry, Mary Beth, I really am," he cut her off, caressing away the tears with his thumbs. "This was too much."

"A normal woman would be really impressed." She hiccupped as her eyes raced around the trailer again.

"You're normal," he reassured her.

"I was, once," she sobbed, curling away from him. "I'm not anymore."

God, it just about broke his heart. There was only one thing to do.

When the first snap gave, she went stiff. When the second snap gave, she quickly flipped back over and grabbed his hand as it hovered near the final snap. The mask was barely clinging to his skin.

"Don't."

He smiled as a sense of peace filled him. "I want to."

A fresh panic seemed to take hold of her. "No, you don't," she insisted.

"Yes, I do," he said as he moved her hand and slipped the mask off. "Today's the day. I've got nothing to hide from you, Mary Beth. I've got nothing I *want* to hide from you."

Her mouth gaped as she stared at the face Buck had left him with, but the dread he'd always feared didn't materialize. The only thing he felt was that this was right.

"This is who I am. You want to talk about not normal?" He smiled, never more sure of who he was. "I'm a Lakota warrior who sends others to fight in court. I'm the surrogate father to an albino girl who's only seven. I'm an Indian missing half his face in love with a white woman. Nothing about me is normal, except when I'm with you."

"Me?" she squeaked, unable to tear her gaze away from the scarred skin that covered the place where his eye had once been.

"You. When I'm with you, I'm normal. I'm just a man in love with you. That's what you do, and not just for me. You give that to Kip too. She's just a little girl with butterflies on her bed to you. You make us profoundly, deeply normal, all because you love us."

She choked a little, covering her mouth in shock as her eyes danced around his face, jumping back and forth from his eye to the scars on his nose.

"You don't have to be normal to be with me. I love you because you're not normal. I love your smart mouth and how Kip always trusted you from the start, and I love how you don't let me get away with being a jerk."

"You love my smart mouth?"

"Yup. It's all part of who I love. You."

283

Her hands snaked back up to her throat. "But—but—"

Deliberately, he moved her hands and undid the Velcro holding the brace on her neck. She went rigid beneath his fingers, closing her eyes as if she could pray him away, but she couldn't.

Her neck laid bare, he traced his fingers lightly over the still-angry flesh. His scars were old, flat and faded in the almost-four years that had passed, but hers were still fresh, the pain still new. "I'm trying to tell you that it doesn't matter to me, but I know I'm not very good with this talking thing." She forced a little grin, but he could see she was still mortified. "I'm sorry I didn't understand how much this bothered you, babe. I should have known. It will get better, I promise. You can wear the brace or a scarf if you want to, but you don't have to."

"But I'm—it's so ugly," she whispered, turning away from him again.

He couldn't stop the chuckle that broke loose. "Compared to what? Have you seen my face?"

"Don't laugh at me," she sobbed. "Please."

"Babe, please. What do you think of when you think of me?"

"What?"

He asked slower this time, enunciating all the words. "What do you think of when you think of me? Am I just a guy in a mask? Is that all you ever think about?"

"Um, at this exact moment, it's kinda high up there," she whispered, swimming in the guilt.

He beamed, so relieved she sounded almost normal. "But not always."

"Jacob, what does—?"

"You think that when I look at you, all I'll ever see is the scar, right?"

She started to suck in air as she squeezed her eyes shut.

"Babe, please, hear me out. It's a part of you, but it's not who you are now. You know what I think of when I look at this?" he asked as he stroked the length of the scar, his fingers memorizing every pinhole and every ridge. "I think of love and honor and sacrifice. I think of everything you willingly almost gave up to save Kip. I think of how brave you were—braver than I ever was. I think of a warrior who fell down and accepted her scars for her family."

"I'm not—" she protested.

He pressed a finger to her lips to quiet her. "You don't have to hide from me, because you've got nothing to be ashamed of. It's not an ugly scar, not to me and not to Kip. It's a badge of honor." And slowly, he leaned down and kissed all three-plus inches of it as he wrapped his fingers through her waves of hair. By the time he finished, she'd gone from board stiff to relaxed, leaning her head back to give him better access. "It's not the worst of you," he murmured as he held her to his chest. "It's the best."

She began to cry again, but he could tell this was different. These were tears of relief. So he let her go as she wrapped her arms around him and held him tight. He glanced around and finally saw where the ring had landed, just behind her.

They were almost to *yes*.

When she finally leaned back, she looked lighter, a silly smile waiting for him. "And I'm sorry I didn't

285

figure out how much your mother was getting on your nerves," he said with a smirk. "I would have sent her home with Kip sooner if I had realized you needed such a break."

That did it. "You really bought this trailer for me?" She looked around at all the newness that was hers for the taking.

He smiled. It felt different without the mask on—his face unencumbered by the leather. He didn't need that piece of leather to hold him together anymore. That's what she was for. "Manufactured home, actually. Trailers have apparently gone the way of all things. And I want you to pick out whatever you want. Even if you wanted to haul that ugly couch out of your house and bring it up here, that'd be okay with me." She giggled again, and he couldn't help but lift her to his lips. "I did already get the mattress…"

"Uh huh," she said, her voice still shaking. "When did you do all this?"

"It was delivered two weeks ago. I decided to ask your mother for permission, and then she called your uncle, so I asked him too, and then I asked Kip what she thought, and she said you'd say yes. But she asked me where we were going to live. So I bought us this trailer."

She rolled her eyes as she smiled, real joy radiating from her eyes. "Uncle Hank knows?"

"He gave his permission. So I think everyone's said yes but you." He leaned down and kissed her. It felt different now that he wasn't wearing the mask. "I love you. Kip loves you. Stay here with me. Stay here with us. You belong here."

She reached up and traced a finger down the pale

scar tissue that had once been his eyelid before it circled the scars where his nose had been reattached to his face. "This—it never really mattered to me."

"I know." He leaned far over, trying to reach the ring without squishing her. "So you want to get married?"

She beamed as he slipped the family diamond on her finger. Her eyes got all misty, but she pulled him down and kissed him hard, setting him on fire again. It wasn't the easiest way to yes, but they'd gotten here all the same.

"*Techihhila,*" she finally managed to say, not quite getting the pronunciation right. But close enough. Jacob hugged her tight before he tasted strawberries in sunshine again.

"I thought you might."

About the Author

Award-winning author Sarah M. Anderson may live east of the Mississippi River, but her heart lies out west on the Great Plains. When she started writing, it wasn't long before her characters found themselves out in South Dakota among the Lakota Sioux. She loves to put people from two different worlds into new situations and see how their backgrounds and cultures take them someplace they never thought they'd go.

With over 1.2 million copies published in over twenty-one countries, Sarah has published over 40 books. Sarah's book *A Man of Privilege* won a RT Book Reviews 2012 Reviewers' Choice Best Book Award. *The Nanny Plan* was a 2016 RITA® winner for Best Contemporary: Short. Additionally, Sarah has given workshops at national and regional conferences, taught craft classes online, spoken at libraries and book clubs, and published articles in the Romance Writers Report. Find out more about Sarah's books at www.sarahmanderson.com. and sign up for the new-release newsletter at http://eepurl.com/nv39b.

Readers can find out more about Sarah's love of cowboys and Indians at:

Her Newsletter: http://eepurl.com/nv39b

Her Website: www.sarahmanderson.com

On Facebook: www.facebook.com/pages/Sarah-M-Anderson-Author

On Twitter: @SarahMAnderson1

On Goodreads: www.goodreads.com/author/show/4982413.Sarah_M_Anderson

By Snail Mail at: Sarah M. Anderson, 200 N 8th ST #193, Quincy IL 62301-9996

Other Books by Sarah M. Anderson

Men of the White Sandy
The Medicine Man
The Rancher
The Shadow
The Medic
The Sheriff
The Wannabe Cowboy

Lawyers in Love
A Man of His Word
A Man of Privilege
A Man of Distinction
Pride and Pregnancy

The Boltons
Straddling the Line
Bringing Home the Bachelor
Expecting a Bolton Baby
Little Secrets: Claiming His Pregnant Bride

Rich, Rugged Ranchers
A Real Cowboy

The Texas Cattleman's Club
What a Rancher Wants
His Lost and Found Family
A Surprise for the Sheikh

Dynasties: The Newports
Claimed by the Cowboy

Rodeo Dreamers
Rodeo Dreams
One Rodeo Season
Crushing on the Cowboy

The First Family of Rodeo
His Best Friend's Sister
His Enemy's Daughter
His for One Night

The Beaumont Heirs
Not the Boss's Baby
Seduced by the Cowboy
A Beaumont Christmas Wedding
His Son, Her Secret
Falling for Her Fake Fiancé
His Illegitimate Heir
Rich Rancher for Christmas
Billionaire's Baby Promise

Billionaires and Babies
The Nanny Plan
His Forever Family
Twins for the Billionaire
Seduction on His Terms

Holiday Novellas
The Christmas Pony

NotMyFirstRodeo.com
Something About a Cowboy
Roping a Rancher

Writing as Maggie Chase

The Jeweled Ladies: The Mistress Series
His Topaz
Their Emerald
Her Ebony
His Sapphire
His Crown Jewel

The Jeweled Ladies: The Rogues Series
His Diamond
Their Amethyst

The Shadow
(Men of the White Sandy #3)

© 2014 by Sarah M. Anderson

Nobody Bodine is a nobody who came from a nobody and will always be a nobody.

He disappears into the shadows—no one sees him if he doesn't want them to. He exists in neither the white man's world nor the tribe's, dispensing vigilante justice when he sees fit. There's no other place for a man like him in this world.

Until Melonie Mitchell shows up on the rez. From the first moment he lays eyes on her, he can tell there's something different about her. For starters, she's not afraid of him. She asks where his scars came from, and why he has so many. But more than that, she sees him. For the first time in his life, Nobody feels like a somebody in her eyes.

Melonie has come west to run the new day care on the White Sandy Reservation. She's intrigued by this strange man and his tattered skin, and when she discovers that he's a self-appointed guardian angel for the boy in her care, she realizes that there's more to Nobody than meets the eyes. But how far will he go to keep the boy safe? And will she be able to draw him into the light?

Excerpt from *The Shadow*

Nobody stood in the shadows, watching her.

She wasn't leaving. Melonie Mitchell normally closed up shop and drove off by this point in the evening, but not tonight. It had to be close to eight—two hours after she normally left. Was that because it was Friday?

What was she doing? Light streamed out of both the front and back doors of the center as she did something inside. He was tempted to edge closer and steal a look in.

She couldn't be painting. In the two weeks since she'd left him the last note, the inside of the center had gone from concrete gray to plain white to rainbows. Maybe that's what she'd meant by creative chaos? Because it was still chaos. He wasn't sure if it was beautiful, but it was definitely wild.

The rainbow colors went vertically up over the walls—even over the foam she'd managed to hang from the ceilings. The foam covered the top four feet of the walls. Not that Nobody made a lot of noise, but even he could tell that the center was more hushed now. Less echo-y.

At the height he'd come to think of as her eye-level, she'd hung bulletin board strips. Papers, splashed with finger paint and crayon scribbles, were tacked up along the wall now, some with kids' names neatly printed at the bottom, others with names that were barely readable.

Then, at kid level, the wall had been covered with tiny handprints. Each set of prints had a name and an age painted onto the wall underneath it. Jamie's hands were up there—no last name, though.

He'd been right. Melonie had taken the boy in. Good.

But that didn't explain what she was doing here now. Didn't she know this wasn't the safest place on the rez? True, he hadn't caught any junkies trying to break in recently, but that didn't mean they wouldn't try again.

She appeared in the front door. Light streamed from behind her, giving her an otherworldly glow.

He felt himself breathe at seeing her again. The two weeks since she'd almost walked right into him at Rebel's place had felt long. Time, as marked by days and weeks, didn't have much meaning for him. His world was divided into light and dark, warm and cold. He cleaned the clinic every day. There were no Mondays, no weekends.

But the last two weeks had moved by at such a slow pace that he'd begun to feel... uneasy about it. Not his usual sense of when someone was in trouble. This had been different. He'd wanted to see her just because. Not because he had to keep her safe or anything. Just... because.

But he'd forced himself to stay away from Rebel's. She'd looked right at him, walked right toward him as if he were standing in broad daylight. If she hadn't gotten distracted... no. He didn't believe she could actually tell he was there. Something else had attracted her attention. That was all.

Backlit, she stretched, her body reaching for the dusk sky. Something else began to make Nobody feel

295

uneasy and that something was obvious—Melonie Mitchell had a hell of a body. Part of what had been bothering him had been those curves—those generous breasts, those hips.

How would her body feel? Would she be terrified if he filled his hands with those breasts? Would she be afraid of him if he grabbed her hips and pulled her into him?

Onto him?

Or would she like it? Would she think it exciting to do it with someone dangerous? Would she moan or cry out?

He got hard just thinking of it. Of her.

Then she did something that snapped him out of his thoughts.

She looked at him.

There was no mistaking this—she looked right at him. And smiled.

What the hell?

He started to shrink back, but she turned away from him, gathering up something off the floor. Did she know he was here or not?

He should go.

He didn't.

www.ingramcontent.com/pod-product-compliance
Lightning Source LLC
Chambersburg PA
CBHW070654180626
46817CB00006B/2367